SCOTT
AND A

It was so natural to move into his arms and dance cheek to cheek. Sharon's forehead brushed Scott's chin. His after-shave was subtle and provocative, and its musky scent went straight to her libido. She pressed closer to him, swaying in time with his every move. She felt his lips press lightly against her temple, combining promises of passion and tenderness....

When the music stopped, Scott guided Sharon back to their table, his touch burning her skin. There was no sense in pretending that this man wasn't someone very special, Sharon knew. No way to deny that he would be very easy to fall in love with.

Sharon recognized the danger in that, and her heart beat faster. Loving him would be opening herself to the promise of heartache...but how could she resist?

ABOUT THE AUTHOR

Chance Meeting is the fifteenth Superromance by
veteran romance writer Meg Hudson. Her legion
of fans will be happy to know that Meg's love of
travel and romantic settings shines through in this
novel's Miami locale.

Books by Meg Hudson

HARLEQUIN SUPERROMANCE

HARLEQUIN AMERICAN ROMANCE

Don't miss any of our special offers. Write to us at the
following address for information on our newest releases.

Harlequin Reader Service
901 Fuhrmann Blvd., P.O. Box 1397, Buffalo, NY 14240
Canadian address: P.O. Box 603,
Fort Erie, Ont. L2A 5X3

Meg Hudson
CHANCE MEETING

Harlequin Books

TORONTO • NEW YORK • LONDON
AMSTERDAM • PARIS • SYDNEY • HAMBURG
STOCKHOLM • ATHENS • TOKYO • MILAN

Published September 1987

First printing July 1987

ISBN 0-373-70274-4

Printed in Canada

For Candy...
the bride Steve found in Florida

CHAPTER ONE

HE WAS SITTING by the window, frowning slightly as he studied a timetable. Sharon, poised in the doorway, photographed him mentally. He made a picture she wasn't apt to forget. He was wearing jeans and a bulky blue sweater, and he was definitely attractive. But that wasn't why he was making such an intense impression on her. It was because he was occupying her compartment.

This train she'd just boarded was already an hour late leaving New York's Pennsylvania Station. People were cramming the narrow corridor behind her, jostling each other and bumping her with their suitcases. Tempers were frayed, irritability acute. There was a thickness in the air compounded of annoyance, trails of smoke from recently snuffed out cigarettes, and a sudden need for haste after the long wait in the crowded, noisy station.

Sharon had two choices: to enter the compartment and confront this stranger, or leave and risk being battered and bruised—figuratively, at the least—as she tried to find an attendant who could straighten out her predicament.

She glanced, for about the fifth time, at the number on the door in front of her. No doubt about it, this was bedroom four, car 714.

The classic cry, "All Aboard!" blared through a scratchy loudspeaker system. The handsome man at the window looked up and, across a space of a few feet, his eyes met Sharon's. Shocking blue eyes, a startling contrast to his deeply tanned skin and dark brown hair.

He smiled, and this lit up a face that was rather stern in repose. Then he asked pleasantly, "Looking for someone?"

"Not exactly," Sharon hedged. He waited expectantly for her to say more, and her throat went dry. "I'm sorry," she managed somewhat hoarsely, "but . . . you have my room."

Whatever this man might have expected to hear from her, it wasn't that. He looked at the suitcase propped in the narrow space between his seat and a second seat that faced the window. His bag was a canvas carryon, nearly identical to the one Sharon was holding. He glanced from her bag to his, then shook his head slowly.

"Sorry," he said. "This is bedroom four, and it's mine."

Suddenly there was motion. The train got underway, sliding through the station's underground labyrinth, a vast, cavernous area of lights and shadows. Sharon let out an exasperated sigh and tried to put a rein on her impatience.

"Look," she said, forcing a slight smile. "Obviously there's been a mix-up. Bedroom four, car 714 is mine."

She fumbled in her handbag for her ticket, verified the numbers, then held the ticket out to him. "Here," she said, not unpleasantly. "See for yourself."

He got up slowly, reluctance stamped on his face. Clearly he didn't like this any better than she did.

Scanning her ticket, he scowled. Then, with visible difficulty, he converted the scowl into a falsely cheerful smile. "Guess we'll have to call the conductor to settle this," he decided. He pushed a small button on the wall, and added, "It'll probably take him a couple of minutes to get here. Meantime, come in."

It was not an enthusiastic invitation, and Sharon bit back a potentially stinging comment. She stepped into the small compartment, booked by the railroad as a "bedroom" that could accommodate two people. Her unwilling host motioned her to the seat by the window, then took the other seat himself. Every inch of the compartment had been designed for maximum space utilization and efficiency, and there really wasn't enough room between seat and window for him to stretch out his long legs comfortably.

Grimacing, he commented, "Cramped quarters, aren't they?"

Sharon nodded without speaking. This trip was getting off to a dismal start...and she'd yearned for the next twenty-six hours to be peace filled, relaxing and free of intrusion from the outside world.

She loved trains. She had a whole memory book of train trips taken around the country with her parents and her twin sister, years ago. Her father had been a sales representative for a large pharmaceutical firm and, because he'd been very good at his job, they'd relocated him many times. Whenever he'd been able, he'd taken his family with him.

In some ways, that had been good. In other ways, bad. Sharon had grown up feeling that she'd never had a real home, and that she'd missed something very valuable by lacking "roots."

It had been a while since she'd been on a train. Usually, she traveled by bus, because she *never* flew. But taking the train was the perfect choice for this particular trip. She needed time by herself without the distraction of traveling companions. So, she'd booked a bedroom, willingly paying the considerable extra tariff for the privilege of solitude. She didn't expect to solve all her problems between New York and Miami, but she did hope to get a good head start on them.

She'd wangled a month away from her job. By the time she began the return trip north, Sharon wanted to have a firm grip on her own sense of direction. She needed to make career decisions, she needed to make personal decisions. And it was necessary, *now*, to lay the groundwork for doing both. There would be diversions in Miami—welcome ones, certainly—but that wouldn't make them any less time and emotion consuming.

This train compartment, she decided resolutely, was worth fighting for!

She glanced at her companion. He was staring moodily out the window, though there was nothing to see. At the moment, everything beyond the glass was blacker than midnight. They were passing under the Hudson River, Sharon realized, going through the tunnel that connected Manhattan with New Jersey.

She heard a discreet knock and looked up to see a man standing in the doorway. A black man, immaculately clad in dark slacks, a bright red jacket, crisp white shirt and a dark bow tie.

He smiled broadly and said pleasantly, "Good afternoon. I'm Thomas Chalmers the Third, and I'll be your attendant on this trip. First, let me explain the features of your bedroom. Then, if there's anything you need—"

Sharon's companion interrupted Thomas Chalmers the Third's welcoming speech with, "I'm afraid there's been a mix-up."

"A mix-up, sir?"

"That's right. It appears that this lady and I have been assigned the same compartment."

Thomas Chalmers the Third looked properly shocked, then he rallied. He said, politely but firmly, "Don't see how that could be, sir." He took a neatly folded piece of paper out of his pocket and consulted it. "Bedroom four," he read aloud. "Mr. and Mrs. S. Williams. You are Mr. Williams, sir?"

"I'm Scott Williams, yes. But there *is* no Mrs. Williams. Not traveling with me, anyway."

The train attendant turned to Sharon. "Would you give me your name, please, ma'am?"

Sharon felt a premonition of disaster as she answered, "Sharon Williams."

"Mmm," Thomas Chalmers murmured, perplexed.

Sharon and Scott Williams exchanged long glances... and reached a mutual conclusion. By some inexplicable quirk of fate, they'd been given the same accommodations.

Ten minutes later, the conductor appeared, plainly harried. "I can't figure out what went wrong," he admitted unhappily. "Probably another computer error. Some robot latched on to you two having the same last name and first initial, and put you together."

Scott Williams nodded. "I'll buy that," he said. "And I'm willing to bow out and let Miss Williams have this compartment. If there's another bedroom available, I'll take it. If not, I'll settle for a roomette."

The conductor shook his head and stated flatly, "There's nothing else available, Mr. Williams. This is an all-reservation train, and we're sold out."

Scott's lips tightened. "Are you telling me there's no place else you can put me?" he demanded.

"That's exactly what I'm telling you," the conductor retorted. He added, more mildly, "Look, we'll arrive in Newark shortly. We're scheduled to board several more passengers there. If someone doesn't show, I'll take care of you. Meantime, will you please just sit tight?" With this the conductor left, closing the door of the compartment behind him.

"Sit tight," Scott Williams grumbled, resuming his seat and trying to do something with his long legs. He looked across at Sharon and smiled apologetically. "I'm sorry about this," he said. "You look as if a little privacy right now means as much to you as it does to me."

Sharon didn't disagree with him.

For the next few minutes they were silent. Scott Williams stared morosely out the window at the winter landscape, and Sharon followed his gaze. Soon the light would be fading on this early March afternoon. Meanwhile, she had the uncanny feeling that this world through which they were traveling was entirely alien. The snow, the sky, and the frozen streams that cut through ice-cotton meadows were all milk white. Occasionally there was a touch of color—burnt rust or dull gold green—in the spiky twigs and dried grasses that thrust through the snowy banks along the edge of the train tracks. Mostly, though, this was a monochromatic Arctic scene.

Abruptly, Scott Williams asked, "How far are you going?"

"Miami," Sharon said absently, concentrating on the landscape and wondering if she could translate that mood to canvas. Painting was her favorite avocation and would have been her vocation, could she have afforded it. As it was, she needed to make a living, and did so doing layout and design for a small printing firm in Providence, Rhode Island.

"Miami," Scott Williams repeated. "The end of the line. As it happens, I'm going all the way, too."

They lapsed into another silence. The heat was on in the train, and Sharon wished she hadn't opted to wear such a heavy sweater. She'd chosen the clothes she was wearing primarily for climate transition. The sweater matched the gray in her plaid skirt and complemented the darker shade of her jacket. Later, she planned to switch the sweater for a blouse and hoped to do something with her hair. At the moment, her thick, copper-red tresses were twisted into a bun. Practical, yes. But it made her look older than her twenty-nine years.

Brooding about her appearance—she was only too conscious that she wasn't looking her best—Sharon wasn't immediately aware of Scott Williams watching her closely. He captured her attention when he said, "Don't worry. I'm sure the conductor will get things straightened out, if we give him a little time." He hesitated, then asked, "Would you care to join me for a drink?"

The suggestion was unexpected. "A drink?" Sharon echoed.

"It might not be too crowded in the club car yet," Scott told her. "Why don't we amble along and hole up there until we get past Newark? Then we can check with the conductor again."

Sharon thought for a second, then admitted, "That's not a bad idea."

Getting to the club car proved a long and rather difficult safari. Difficult for Sharon, at least. The train was swaying from side to side, and she had a hard time keeping her balance. They had to pass through three bedroom-roomette cars and three coach cars before they reached the club car, and it wasn't easy. But the worst, from Sharon's viewpoint, was the area between the cars where the motion was particularly bad. Stepping across the metal floor that covered the coupling mechanism gave her the carnival ride feeling that she was suddenly going to hurtle out of control. At those moments, she was grateful for Scott's firm hand on her arm, steadying her.

The club car was decorated in an attractive black, red and gold motif. A semicircular bar curved in one corner, and there were tables for two and four. Scott selected a table for two and, once they were seated, asked Sharon, "What's your pleasure?"

"Oh, perhaps some ginger ale," she said vaguely.

He grinned. "Under the circumstances, I'd prescribe something a little stronger."

"Well...maybe I'll have a whiskey sour," she decided.

As she spoke, Sharon told herself she would have exactly *one* whiskey sour. She was weary, and she'd had almost nothing to eat all day. Both were conditions conducive to letting alcohol rush to her head, especially since she seldom drank much beyond a glass or two of wine.

A waiter brought their drinks and Scott Williams raised his glass. "Here's to your good sportsmanship," he toasted. Noting Sharon's surprise, he added, "You have been a good sport, you know. You could have pushed the panic button a lot harder when you saw me already established in your compartment."

Sharon laughed. "Aha!" she challenged. "So you admit it's my compartment?"

"Our compartment," Scott said, grinning. Then, instinctively, he backed off.

Fortunately, she let his comment pass and Scott, relieved, took refuge in his drink. Sharon, he noted, appeared to have become lost in her own thoughts, which gave him the opportunity to study her over the rim of his glass.

She had an interesting face, pretty and unique. Her green eyes slanted in a way that gave her a slightly elfin quality, though she certainly was not a pixie type. Her high cheekbones accented the slant of her eyes, and her other facial features were well-defined and firm. She had potentially beautiful hair, though the way she was wearing it now didn't do much for her. And, from what he'd observed as they'd lurched through the train together on their way to the club car, she had an excellent figure.

She was an attractive woman, definitely intriguing. But regardless of her attributes, Scott didn't want to share his space on this train with her.

It was rotten luck that this had happened. He hadn't been on a train since he was a kid, when he'd traveled with his father from New York to Chicago. This trip was to have been special in a number of ways. A nostalgia trek, admittedly, but much more than that. This was a chance to be totally alone for twenty-six hours, during which time Scott hoped to start putting his act together again.

The parts were still not all there. The things that had happened to him, happened too quickly. No man, he thought wryly, should have to recuperate—at the same time—from the breakup of a messy marriage and career-threatening surgery.

The divorce was final. This past week in New York with his wife and her lawyers had assured that. The outcome of his surgery wasn't nearly as definite. It would be several months before the people in charge knew for sure whether or not he'd be able to fly again.

The thought that at thirty-four he might have to give up forever the thing he loved doing most was... traumatic. Nevertheless, he knew he'd have to get used to the feeling of being grounded—for now, anyway— and to being a bachelor, after many long years of marriage to Claudia. Neither was easy.

Musing about that, Scott noticed that though he'd already downed most of his drink, Sharon Williams had scarcely touched hers. From Scott's viewpoint, that was entirely to the good. He'd had enough of women drinking too much, with Claudia. Claudia, who could never come home from a party sober.

Remembering this, he wished he could throw away all his negative recollections of his wife and keep only the happy memories. Unfortunately, those happy memories were of times so far in the past they'd long ago been eclipsed. That June afternoon when he'd married Claudia under the blazing Colorado sun, the day after his graduation from the Air Force Academy, could have been in another life. Twelve years had passed since that day when he'd honestly believed he and Claudia were embarking on a journey together where they'd live happily ever after.

The first two years, Scott recalled, had been blissful enough. The next four had been indifferent. Then...the final six years had ranged from merely spending time in a mythical purgatory to being burned in the deepest recesses of hell.

Claudia's resentment of his career had passed the saturation point. She'd taken to drinking too much and to playing around with other men every time he went off on a mission. By the time they agreed, after a final blowup, that divorce was their only answer, Scott accepted that he'd been the proverbial last to know about Claudia's infidelity. Half of the Air Force, he thought bitterly, had been far better informed about his wife then he'd been.

The train slowed, and Scott came out of his reverie.

Sharon was coming out of hers, too. Glancing out the window, she said, "I think this must be Newark."

Scott nodded. "Once we're under way again, I'll go check with the conductor."

A few minutes later, with the Newark station receding behind them, he suggested, "Why don't you stay here and hold the fort while I find out what the score is?"

Sharon agreed, and watched Scott walk through the swaying club car with an ease she envied.

He was a very attractive man, and she suspected he was equally as interesting. In art, Sharon divided her available time between painting landscapes and portraits, with the accent on painting portraits. Perhaps because of that, she instinctively tended to "see deep" into people, even after only a brief acquaintance. Inevitably, she'd find herself bypassing surface appearance and outward charm in favor of what lay beneath.

Now, she was doing this again. She'd spent very little time with Scott Williams, but she was already certain of several things about him.

The lines on his handsome face revealed a past that might not have been apparent to most people, but were to Sharon. She would have sworn that something was haunting him, and this conviction needled her curiosity. Had there been a bad experience with a woman he'd cared for? Or a career problem? Or an illness? There'd definitely been something, and not too long ago. Despite his appealing smile and a polite attentiveness she imagined came naturally to him, Sharon detected some very deep shadows darkening Scott Williams's world.

Finishing her drink, she fished the cherry out of the bottom of the glass and ate it. The club car was beginning to fill up, and the waiter stopped by to ask if they'd want another round. Somewhat abstractedly, for she was still thinking about Scott, Sharon nodded.

Finally, he slid into the seat opposite hers. Sharon saw that he looked perturbed, and her heart sank. "No hope?" she queried.

"Not a prayer," he answered tersely.

"So, what do we do?" She tried to inject a light touch. "Draw straws, maybe?"

The waiter brought the second round of drinks. When Scott looked at his glass in surprise, Sharon said quickly, "I ordered them."

"Fine."

Scott took a healthy swig of his Scotch before vocalizing an idea that had been germinating in his mind. "Look, this will probably sound crazy to you, but the fact is, I'm bushed. I suppose I could spend the night here in the club car, but that's not a happy thought. I have no desire to get drunk, nor to listen to the sad tales of people who've already gotten drunk. I don't want to get up a foursome to play poker, or try to read a book when I'd be so bleary-eyed I couldn't see straight."

He drew a long breath. "I'm not saying this very well," he admitted, "but...there *is* space for two in that compartment. I could take the upper berth and you could take the lower berth. We'd both get some privacy and, hopefully, could sleep in the bargain.''

He looked across at her, his blue eyes darkening, his expression strained. "Couldn't we share the room?"

There was a long pause before Sharon blurted, "Are you out of your mind?"

Scott grinned, and there was something very boyish and appealing about him as he said, "I hope not." He hesitated, then stated, "Believe me, Sharon, all I want is a bed for the night."

"It's not that I don't believe you, Scott. It's just . . . well, I hardly know you."

"I'm aware of that, and . . . I don't really know you, either."

Despite herself, Sharon was amused. Scott, she had to concede, was refreshingly forthright. She said with a smile, "I suppose that's true enough."

He smiled back at her. "So," he commented easily, "we'd both be taking a chance."

The expression in his deep blue eyes told Sharon he was teasing. She felt a sudden impulse to go along with him, but her natural caution held her back. She said seriously, "To be truthful, Scott, I'd be uncomfortable with an arrangement like that. Nothing personal, of course," she added, as lightly as she could.

"No?" he shot back, and was gratified when she flushed.

"Look," she temporized. "I don't mind sitting up in the club car. I brought along a good book—"

"Don't be ridiculous!" Scott interrupted. "Do you really think I'd consider having you sit up while I sleep in the lap of luxury?"

Sharon smiled impishly. "I'm not sure you'd be in the lap of luxury," she told him. "Trains do jounce around in the night, you know."

"No, I don't know. It's been a long time since I last rode on a train. Regardless of that, if we can't share, the compartment is all yours."

Sharon tried to bite back a giggle just a shade too late. She realized that the second drink was getting to her, and she wished she'd asked the waiter to bring some tortilla chips, pretzels, anything she could have munched on to offset the effect of the alcohol.

She was aware that Scott was watching her very closely, the expression in his eyes so intense that yet another giggle bubbled forth. Mischievously, she accused, "I can hear your armor clanking."

"What?"

"Your armor," she repeated. "Looks good on you, too. So does that white horse you're riding."

Scott studied her closely, then got the allusion. So, he was coming on like a knight in shining armor. Scott Williams, who'd long since declared chivalry dead and buried!

The concept was interesting, but something else struck him. Something considerably more important.

Sharon was getting tipsy.

The distaste that soured Scott's mouth was automatic. Long ago, Claudia had turned him off women who lost control when they drank. He vividly remembered her escapades at too many of the military functions he'd taken her to, occasions when an officer was apt to be noticed, if not judged, by the behavior of his wife.

He reminded himself sharply that Sharon Williams was not Claudia. It was unfair to judge her in the same light. Nevertheless, he wished he wasn't seeing this side of her.

She smiled at him—she did have a beautiful smile—and said lightly, "Hey, I've solved the problem."

Scott was still tasting his own bitterness. With an effort, he forced a weak smile and queried politely, "You have?"

Sharon nodded solemnly. "We can switch. You can have the bedroom part of the time and I'll stay here in the club car. Then we'll change places."

"Every hour, every two hours, or every four?" Scott asked casually, submerging both his memories and his fears.

She laughed. "Well, I don't know," she admitted.

"I do know," Scott stated. "And *you* should know you wouldn't have a minute's peace in here by yourself. There are quite a few men traveling by themselves. Most would take just one look at you, and you wouldn't be alone any longer."

Sharon's face twisted skeptically, but Scott knew that what he was saying was true.

A few wisps of Sharon's beautiful coppery hair had escaped the confining bun, the tendrils curling against her milky white neck. There was a sprinkling of freckles across her nose, a nose that begged to be kissed. Scott averted his eyes from the freckles and found himself focusing elsewhere. Sharon's bulky gray sweater only hinted at what must lie beneath it, but he envisioned upthrust breasts as creamy white as those portions of her skin already visible. And the vision was incredibly erotic.

He swallowed hard and took a hasty sip of his drink, suppressing images that had no place in his consciousness. The last thing he needed at this stage in his life was involvement with a woman...especially a woman who had a low tolerance for alcohol.

He made a decision, and clipped it out as he would a military order. "Let's go back to the bedroom," he said brusquely.

Sharon had been feeling surprisingly relaxed with him, but his tone and request brought her up short. Trying to fathom what caused the change in him, she murmured, "That wouldn't solve anything."

"It might," Scott disagreed. "Once we're back in the compartment, I'll get hold of the conductor again. He'll have to come up with something, even if it means giving up his own bed. I presume he has a place on this train where he can put his head."

A memory flashed, and Scott couldn't repress a grin. He hadn't intended to tell Sharon this, but now he found himself saying, "Frankly, I have a feeling the conductor thinks we're putting this on."

"Putting what on?"

"I think he thinks we're married, and that we've had a fight," Scott informed her. "Without actually coming out and saying so, he inferred that we should make up and leave him in peace."

Sharon frowned. "I don't think we should leave him with that...delusion," she said coldly. "We'd better both speak to him." She pushed back her chair and got to her feet as she spoke, and only then did she realize how unsteady she was.

The train was lurching, she was swaying. She thought of the long safari back to car 714 and knew it would take all the self-control she could muster to make the trek without falling flat on her face. Scott, she sensed, knew it, too. He was right behind her as she wove her way up the aisle of the club car, trying not to clutch at every chair she passed.

By the time they reached the first of the treacherous stretches between cars, Sharon was afire with chagrin and embarrassment. And, despite her best efforts, she swerved.

Her arms were instantly grasped by two strong hands. Scott urged, "Take it easy."

"I . . . I'm giddy," Sharon confessed.

"So I noticed."

He tried not to sound condemnatory, but knew he'd failed when he felt Sharon stiffen.

"I'm all right," she said, her voice quavering slightly. "I can manage on my own."

Her message was clear, and Scott reluctantly let go of her, even though he felt it might be a mistake. It was. At once, Sharon swayed and had to grip for the metal handle fastened to the wall of the next car.

"Please," Scott said more gently. "Let me help you, okay?"

Sharon was brimming with resentment, working herself toward outrage, but the gentleness in his tone reached her. Still, she wasn't mollified, yet she had the sense to know that she didn't have too many viable options if she hoped to make it back to car 714 successfully.

Scott felt her tense again as he placed a hand on her shoulder. He wished he'd been a little kinder—at least in his thoughts about her. He reminded himself that there could be extenuating circumstances to just about everything.

The journey through the train proved to be exhausting for Sharon, and by the time they reached bedroom four, she was more than ready to collapse into the cushioned seat by the window.

"Excuse me, will you?" she said shakily. "I need to close my eyes for a minute."

Watching her narrowly, Scott was alarmed by her pallor and her obvious weariness. Maybe something had happened to her that had tired her out, he reasoned. Or maybe she'd downed those drinks on an empty stomach.

He started to ask her if she'd like to have Thomas Chalmers bring her a sandwich or coffee, but he was too late. Sharon had already pillowed her head against the back of the seat and folded her hands against her cheek like an innocent child. In fact, she had fallen fast asleep!

Time passed. Scott sat stiffly in the other seat and dozed a little himself. Then there was a discreet knock at the door. He glanced quickly at Sharon, but she didn't even stir.

"It's open," he said softly.

Thomas Chalmers the Third peered in. "You folks had dinner yet?" he asked quietly.

Scott shook his head and motioned for silence. Then he got up, stepped out into the corridor and closed the door behind him.

"Your wife asleep?" the attendant queried.

Scott nodded, not denying the relationship.

"Well, maybe it's best you should wake her up," Thomas Chalmers advised. "They'll only be serving in the dining car for the next thirty minutes or so."

Hearing this, Scott realized he'd dozed off for longer than he'd thought. "Thank you, I'll do that," he agreed.

"While you're eating, I can fix up the beds if you'd like," Thomas Chalmers suggested. "Just be careful if you use that upper berth. Make sure and strap yourself in tight. It's okay when we're traveling straight, but when the train goes around a curve you can fly right out," he concluded, graphically demonstrating the flying process with his hands and body.

"I'll be careful," Scott promised.

He spent a final moment trying to think things through clearly, while Thomas Chalmers patiently awaited his decision. Then, knowing that he was casting a considerable die, he said, "Yes, go ahead and make up the bunks while we're having our dinner."

CHAPTER TWO

SHARON WAS SLEEPY but sober as she and Scott made their way toward the dining car. She negotiated the tricky between-car stretches herself this time, ignoring the loud clacking of the train's wheels and grasping the metal safety bars to help keep her balance.

She didn't want Scott to think that she again needed his assistance, and yet, paradoxically, she found herself wanting to lean on him, wanting his touch. Her memory of their earlier safari back from the club car was somewhat hazy, but she knew his strong hands on her shoulders had felt good. Very good. His nearness and warmth . . . his scent.

Sharon blinked and forced herself to concentrate on the task at hand, as she still felt shaky. Part of her problem, she knew, stemmed from the fact that she'd been eating too little of late, and working too much. She'd wanted to leave things in the best possible shape for Gary Freeman, knowing there was a chance that she just might not go back to work for him. But as a result of her overtime hours, her energy level was presently at an all-time low.

For the umpteenth time, she chided herself for ordering a second drink and then polishing it off much too quickly, knowing herself as she did.

The dining car served meals "buffet style," which proved to be a euphemism for cafeteria service. A steam table was presided over by a chef wearing a towering white hat. Salads and desserts, fruit juices and small bottles of wine were kept in refrigerated cabinets. Sharon meticulously bypassed the wine.

Waiters conveyed the food-laden trays to the tables, which was fortunate. Sharon could easily imagine the mess she might make were she obliged to carry her tray herself!

The decor in the dining car was cinnamon and beige. The tables, all seating four, were covered with beige plastic cloths, and a yellow silk rose in a small vase was placed in the center of each. Though this was the last call for dinner, quite a few people were still eating.

After setting Sharon's tray on a vacant table, the waiter pulled out the chair by the window for her. Then, Scott's tray was placed next to hers. When Scott indicated he would prefer the opposite window seat the waiter stated, politely but firmly, "If you don't mind, sir, we're crowded tonight and the tables must be shared. So we would appreciate it if couples sit side by side."

Again, Sharon was forcibly made aware of Scott's proximity. He was very close to her. So close, it was impossible not to bump elbows as they ate.

After a particularly jolting nudge, Scott laughed. "Tight quarters, I'd say," he commented dryly.

"Yes," Sharon agreed, awkwardly trying to slice her chicken filet without jabbing him.

She poked him anyway, and gritted her teeth. It was ridiculous, but she couldn't relax with Scott so near. She was sure her face looked flushed. She actually felt hot. She tried to put down her reaction to her recent embarrassment over the drinks that had gone to her head. And she wondered how long she would keep cringing at the idea of how silly Scott must have thought her!

Still, honesty compelled Sharon to admit that it wasn't only chagrin evoking this flustered feeling. A lot of it could be attributed directly to Scott himself. She had a tingling awareness of him. He made her feel the way she did in spring, when she watched the trees budding after their long, dormant winter. She'd gone through an emotionally dormant winter herself—several, actually—and it was a shock to realize she could feel so...stimulated. Especially about someone she'd just met, and by chance at that.

Abruptly, she asked, "Did you speak to the conductor again?"

Scott looked at her blankly. "About what?"

"You said if he couldn't find a place for you, you'd take his bed," she recalled.

It was time for the moment of truth, but Scott wasn't ready. He drained the last of his coffee, saw that Sharon had finished eating, and muttered, "Look, Sharon, let's go back to the compartment. Everything will work out, I promise."

The train was moving at a real clip now. Cautiously, they headed in the direction of car 714. Sharon cast ego aside and accepted Scott's guiding hand on her arm. It was good to know that if she started to fall, he'd catch her.

When they finally reached bedroom four, Scott pushed the door open. He stood back to let Sharon precede him into the room, but she took only a single step before she stopped, thunderstruck.

A transformation had been effected while they were at dinner. A lower berth, made up with crisp white linen, occupied the space where the two seats had been. Above it, an upper berth had been swung down into place. A ladder was hooked to one end of the berth, for easier ascent, and both carryon bags, bearing those telltale initials SW, had been placed neatly together on the floor.

Bedroom four was, indeed, now a bedroom. The small compartment was even smaller with the bunks in place. For Sharon, at least, the intimacy created was shocking.

She turned to Scott, sputtering her words. "You'll have to call the attendant, and have him . . . undo this!"

Scott stared at the bunks speechlessly, more than slightly shaken himself. He hadn't realized just how *familiar* an atmosphere would be evoked by converting the compartment from parlor to bedroom.

"Please, Scott," Sharon urged. "Ring the bell for Mr. What's-his-name, and tell him he's made a mistake."

Scott shook his head. "No," he corrected gravely. "He hasn't made a mistake."

"I don't understand. What are you saying?"

"I asked him to make the beds up."

"You *asked* him to make the beds up?" Sharon couldn't believe what she was hearing. Affronted, she demanded coldly, "Don't you think you should have consulted me?"

"I would have, but you'd fallen asleep."

"Regardless, you had no right to take things in your own hands this way!"

"That's true," Scott admitted. "But honestly, Sharon, I didn't have much choice. I couldn't see any other practical route to follow. I know you wanted your own compartment, but so did I. And . . . here we are. The train's booked to capacity. There's nothing we can do about it. Fortunately, I'd say we're compatible."

Sharon's glance bristled with suspicion.

Scott quickly continued, "We *are* both adults, you know. Responsible adults. Certainly we can respect each other's right of privacy. I can take the upper berth, you can take the lower one. There's no reason why we should get in each other's way.''

Sharon hesitated. There was such a thing as protesting too much. Also, she was beginning to see that there was no point in making a federal case over this. Common sense told her Scott's logic was sound. To add to that, she was very tired. She had no desire to move another inch until she'd had some rest.

Reluctantly, she conceded, ''You may be right.''

''Definitely, I'm right.''

Scott smiled, a self-mocking, crooked smile that was very endearing. ''Maybe we could persuade the conductor to stop at the next station long enough so you can call my mother,'' he suggested. ''She lives in Chicago, and I guarantee she'd give me a sterling character reference. And then there's my brother. He's an architect in Los Angeles. I think he'd say some fairly decent things about me, though you never know about brothers.''

Despite herself, Sharon laughed.

''If you want to check up on me,'' she ventured, deciding to play the same game, ''you could call my twin sister Diane, in Miami. She's the person I'm going to visit.''

''I'm sure we'd both come up with top-notch references,'' Scott assured her. Turning practical, he added, ''Our bathroom, as you've probably observed, isn't big enough to undress in comfortably. So why don't I wait in the corridor while you get ready for bed, okay?''

Sharon nodded agreeably. But while she was slipping out of her clothes and into her lace-trimmed lilac satin nightgown, she was painfully conscious that Scott was standing only a few feet away on the other side of the door to bedroom four.

She washed her face, then took down her hair and brushed it. Finally, her nerves on edge, she dove for the sanctuary of the lower berth and called out, "Your turn."

She snuggled under the blankets as Scott opened the door and squeezed into the room. She had her reading light on and her book in hand, but the blanket didn't cover the nightgown's lacy straps. Nor did it hide a beautiful, creamy portion of Sharon herself.

Scott noticed this, and drew in his breath sharply. In these cramped surroundings, there was no way he could avoid looking at her. She'd washed off the little bit of makeup she used and, *au naturel*, she was especially lovely. As for her hair, it was dazzling.

Scott briefly used the bathroom. Then he approached the berths thinking, with each step, that this was the way a moth must feel being drawn to a flame. He smiled awkwardly and said, "Well, I'll be off for the upper regions."

"Take care," Sharon said lightly, her pulse pounding.

"You, too," Scott replied huskily.

He climbed up the ladder and, maneuvering like a giant in a playpen, managed to undress down to his shorts. Then he piled his clothing at the far end of his bunk and slid his long length under the covers. Lastly, he fastened the belt that supposedly would keep him from falling into space during the night.

He couldn't remember when he'd felt more weary. But now that the moment had arrived when he might actually relax and get some sleep, Scott found himself wide awake . . . and overwhelmingly conscious of the woman occupying the berth just under his.

He knew almost nothing about her, except that she had a twin sister named Diane in Miami. Still, she'd made a deep impression on him.

His lips tightened and his face was grim as he considered this. He wouldn't have believed that a woman—any woman—could have left more than the most ephemeral touch on him just now. He was admittedly gun-shy. Even a casual involvement was the last thing in God's world he wanted!

Scott was reminding himself of that as he drifted off to sleep. Yet it was Sharon, rather than the problems he'd intended to cope with, who invaded his dreams and occupied the fantasy corners of his mind.

Toward dawn, with a dim gray light infiltrating bedroom four, a sudden loud noise made Scott sit bolt upright so suddenly he bumped his head on the low ceiling. He swore softly and was rubbing his head when he heard Sharon exclaim, "Good grief!"

Peering over the edge of the berth, he saw her standing in the middle of the small floor space still left in bedroom four. From this vantage point, he had an intoxicating view of her. Clearly visible was the rise and fall of her chest and the creamy swell of her breasts inside the nightgown's deep vee. The satin clung to her, outlining her slender waist and curving hips and leaving little to the imagination. She made such a provocative picture that Scott's physical reaction was prompt and manifest.

He gritted his teeth as he tried to fight down his swelling desire. Then he asked, hoarsely, "What's the matter?"

In answer, Sharon stooped and picked up his trousers, shirt and shoes. "You dropped something," she told him.

"Damn, the train must have swung around quite a curve for that stuff to fall off," Scott marveled, and added apologetically, "Look, I'm sorry this woke you up."

Unexpectedly, Sharon grinned. "Take it easy," she said, holding up his possessions to him. "No problem."

Once he'd grasped them, she climbed back into her berth. Then she realized the picture she must have made standing there in her nightgown, and suddenly felt hot all over. She'd seen Scott's face only dimly in the gray dawn light, but she'd felt his eyes on her and was sure he hadn't missed a single detail.

Jerry had never missed anything, either, she remembered sadly. Like Scott Williams, Jerry had been alert, sure of himself . . . and always ready to take a chance. In that, she suspected the two men differed. She couldn't imagine Scott being possessed of Jerry's brand of restlessness. He seemed too controlled a person.

She and Jerry, she mused, had been so totally different. Sometimes it seemed strange to think that she'd fallen so deeply in love with him. And even more strange that the love had endured as it had.

Jerry had been ten years older than Sharon; she'd been twenty-one when they married, and he'd been almost thirty-one. It had come naturally to him to take the lead in their relationship, and she'd gone along with that— she'd pretty much let him control their lives. Now she sometimes wondered what their marriage would have been like had she been more assertive. Had she insisted, for example, that they settle down and buy a house that could become the kind of a permanent home base she'd always wanted.

Jerry, though, had been such a free spirit. He'd never stayed chained to anything for very long, and with his carefree nature, outgoing personality and zest for life, things had always come easily to him. Jobs, for instance. Sharon had learned to expect that six months was the longest she could ever hope Jerry to remain happy in a job. Then he'd begin to get restless, complaining that the challenge had gone out of his work.

Inevitably, he'd be offered something else, something that would become an instant lure. Jerry would come home, full of an excitement that could be very contagious. And, even though she knew she'd once again be turning her back on the kind of permanence she wanted so much in her life, Sharon would begin to pack up china and glassware and get their things together so they could move to wherever this latest "opportunity" beckoned.

Through the five years of their marriage, life with Jerry had been exciting. Sharon couldn't deny that. They'd ridden on a constant merry-go-round with Jerry always reaching for the brass ring. Many times he'd come close to grabbing it, teasingly close. He'd made enough money for them to get by on—usually—but never enough so they could rid themselves of all their debts and stash away something for the future.

As it turned out, the span of Jerry's future had been so limited.

Pain still twisted when Sharon thought about that. She'd shared a lot with Jerry, but one thing she'd never embraced was his love of flying. She especially disliked small planes. And when Jerry went out on a financial limb after they moved to Rhode Island, and bought half interest in a Cessna with a friend, they'd come close to having a real battle.

In the end Jerry won, and Sharon had felt downright cruel about trying to dampen his wonderful enthusiasm. Still, each time he insisted she go up with him became an ordeal. And they only got worse instead of better. She'd be trembling as she climbed into the cockpit, and violently shaking by the time they touched down on firm ground.

More often than not on those aerial excursions with Jerry, she'd become nauseated. Eventually, this really annoyed him, and she couldn't blame him. Jerry was a natural-born flyer, in his element in the sky. It was difficult for him to understand that not everyone shared his love for that pursuit.

Finally, after a year of these episodes, Jerry began to accept the excuses she'd made when he asked her to "visit the sky," as he liked to say. But for that, she would have been with him in the air that day in Newport, instead of on the ground waiting....

Sharon shivered, pushing away her memories, and forced herself to concentrate on the scenes emerging with daylight outside her window. They crossed a bridge over the pewter waters of a swollen river. Then, from earlier trips south with her parents and Diane, she recognized the spreading silhouettes of pecan trees etched against the charcoal-clouded sky. She saw cotton fields left fallow through the winter, occasional clumps of white still clinging to the plants. Low growing, spiky palmettos edged the railroad bed, reminding Sharon of the fronds passed out in church on Palm Sunday. And Spanish moss rimed the tree branches with trailing, silver-gray wisps.

They were really in the deep South now, judging from what she was seeing. Probably South Carolina, possibly Georgia.

There wasn't a sound emanating from the upper berth. Apparently Scott had fallen asleep again. Sharon, wide awake, took advantage of the opportunity to get up, use the tiny bathroom, and dress. She put on the same plaid skirt she'd worn yesterday, but teamed it with a lighter, lavender sweater.

She was reclining on her bunk, reading, when she heard Scott stir. "Sharon?" he asked in a very low voice.

"Yes," she answered softly.

"Just wanted to be sure you're conscious."

A minute later, after an obvious struggle to get into his clothes, Scott climbed down the ladder and stood before her. His dark hair was mussed and, running a hand over the stubble on his chin, he muttered, "Guess I need a shave."

Sharon couldn't possibly have answered that. She'd never seen a man who looked as sexy as Scott did, rumpled but magnificently masculine, a lazy sleepiness still clouding his deep blue eyes. It was all she could do not to stare at him in wonder.

She tried focusing her attention on her book, but to no avail. Her concentration had been completely shot down by Scott. Then, when he emerged a few minutes later freshly shaven, he smelled of an after-shave lotion that could have done double duty as an aphrodisiac.

Sharon inadvertently held her breath as he asked cheerily, "Ready for breakfast?"

"Sure," she managed, seeking any diversion—any action—that would help get her mind off him.

It was early, and the dining car was uncrowded. This time, Scott sat opposite Sharon before the waiter could spell out the preferred seating arrangements. Glancing at the overcast sky outside, he observed, "Looks like the sun's waiting for the Florida border."

"Looks like," Sharon echoed lamely. She was thinking that she'd just spent the night in the same room as this handsome stranger, and had been treated with the utmost respect. She couldn't decide whether his deference toward her was a plus or a minus!

He stirred cream into his coffee, then asked, "Are you going to be in Miami very long?"

"Probably a month, maybe more."

"You said you'll be visiting your twin sister?"

"That's right."

"Are you identical twins?"

Sharon chuckled. "Yes, but you'd never know it. I mean, we look alike, though not as much as we did when we were younger. Our styles, though, are so different that more often than not people don't realize we're sisters."

"Diane, wasn't it?" Scott queried.

"Yes, that's right."

"Is Diane in Miami for winter warmth, or does she live there?"

"She's lived in Miami—Miami Beach, actually—for the past four years," Sharon told him. After a moment's thought, she added hesitantly, "She and her husband are waiting for their divorce to be finalized."

"I see," Scott murmured. The subject of divorce was still painful to him, and he didn't want to get into a discussion of either his own divorce or anyone else's.

"Tony, my brother-in-law, owns a nightclub in a small hotel on Collins Avenue," Sharon continued. "Evidently it's become a very popular spot. And Diane . . . Diane's in the real estate business, and I gather doing quite well." She paused. "Are you going to Miami on business, or is this a vacation?"

He settled for some of the truth, but not all. "As it happens," he said, "I'm convalescing from surgery. For the next few months, I've been told to take it easy."

"Really?" Sharon asked, her apprehension showing.

"Yes." *Only then,* he thought silently, *will I know whether I'll ever be able to live life fully again, and fly.*

He couldn't imagine life without flying. He'd always loved being airborne, ever since the first time he'd gone up in his older brother's small plane. He'd been in his early teens and Hugh had let him handle the controls, guiding him along and only taking over when it came time to make the approach for a landing.

Funny, but he'd thought Hugh would be the one to become an Air Force pilot. Instead, Hugh had chosen architecture for his career, and had kept flying as a hobby.

It was Scott who'd aimed for the Air Force Academy, and the day he'd received his appointment had been the high mark of his life. He'd been eighteen and just out of high school. Within days he'd flown to Colorado and embarked on an air cadet's strict training. Later, there'd been pilot school, and the accompanying shock of seeing many of his classmates wash out—sometimes for what appeared to be extremely trivial reasons.

Many types of perfection were required of a jet pilot, he'd realized soberly. Not only physical perfection, but a special blend of coordination, superb reflexes and steady nerves that weren't apt to fray under pressure. The list went on. And Scott met all the requirements.

There'd been no conceit in Scott in meeting those standards. He'd only been grateful that he was possessed of the necessary attributes enabling him to do what he wanted more than anything else.

Ever since, he'd flown. He'd been stationed around the world, most recently at a base in England. There, he'd been tested to the maximum—called upon to fly several controversial missions about which he'd personally felt ambivalent. The truth of the old axiom, "Yours is not to question why, yours is but to do and die,'' had been forced home to him. But like any professional, like any career officer, he'd done what was required of him when the necessity for doing so had risen.

Now, quite suddenly, there was better than a fifty-fifty chance his flying days were over. Worse, he wouldn't know the verdict for at least three months, when he had the first of two all-important physicals.

All of this flashed through Scott's mind while he watched the speculation in Sharon's eyes. He knew she was trying to find a way of framing her questions without appearing too inquisitive, so he bailed her out. "My problem was something called 'acoustic neuroma.'"

"I have no idea what that might be," Sharon admitted.

"I wouldn't expect you to," he said lightly. "I'd never heard of it myself, until one day I had it!"

He doubted he'd ever forget the first episode. It happened in England, right after his return from one of those special missions he'd flown. He was taking a shower. Suddenly, without warning, he'd felt so dizzy he'd nearly fallen. Unnerved, he'd groped his way to his bed, dizziness mixing with nausea as he sank back against the pillows.

Once the spell passed, he tried to imagine why it had happened. He'd been under a lot of strain recently, he realized, both professionally and personally, with Claudia. But that was nothing new, so he put the episode down to something he'd eaten that had disagreed with him, then blocked it out of his mind.

A couple of weeks later, it happened again. This time, he'd just returned from a routine flight and was in his office filling out a report when dizziness struck. It had been all he could do to camouflage what he was experiencing and leave the base. But beyond the gates, at the wheel of his sports car, he'd known that if he tried to continue driving he would lose control and crash.

He'd pulled over to the side of the road until the spell passed. Then, shakily, he'd driven to his flat a couple of miles away, knowing he couldn't pretend that this wasn't happening.

The next morning, Scott consulted a doctor on the base. That had been the beginning. Test after test followed—first at a hospital in England, then at Walter Reed Hospital in Washington. There, surgery was performed by an astute young Cuban-American neurologist who was finishing his surgical residency as an Army captain, paying back the government for the medical school scholarship he'd been advanced.

He'd been Ricardo Fabrega's last patient at the massive Army medical complex, Scott remembered. While he was still a bed patient, Rick had finished his stint in the service and had returned to his home in Miami.

Because of Rick Fabrega—whom he'd liked and trusted from day one—Scott had put in for temporary assignment at Homestead Air Force Base just south of Miami, where he would be on very limited duty for several months. The powers that be in the Pentagon apparently had been glad to grant his request. During this time in limbo, he thought cynically, they were probably happy to have him within hailing distance of the surgeon who'd done the operation.

Suddenly, he became sharply aware of Sharon. She was looking at him in an odd way, her beautiful green eyes hazy. He had the feeling he'd lost her in a reverie of her own, and not a happy one.

He said apologetically, "I'm sorry. I just got to thinking, that's all."

"If you don't want to talk about ... whatever it is, Scott, I'll understand."

Was he right in sensing that she didn't want him to say more? That she didn't want to be involved in his problems? He couldn't blame her, if that was the case. Hell, she hardly knew him!

"There's really not that much to talk about," he decided. "My problem involved the inner ear, and it's been surgically corrected. There isn't even any hearing loss, and with a little more time to recuperate I'll be good as new."

The clouds vanished from Sharon's lovely eyes, and a genuine smile transformed the gentle curves of her mouth. "I'm glad to hear that," she said. "And I must say, you certainly look the picture of health."

"Do I, now?" He grinned.

Scott liked the way his teasing flustered her. He liked *her*, and the honest friendship that had been building between them on this unusual trip south. And he knew, quite suddenly, that he wanted to see her again in Miami. He wanted them to have the chance to know each other better. Because even though the mere idea scared the hell out of him, these vibes between them, incessant as twanging harp strings, were too persistent to ignore.

CHAPTER THREE

THE TRAIN, once it passed Jacksonville, virtually became a local, wending its way through central Florida and stopping at almost every station along the way before veering over to the east coast.

This induced a lazy, vacation atmosphere. Looking out the window at each stop, Sharon saw pale people in winter clothes disembarking, greeted by tanned people in summer clothes. Watching their hugs and kisses and seeing mouths form words she couldn't hear was like viewing a pantomime.

These touching scenes made her feel lonely. Diane would be meeting her in Miami, but she and Tony were divorcing. There'd be no feeling of family unity at Diane's house in Miami Beach, and Sharon sighed. Since their mother's death from cancer five years ago, their father had remarried. He and his new wife—many years his junior—lived in San Diego. So there was no sense of family there, either.

She should have been brought up in a two-hundred-year-old house in a family of ten kids, Sharon thought wistfully. Then, perhaps, she would have had enough togetherness.

Or, if Jerry and I had had a child...

With the self-discipline she'd learned during the three years since Jerry had been killed, Sharon shut off that line of thought.

The train was between stations, traveling at a relatively slow speed compared to the hurtling rate that had caused Scott's clothing to tumble from his berth near dawn. Again, Sharon tried to concentrate on the book she'd been attempting to read throughout this trip, and again she couldn't get past a few pages. Thoughts of Scott kept forcing their way between her eyes and the printed words.

He'd headed off to the club car in search of a pre-lunch Bloody Mary. She'd declined his invitation to go along with him, telling him she wanted to read for a while and maybe snooze a little.

Those were valid excuses, but there'd been a much stronger reason, not expressed. She needed space from Scott, simple physical separation. They'd had so much proximity at this point that Sharon felt saturated with him in a peculiar yet pleasantly intoxicating way. Also, all the small things that had happened between them were beginning to be impossible to wash out of her system. Not that she wanted to do that, but . . .

The scent of his after-shave lingered in the air. When Sharon closed her eyes, she had the crazy feeling that Scott's handsome face had been sketched in the front of her mind and threatened to become permanently engraved there. It was like pulling down a movie screen, then projecting an image. She could mentally trace the shape of his face, the arch of his eyebrows, the curve of his mouth—a mouth that tended to quirk slightly upward whenever he was annoyed or amused.

She saw his eyes, as deep blue as a mountain lake. She remembered the feel of his touch on her arm as he'd guided her through the train, the way he'd held her when they'd negotiated the tricky areas between the cars. She missed that small, personal contact with him, she admitted, shivering a little. She missed him!

Sharon faced this fact with considerable dismay, especially as it dawned on her that in a few hours they'd literally be reaching the end of the line. They'd go their separate ways in Miami, and...

The subject of her daydreams appeared before her so suddenly, Sharon blinked. She felt as if she'd rubbed an Aladdin's lamp, and the genie had promptly granted her wish.

Scott glanced over her shoulder at the passing countryside and commented, "It's turned into a real Florida day, hasn't it?"

"Yes, it has," Sharon agreed, following his gaze.

The sun had finally asserted itself, and the day was gold and blue, all sunlight and sky. There wasn't much breeze, Sharon realized. The fronds on the ever-present palms stood out in sharp, tropical silhouette. But a good bit of the scenery really wasn't that attractive. As they approached another town, the view became one of backyards and vacant lots. Then the rear of a shopping center went by, followed by the alley side of scattered buildings along a main business street.

Scott observed, "When you travel by train you really see behind the scenes, don't you? I hadn't realized that."

"Not very pretty, is it?" Sharon murmured, still reacting to his sudden appearance, still concentrating mostly on him.

He glanced at his sleek chrome wristwatch and frowned. "We're crawling," he complained. "I think I could walk faster!" Sharon chuckled, and he added, "I was looking at the timetable again in the club car. Did you know the name of this train is the *Silver Comet*?"

"Quite the misnomer, I'd say."

"Isn't it, though?" He sat down awkwardly, trying to find a comfortable position for his long legs. "I'm beginning to feel like a pretzel," he joked. Then he asked, "How do you suppose they ever decided on that title for this train?"

"Oh, to give the illusion of speed, probably."

"Well, we're not exactly streaking along the ground, to say nothing of the sky."

"As long as we stay on the ground, that's all I care about," Sharon responded, her voice tightening despite herself. Thinking of *anything* streaking through the sky transported her back to that summer day at the airport in Newport where she'd stood, screaming, as she'd watched Jerry's plane plummet earthward, to crash and explode in flames....

She shook herself, mentally and physically. "I'm sorry," she said weakly. "I was thinking of something else."

Scott stared at Sharon, appalled. For a frightening instant there'd been a strange, glazed look to her eyes, and she'd turned so pale he was afraid she might pass out on him. He asked tightly, "Do you suppose you could tell me what brought *that* on?"

Sharon glanced across at him, still shaken. Scott demanded gently but anxiously, "Are you all right?" When she nodded, he urged, "Please, tell me. What came over you to make you look like that?"

She moistened her lips and said, "My husband was killed in a plane crash three years ago, Scott. I was waiting on the ground...I saw him crash." She paused, trying not to relive the whole thing for perhaps the thousandth time. She finished quietly, "Since then, I hate the thought of anything streaking through the sky. I hate planes...I hate flying."

Scott froze, overwhelmed with shock. Inadvertently, he shut his eyes, blotting out a traumatic memory of his own. One of his best friends had been killed in a plane crash. He'd watched the accident from the air—he was right behind Tim's jet, scheduled to land next—and knew all too well the terrible, helpless agony Sharon had endured.

There'd been a couple of other incidents, but witnessing Tim's death had been the worst. Thinking about it still made Scott feel rocky.

That feeling slowly passed, though, as Sharon's proclamation echoed in his head.

"I hate the thought of anything streaking through the sky. I hate planes... I hate flying."

Few other things she might have said could have been more devastating to Scott. Sharon reached for a handkerchief and, as he watched, she wiped a tear from the corner of her eye.

Shakily, she asked, "Did you have your Bloody Mary?"

He respected her valiant effort to change the subject, and shook his head. "I decided on another cup of coffee," he said. "Look, they're serving lunch by now. Are you hungry?" He certainly wasn't hungry, he thought wryly, but he had to get out of this compartment. He had to physically leave.

As they started back toward the dining car, Scott knew one thing was obvious. Wisdom was dictating that he watch what he said to Sharon for the remainder of the trip. It would be best to let her think he was going to Miami only to take it easy for a while, per doctor's orders. Eventually, of course, he would have to tell her what he did for a living. But he wanted to give her the chance to get to know him much better before he lowered that particular boom!

The *Silver Comet* fell further behind schedule as it poked its way down through Florida. Sharon and Scott ticked off the stops: Sanford, Winter Park, Orlando, Kissimmee, Winter Haven, Sebring, West Palm Beach....

"I feel like I'm back in geography class," Scott said. But his grin faded when he consulted the timetable again and discovered they were running nearly two hours late.

In the middle of the afternoon, Thomas Chalmers the Third surprised them with a complimentary basket of cheese and crackers, plus a small bottle of wine. Thomas didn't seem to be his usual self though and, perceiving this, Scott asked, "Something wrong?"

The attendant hesitated, then confided, "Well, this is initiation night at my lodge, and I'm supposed to be inducted into a high office. But the way we're going, I'm afraid I'll miss the ceremony." He added reluctantly, "Seems like we got off to a slow start this trip, and just haven't been able to catch up."

They'd been due in Miami at six o'clock, but it was slightly after eight when the *Silver Comet* crawled into the station. Passengers thronged the corridor, eager to disembark onto solid ground. As she preceded Scott out of bedroom four, Sharon was at once caught up in a mob of people. But Scott managed to squeeze in behind her, and they pressed forward slowly.

They were nearly at the exit door of car 714 when Sharon heard him mutter, "Damn it!"

She managed to look back over her shoulder, despite the fact she could hardly move. "What's the matter?"

"I can't find my wallet. I must have dropped it back in our compartment. You go on, Sharon. I'll only be a minute."

She didn't envy Scott having to make his way back to bedroom four against the traffic. She inched along toward the exit, planning to wait for him on the platform. Stepping off the train, she nearly bumped into Thomas Chalmers. The affable attendant had already doffed his uniform and had on a sharp looking Hawaiian sport shirt.

"Are you going to make it to your induction?" Sharon asked him.

Thomas flashed her a grin. "Got just enough time to get there," he stated confidently. "Nice to have met you, Mrs. Williams," he added sincerely, then strode off down the platform.

Sharon felt strangely bereft as she watched him go. He'd been such an integral part of this experience. Then, as a heavyset man carrying a briefcase jostled into her, she decided there were a few aspects of train travel she could do without. She hated crowds, and people were pressing in all around her.

Where was Scott?

She stood by car 714, irresolute. She thought of trying to buck the tide and go after Scott, but there was also the matter of remaining visible so that Diane could find her. She knew her sister planned to meet her, but the train had been so late there was a chance Diane might have decided to return home and await her call.

She hadn't. Sharon spotted her twin hurrying down the platform toward her, and briefly had the uncanny feeling of watching herself. She and Diane didn't look like exact copies of the same person, as they had when they were younger. Still, the resemblance was strong enough to make heads turn as coppery hair merged with coppery hair when they hugged.

Then a slim, dark-haired man stepped out from behind Diane, and Sharon felt a sharp twinge of déjà vu. The last person she'd expected to see here was Diane's soon to be ex-husband, Tony DeLuca.

Tony, a wide smile on his face, moved forward and clasped Sharon's hands as he kissed her cheeks. "Welcome to Miami," he greeted her.

Diane tugged Sharon's arm. "Come along," she urged. "You must be starving or dying of thirst or exhausted, or all three. I thought you'd never get here!"

Sharon started to draw back, again wondering what was taking Scott so long. The crowd was thinning out, and the section of platform between her and car 714 was quite empty. But there was no sign of her handsome companion.

"Is this all you brought?" Tony asked, relieving her of her carryon.

"Diane insisted it would make sense to travel light," she answered absently. "Anyway, I want to buy some new things . . ."

"You can always wear mine!" Diane teased.

Sharon only half heard her sister. She had about decided to go back and look for Scott, but then reasoned that she'd catch up with him inside the station. Meantime, Diane was babbling about all sorts of things in her usual excited way, and Tony was smiling at her indulgently, just as he'd always done. It seemed weird to think that these two had recently gone into court and petitioned for divorce on the grounds of irreconcilable differences.

"Tonette was dying to come meet you," Diane said as they stepped into the lobby of the station. "But she's been home with a bug the past couple of days, so I vetoed the idea. Anyway, Sylvie's with her.''

Sharon had no idea who Sylvie was, but she was sure she'd soon find out. The fragmented pieces of Diane's conversation always eventually came together to form a coherent whole.

There was still no sign of Scott as they moved through the station, which wasn't as big as Sharon expected, considering the size of the city it served. Before she knew what was happening they were walking out the front entrance and heading for the parking lot, and Tony was fishing in his jacket for his car keys.

Sharon tried desperately to think things out and reach a decision. She really didn't want to tell Diane about Scott yet, because she wasn't ready to face her twin's unbounding curiosity. Diane was a natural romantic who loved nothing better than playing matchmaker. And that, at times, could be quite irritating.

Since Diane's move to Miami a year before Jerry's death, they hadn't seen that much of each other. Mostly, this was Sharon's fault. It didn't help that she refused to fly. They'd rendezvoused twice in New York and twice in Providence. They'd also intended to visit their father and their new stepmother in San Diego, but couldn't agree on how to get there, if they were to travel together.

On the few occasions when they had met, though, Diane's matchmaking instincts had surfaced, sometimes to Sharon's embarrassment. In Providence, she'd done her utmost to bring Sharon together with Gary Freeman, ignoring all of her sister's pleas to stop.

Sharon had grown fond of Gary during the three years in which she'd worked for his printing firm. He was in his early forties, an excellent employer and a terrific person. They had a lot in common, and he'd enthusiastically encouraged her to be innovative with her designs. She was sure few places would give her such a free rein.

But with that freedom there had evolved certain problems. Gradually Sharon realized that Gary's interest in her was not entirely professional, nor was it merely friendship that he offered. Gary had been widowed for several years, and it became disturbingly clear to Sharon that he was looking for a new wife and had set his eyes on her to fill that vacancy.

There were moments when she'd come close—maybe a shade too close—to giving him the wrong idea about how she felt. Moments when she'd been lonely and tired and discontent with her solitary life. That was one reason why she'd asked for this month off, using the pretext of visiting her sister in a time of need.

Gary had been understanding. Gary was always understanding where she was concerned. He'd driven her to the railroad station in Providence to catch the train for New York, where she'd changed for the *Silver Comet*. But the expression on his face as he'd kissed her goodbye had poignantly conveyed to Sharon that her relationship with him, as well as her future career plans, were topics she had to address seriously before she returned to Rhode Island. And the reasons that she'd been so anxious to have bedroom four to herself.

Now, thinking everything over, Sharon could vividly imagine what a field day Diane would have with the whole Scott encounter. She didn't want anything to jeopardize what had happened between Scott and herself. Their train experience was still too ephemeral and, potentially, too valuable. They needed to take the next step entirely on their own.

She was beginning to wonder if there'd be a next step, at this point. Scratching her memory, she realized they'd made no definite plans about getting together in Miami. She'd somehow assumed that they would. Now, in retrospect, it seemed that their conversations—especially after her revelation to Scott about the circumstances of Jerry's death—had become increasingly impersonal.

She wondered why.

She knew she wanted to see Scott again here in Miami, and yes, she was confident he felt the same way. Turning to Diane and Tony, she said abruptly, "Would you two hold on for just a minute? There's something I have to do."

Before Diane could frame a question, Sharon hurried back toward the station. She more than half expected to find Scott waiting for her, but there were very few people lingering in the lobby, and Scott wasn't among them. Evidently the *Silver Comet* was the last train due for the night, and the station was already quieting down.

An anxious feeling clutched at Sharon's chest as she moved out onto the platform beside which the *Comet* now rested, its engines stilled.

The platform was illuminated by occasional overhead lights that cast a wan yellow glow against the deserted train and the empty baggage carts parked along its shiny metallic sides. It was an eerie scene, rather spooky and frightening... especially since Sharon was beginning to feel that she'd lost someone, and something, very important to her.

As she neared car 714, a man stepped down from its darkened interior. Scott? Sharon found herself praying that when this shadowy silhouette became substance she'd find herself looking up into Scott's wonderful face.

But it wasn't him. It was the conductor who, according to Scott, had thought they were married.

He walked slowly in Sharon's direction, tired and slightly stooped, the weird yellow light making him appear older than he was. "Looking for something, Mrs. Williams?"

"Have you see Mr. Williams?" Sharon asked him.

He quirked an odd glance at her, and she imagined he was thinking, *This is all I need. First these people drive me crazy pretending they aren't married. Now, she's lost her husband!*

He said wryly, "Guess you know someone apparently stole his wallet?"

"No, I only knew he lost it."

"Well, we couldn't find it anywhere," the conductor told her. "I got hold of a security officer, and then a friend of your husband's showed up. The three of them went off so Mr. Williams could file a report. Could be they're back in the stationmaster's office."

They weren't. Even the stationmaster had left for the night, Sharon discovered. His door was closed and locked. She felt sick, certainly in no shape to face up to Diane and Tony. Incredibly, Scott had left without a final word to her... to become swallowed up in the vastness of Miami.

Slowly, she walked out to the parking lot, her head and her heart both starting to ache.

Tony was pacing near his car, smoking a cigarette. He tossed the butt away when he saw Sharon and came toward her, smiling that affable smile of his that was such a camouflage at times.

"Diane's waiting inside the car," he said. "You know Diane. She's never learned to buy comfortable shoes."

Sharon laughed weakly, knowing Tony was right. Vanity was one character trait, if it could be called that, that she and her twin sister didn't share. Diane loved to dress up and tended to forfeit comfort in favor of style. Sharon liked to dress well, too, but preferred to be comfortable at the same time. When they'd been teenagers and their mother had encouraged them to dress alike, the result had often been a sisterly spat.

Diane was in the back seat of Tony's sleek black sedan, so Sharon didn't see her until she poked her head out the window and said, "You sit up front with Tony, okay?"

Sharon complied, and slid wearily onto the plush passenger seat. As they drove out of the parking lot, Tony said, "We're right next to Hialeah, Sharon. We'll have to take in the races while you're here."

He spoke so normally that she had to wonder if he and Diane had decided to reconcile, but hadn't gotten around to telling her yet.

This wasn't the moment to ask. She wasn't up to asking much about anything. Anyway, Tony was explaining the street numbering system in Miami, telling her how easy it was to get around. "Of course, you'll probably be spending most of your time in Miami Beach," he finished. "Which, incidentally, is a separate city with its own government."

"It's another world," Diane concurred from the shadows of the back seat.

Tony asked, "Do you want me to switch on the air-conditioning, Sharon? This must seem pretty warm to you, coming straight from the frozen north."

"No, it's fine," she said absently, then realized it was warm and quite humid. Still, her mind was on Scott, to the exclusion of minor details. She couldn't believe that he'd vanished so quickly—not merely into the night, but out of her life!

The thought that his actions might have been deliberate began nagging her. Then came the devastating realization that Scott had never asked her for either Diane's address or phone number.

Perhaps he'd quietly planned for Miami to be the end of the line, as far as she was concerned. The facts were there, but Sharon didn't want to accept the signposts Scott had constructed. Although the more she thought about this, the more it seemed that he'd constructed them quite carefully.

Tony turned from one main boulevard onto another, moving in a steady stream of fast-paced traffic. Then they were crossing a wide stretch of onyx water glittering with gold and silver from the lights of Miami's jagged skyline.

"Julia Tuttle Causeway," Tony explained. "This takes us to Miami Beach."

Sharon found a surrealistic quality to the view across Biscayne Bay. Miami Beach loomed ahead, the bright lights and glitz of its numerous hotels and high-rise condominiums contrasting with the dark, star-sprinkled sky. Coming off the causeway into the city proper surprised Sharon even more. There was a lot more here than sand and famous hotels. They passed a huge hospital on the left, then drove along a street lined with fashionable stores and restaurants. Miniature white lights twinkled in many of the bushes landscaping the high rises, creating a festive atmosphere.

"Wow!" Sharon murmured. "It's a real-life TV set."

Tony chuckled. "I guess you could say that. Wait'll you see the architecture around here. This is Deco heaven. And the supersized mural that's been painted on one side of the Fontainebleau is wild." He made a left turn and added, "This is Pine Tree Drive."

The name registered instantly. The street Diane lived on.

"Collins Avenue is over to the right," Tony continued. "That's where all the big hotels are. Collins runs from one end of the beach to the other—five or six miles, I'd guess—then turns into Route AIA after that."

He slowed and made a swooping turn into a semicircular driveway in front of a large, Spanish-style house ablaze with lights. Diane's home. Sharon had known it was attractive from the daytime photos Diane had sent her; at night, it was spectacular.

As soon as they parked, Diane came alive. She opened the big front door carefully, then whispered over her shoulder, "I'm hoping Tonette's asleep."

Sharon followed her into a wide foyer dominated by a curving stairway that spiraled up to the second floor. To the left, two carpeted steps led down to a large living room furnished in black, white and silver. Sharon felt as though she'd stumbled into a nightclub scene from the so-called Roaring Twenties.

Tony set her bag down, then kissed Diane lightly on the forehead. Repeating the caress with Sharon, he said casually, "See you around, girls." To Sharon, he added, "Good to have you in Miami Beach, Sis."

With that, he was gone.

Sharon stifled a choke, and Diane burst out laughing.

"You should see your face!" she chortled.

Sharon smiled slightly. "I'm beginning to feel like the picture I'm seeing is out of focus," she confessed.

"I don't suppose I can blame you," her twin admitted, preceding Sharon into the living room and collapsing, gracefully, onto a low couch upholstered in black velvet.

"Well, is the divorce still on?" Sharon demanded.

"The mail should bring our final decrees any day now," Diane answered seriously. "But...you don't have to hate someone for life because you can't live with them, Sharon. As a matter of fact, I'm extremely fond of Tony these days, in an entirely different way than before."

"I see," Sharon said.

"No," Diane corrected gently, "you don't see at all. Which surprises me. Remember...you and I are twins."

They were indeed. And because of that, they often had the capacity to discern too much about each other, Sharon recalled. When they were younger, she'd sometimes felt that she was inside Diane's skin and Diane was inside hers—they were that knowing about each other. In those days, it hadn't been unusual to find them matching moods, opinions and friends.

They still had an uncanny affinity when it came to a lot of things. But time, distance, and dissimilar life-styles had paved the way for their becoming two separate persons, which was the way it should be, Sharon thought. Still, looking across at her sister from the large white armchair she'd fallen into, she didn't doubt that she and Diane would always possess a special ability to see deeply into each other and truly understand what the other was feeling.

At some point, Diane would ask her why she'd gone back inside the train station. She was sure Diane was already attuned to the fact that something important had gone wrong for her.

Sharon had never tried dissembling with her twin; there'd never been an occasion when she'd really wanted to. But now she knew she would have to conjure up a few fibs until she could think rationally about the handsome stranger she'd shared a compartment with on the *Silver Comet*.

CHAPTER FOUR

"AH," DIANE SAID, "there's Sylvie. I thought she'd probably gotten tired of waiting up for us and decided to take a nap."

Sharon looked up to see a tall, very slim, very blond woman descending the spiral stairway. The woman had the striking figure and willowy grace of a model, and her sleek, red satin lounging pajamas were both a step back into the Deco age and a leap forward into advanced haute couture. Very few people, Sharon thought whimsically, could get away with wearing that outfit. Sylvie, whomever she was, not only could, but did!

"She's here, Sylvie," Diane said, waving toward her twin by way of introduction. "The train was a couple hours late."

"Sharon," the willowy blonde murmured, extending her hand. Sharon took it and found the woman's grasp surprisingly strong. She also found herself the subject of intense scrutiny. Sylvie's eyes were an unusual shade of topaz, and definitely discerning. Sharon had the feeling this woman possessed the ability to read minds, and wondered, only half humorously, if she could see into the future, as well.

"Sylvie Grenda," Diane expanded. "Our treasure." She added hastily, "That sounds so demeaning, doesn't it? But you know that's not at all how I feel, Sylvie *mia*."

Diane smiled disarmingly. "I simply don't know what I'd do without you, that's all," she confessed.

"You would manage very well," Sylvie retorted rather languidly. She sat down in a white chair that matched the one Sharon was occupying, and crossed her long legs. She did everything with a grace to be envied, Sharon thought. Long ago she must have discovered how to make the best of her height.

Sylvie produced a cigarette holder, fitted a long cigarette into it, then lit the cigarette with that same graceful deliberation that appeared to be her trademark. "So," she observed, "your train was late?"

Though her English was fluent, she spoke with a definite accent, and Sharon wondered where she originally hailed from. Were it not for her coloring, Sharon would have guessed she was French. But her coloring was decidedly Nordic, possibly Slavic.

She nodded and answered, "More than two hours late."

"That must have been tedious," Sylvie concluded. She reached out slowly to knock her cigarette ash into an enormous Deco ashtray, and added, "But then, I despise trains. There were too many trains in my childhood, you know. Everywhere, everywhere, going by train. Of course the trains in Europe are quick and efficient. Why didn't you fly?"

The question came quickly, unexpectedly. Sharon heard Diane gasp, though it was a question they'd discussed at length, many times. She answered steadily, "I don't like to fly."

Sylvie shrugged. "Who likes to fly?" she asked rhetorically. "It is speedy, it is easy, that is all. You are here, then you are there." She switched the subject. "Tonette no longer has a fever," she told Diane. "She is fast asleep, so I think she will be fine tomorrow. She asked that we wake her when Sharon arrived, and she will be angry with us, but I think it would be best to let her sleep.''

"Absolutely,'' Diane agreed.

Sylvie inhaled deeply, then blew out the smoke in a long trail. Favoring Sharon with a charming smile, she said, "I should not be doing this, of course. It is a vice. My vice, as it happens, and so if it is bad for me I blame no one but myself. Speaking of blame...blame me when Tonette complains that she was not awakened. Tell her I forgot.''

"You do think of everything,'' Diane said, smiling. "However, I'll tell Tonette the truth. I'll tell her we didn't wake her up because we wanted her well, so she could really enjoy her aunt's visit.''

"Touché,'' Sylvie returned ruefully. "You are proving to me that honesty can sometimes be the best policy. Not always, but sometimes.''

Her arresting face was turned in profile as Sharon watched her speak to Diane. She was not beautiful, but then neither was she young, Sharon saw now. Probably in her mid-forties, and actually looking every bit her age, despite her tremendous personality projection.

Her features were sculptured, but refined. The sensuous droop of her eyelids over those discerning topaz eyes lent a sultriness to her expression. Her mouth was generous. She looked like a person capable of deep feeling and emotion, like a woman who'd experienced her full share of both. Slightly haggard, slightly weary, yet still possessing a marvelous joie de vivre.

She turned back to Sharon to ask, "So, did you meet anyone interesting on the train?''

This time, the question was not merely unexpected, it was like a jolt from the stratosphere. Sharon could feel the heat beginning to rise inside her, all the way from her toe tips to the top of her head.

She knew she was flushing, and that was more than enough to stir Diane's ever ready curiosity. "My goodness," her sister asked, "*did* you meet someone on the train? Was that why you went back into the station?"

Sharon realized she'd be dropping a bombshell if she said, "Yes, I met one of the most terrific men I've ever encountered. Not merely met him, either. We shared the same compartment. I slept in the lower berth, and he slept in the upper..."

A vision of Scott as he'd appeared this morning, upon arising, crossed her memory. Rumpled and wonderfully masculine, exuding an unconscious sexiness....

Remembering, Sharon's flush deepened.

Diane was staring at her sister wide-eyed. Never one to mince words, she said, "I'd say Sylvie had struck pay dirt. Who is he, Sharon?"

"No one. That is...I did meet a man on the train, yes. A very...pleasant person." Her tongue tripped over what was surely the understatement of the century.

"Does he live in Miami?"

She shook her head. "No. At least, I don't think so."

"You don't think so? Don't you know?"

"No. That is, not exactly." As she spoke, she realized she didn't know. She didn't think Scott actually lived in Miami, though it was possible. Trying to recall exactly what he'd told her, she remembered he'd said he was coming to Miami to convalesce from surgery—a rather lengthy convalescence. He'd mentioned it being a matter of several months.

She supposed he could have family in Miami. But he'd said his mother lived in Chicago and his brother—evidently his only other close relative—lived in California, so that didn't seem likely. Maybe he had close friends here in Florida, and they'd invited him to recuperate at their home.

She didn't like to think that the "close friends" might, in fact, be singular. A close friend. A *female* friend. But as she brooded about the chance of that, Sharon was relatively sure Scott wasn't coming to Florida to visit a woman.

She had the impression that he was—generally speaking—wary of women. True, there'd been a growing warmth between them during the trip. But he'd said pretty firmly to Thomas Chalmers, when they'd left New York, that there was no Mrs. Williams. Not with him, anyway.

The more she mused about his statement the more Sharon was convinced that, though there wasn't currently a Mrs. Williams, there once had been. She was equally sure Scott wasn't a widower, or he would have said something about his own loss when she spoke of Jerry's death. That meant he was divorced—and fairly recently, she suspected, though if asked she couldn't have explained why.

Diane said impatiently, "Sharon, I can read your mind sometimes, but not when it's kicking along at a hundred miles a minute. Elucidate, will you?"

"There's not that much to tell."

"Then tell what there is to tell," Diane prompted. "You *must* know whether or not he lives in Miami. You are going to see him, aren't you?"

Diane tended to double up on her comments and questions, and Sharon sighed. "I wish I could be more informative," she said frankly, "but I honestly can't. We got separated at the station, just as we were about to get off the train. He lost his wallet and went back to . . . his compartment to look for it. Apparently, it was stolen. At least that's what the conductor told me when I bumped into him on the platform, after I left you to say good-bye to Scott."

"Scott, eh?"

"Yes." Sharon nodded, and added impishly, "Scott Williams, would you believe it?"

That was as far as she was going to go. In another second, Diane would have the whole story out of her. As it was, Diane chuckled. "Coincidence, coincidence," she said lightly. "Anyway, I could do with a drink. Would a gin and tonic suit you, Sharon?"

"Yes, it would." At this point, she was willing to risk the possible effects of a single drink taken within the sanctuary of her sister's home.

"Care to join us, Sylvie?" Diane asked.

"No, thank you, darling. I must go. In the morning I have an interview for a fantastic job."

"A *fantastic* job? Doing what, may I ask?"

"Selling tawdry Florida souvenirs in a little shop on Collins Avenue." Sylvie smiled.

Diane groaned and protested, "Why do you waste your time on things like that? You know you won't last a day. Why don't you get out and do what you should be doing?"

"Because I don't feel like it," Sylvie stated simply. She stood, her long *faux* rhinestone and ruby earrings glinting in the light of the elaborate Deco chandelier suspended over the center of Diane's living room. She was like a figure out of a thirties movie, Sharon thought. A somewhat tragic figure, despite her outer assuredness and savoir faire.

"I will see you both tomorrow evening," she promised. "Did you say nine o'clock, Diane?"

"Nine or nine-thirty. The show at Tony's place goes on at ten."

So, they were going to Tony's nightclub. Sharon still couldn't get used to the idea of her sister being on such friendly terms with the man she'd just divorced.

Sylvie departed, Diane fixed drinks, and they settled down again, Diane kicking off her shoes and stretching her coral-painted toes luxuriously.

"Ah, that feels good," she said. "And," after a sip of the drink, "this tastes good. Unless you're starving, let's just relax for a few minutes. Then I'll stick some of Maria's marvelous casserole in the microwave."

"Maria?" Sharon queried.

"My mainstay," Diane said. "She cleans for me, washes for me, irons what needs to be ironed for me, does everything for me. She's here till five every afternoon, so there's always someone around when Tonette gets home from school. I can't always be here myself. I have to be at the beck and call of my clients."

"You're really getting into the real estate business?"

Diane looked faintly shocked. "Getting into it? Darling, I *am* into it, and I love it. I think it's the first thing in my life I've ever done that I find totally fulfilling...except having Tonette, that is. I have my broker's license now—did I tell you that?—and I'm working with Greg Dubrinski, a local guy who's been in Florida real estate for almost as long as you and I have been alive. He's really taught me a lot."

It was Sharon's turn to look at her twin curiously. Was there a chance Diane was already interested in another man?

Diane noted the look and laughed. "Ah, but we still are tuned to the same wavelength, aren't we, Shar?" she murmured contentedly. "No, I don't have anything going with Greg. As a matter of fact, I'm trying to get Sylvie and Greg interested in each other, to no avail. I think they're each too independent to tolerate the other. Greg needs a weaker woman and Sylvie needs a milder man."

"Tell me about Sylvie," Sharon invited.

"Sylvie Grenda is one of the most fascinating people I've ever met," Diane said, quickly accepting the invitation. "She's half Lithuanian, half French. She's lived all over the world, been as rich as Croesus one minute and dead broke the next. She's survived revolutions and three divorces and she's as cold as steel in some ways, yet kind and compassionate and wonderful with the people she cares about. She's crazy about Tonette—they're a mutual admiration society. So it's absolutely great to have her available to sit for me nights when I need her, as I often do. Her apartment is within walking distance."

"Sylvie is your baby-sitter?" Sharon asked disbelievingly. The intriguing blonde just didn't fit a baby-sitter image.

"Well, that's how our relationship began, oh . . . just about a year ago. Now we're fast friends, as well. If Sylvie likes you, she likes you. She's a person you can turn to, knowing she'll be there." Briefly, a sad expression shadowed Diane's ebullient facade. "It hasn't been easy, breaking up with Tony," she admitted quietly. "I've had some lonely moments, some very bad moments. Times when I've told myself I was crazy to let him go. Yet I knew it was the best thing to do, for both our sakes. A way down the pike, we'd have been thoroughly hating each other. And none of us—Tonette, especially—needs that. But it was hell living through the tension that kept building, for months, before we made our final, mutual decision."

Diane sipped her drink, then continued, "Any divorce is traumatic, Sharon. Even one as amicable as Tony's and mine. There've been times when I've desperately needed to speak to someone who could really understand. That's when I've turned to Sylvie, and I'll never forget her for just listening to me as she has. She doesn't criticize, she doesn't interject a lot of her own personality or ideas. She just listens and lets you get it all out...and then she makes a couple of comments that go right to the point. Afterward, you feel so completely *soothed*."

Diane broke off with a laugh. "Enough," she decided. "On to the microwave."

They ate their late supper in Diane's kitchen, all the while chattering about a variety of things. Diane's stories of her real estate ventures—several of which had led to profitable sales—were witty, and Sharon found herself frequently breaking into a spontaneous chuckle. She'd almost forgotten how funny her twin could be.

Then Diane drew Sharon out about working with Gary Freeman, only to observe, "I don't catch quite the zest in your voice I'd like to hear, you know."

"Oh, I really enjoy working for Gary," Sharon said hastily. "I like doing layout and design, you know that. And Gary gives me free rein with just about everything. Only when a customer actually insists that we follow his outdated instructions do I have to conform and maybe do something stodgy I'd rather not do."

"Even so," Diane said sagely, "layout and design aren't your real thing, Shar. You should be painting, just as Sylvie should."

"Sylvie's an artist?"

"An excellent artist," Diane said seriously. "She has a crazy studio not far from here, and the walls are lined with her paintings. I've pleaded with her to let me take them to a few of the local galleries. I think they'd sell before she had a chance to hang them straight, but she won't hear of it. She dismisses the whole idea with a wave of the hand and a languid, 'No one would wish to own my work.' At such moments, I could throttle her. It's the one thing she makes no sense about . . . just like you."

Sharon smiled sadly and said, "I love to paint, Di. But I also have to make a living."

Diane, she knew, was well aware that Jerry had left her with no insurance and a batch of minor debts. She'd managed to pay off the last bill only recently.

Diane nodded and conceded, "I know." Then she brightened. "Anyway, you can paint for the next month, paint every day, if you like. Maybe you can even persuade Sylvie to go off on an expedition or two with you. Once she decided to stay down here, she bought an old jalopy I sometimes think is held together with giant sized paper clips. But it gets her around, I can't argue with that."

"How did she happen to move to Miami?"

"A man," Diane stated, "considerably older than she is, and very wealthy. He wanted to install her in a penthouse over on Collins Avenue. But before that happened, they came to a rather abrupt parting of the ways.

He'd told Sylvie he was divorced, but she discovered he was very much married. Although she's very liberal about some things, she flatly refuses to become involved with married men. So she told him none too politely what he could do with his penthouse, flung the expensive jewelry he'd given her in his face, and walked out.''

"And?"

"And she's been doing all sorts of odd jobs since then. She doesn't stay at anything very long. Like I said about you, she should be painting."

The twins put their dinner dishes in the dishwasher, then Diane led Sharon up to the room that was hers for her stay. It was a spacious corner bedroom with pale pink walls, a deep pink ceiling and an enormous bed upholstered in rose velvet.

"I'm going to feel like Madame de Pompadour, sleeping in that," Sharon teased.

"There's a screened-in room through those French doors where you can relax and catch the sun," Diane advised. "Your bath's through there," she added, pointing.

Sharon felt her heart swell and whispered, "Thanks, Diane. Your home is really terrific."

"I'm glad you're here, Sharon. Now...sleep as late as you like." So saying, Diane left her with a sisterly kiss on the cheek.

With her departure, Sharon felt a sudden, sharp loneliness. She went to the front windows to find that her room looked out over Pine Tree Drive. To her left, she saw the dark silhouette of a large building that Diane had already explained was a hospital. Up in the night sky, the famed moon was hovering over Miami. Across the street, palm fronds waved gently. She caught a waft of sweet-scented flowers. Gardenias, she thought.

She found herself wishing she knew where Scott Williams was. Was he here in Miami Beach, or across the glittering waters of Biscayne Bay, somewhere in the city of Miami itself? Such a big area, so many people. Could she possibly expect that in the course of a month they'd bump into each other? It was most unlikely.

Trying to find him, Sharon reasoned, would be as futile as searching for the proverbial needle in a haystack. She had absolutely no clue to go by. Nor, more's the pity, did he.

SEVEN-YEAR-OLD TONETTE was normally a bundle of energy, but yesterday's "bug" had left her rather subdued. She poked her head around the corner of Sharon's bedroom door the next morning, shyly investigating. Then, seeing her aunt awake, she scampered across the room and collapsed onto the bed and into Sharon's arms.

Tonette had Diane's features, Sharon mused—her features, too, she amended—but Tony's coloring. Her dark eyes were eloquent mood conveyers, and they shone with excitement as she plotted out all the things she and Sharon could do together during the next month.

"Think you'll have any time left over for school?" Sharon asked.

Tonette made a face and tossed her head from side to side, her thick black curls bouncing with a life of their own. "School!" she protested.

"It happens to all of us, little girl. Anyway, we'll get it all in somehow."

"Starting with right now!" Tonette insisted. "Let's go to the beach."

From the doorway, Diane said, "If you're well enough to go to the beach, cherub, you're well enough to go to school."

"Mommy!"

"Maria's fixing your breakfast, so run along," Diane advised. "Sharon and I will be down as soon as we've had our first cup of coffee."

With Tonette gone, Diane invited, "Come over to my room, Sharon. I have my own personal coffee maker there."

The master bedroom was huge, dominated by Diane's giant brass bed piled high with bright blue satin pillows. Diane produced coffee, and Sharon ensconced herself comfortably on one corner of the bed as she sipped the fragrant, steaming eye-opener.

"I can see why you like Florida life," she told her sister. "Up north, the winter winds are blowing and it's probably snowing."

"And you're a poet but you don't know it?" Diane teased.

Sharon laughed. "Well, this really is like life on a movie set. Palm trees and pelicans and splashes of Deco everywhere you look. Was that an honest-to-God orange tree I spied in the yard next door?"

"Most definitely," Diane assured her. "But you don't have to go after forbidden fruit, sister mine. I have two orange trees, two grapefruit trees, an avocado tree and even a kumquat tree right in *my* back yard. You can pick oranges to your heart's content, and Maria will squeeze them for you. The fresh juice is marvelous."

"I'm sure it's delicious."

It was, she discovered a while later, after she picked half a dozen oranges and Maria—a plump, ebullient Cuban woman with the most gorgeous brown eyes Sharon had ever seen—converted sliced halves into juice, which she presented to Sharon in a tall frosted glass.

"I am going to become hopelessly spoiled with this kind of treatment," she complained to Diane, as they sat out on the screened patio behind the house sipping Cuban coffee and munching almond breakfast pastries.

"You could stand a bit of spoiling," Diane replied rather shortly. "Sometimes I think I'm the twin who's had all the breaks, and you've gotten all the rough spots."

"I wouldn't say that."

"Well, I suppose it's a matter of viewpoint." Glancing at her watch, she added, "Look, Shar, I have to run pretty soon. I have my eye on a small apartment complex I'm thinking of buying."

"For yourself?" Sharon asked, astonished.

"As an investment. There are four rental units in the building, and a sister building across a small courtyard that might also be on the market before long. It's a nice property for the money, with a good rental income."

Sharon shook her head in wonder. "You really are into this, aren't you? Funny, I never expected you to turn out to be a businesswoman."

Diane laughed. "Don't you remember how I used to do your math homework in exchange for your doing my art assignments?" she queried. "Anyway...I have to run, but if Tonette feels up to it she can walk over to the beach with you after a while. She'd love to show you around. And don't forget, we're going to Tony's club tonight. He has a new show he says is absolutely smashing."

"Terrific."

Diane paused, thinking. Then she said, "There's just one other thing…"

"Yes?"

"Well, I'm not trying to map out an agenda for you, Sharon, but I do want to have a cocktail party this weekend, to introduce you to some of the people I know around here. Saturday evening, I think."

Sharon immediately backed off. "Di, I'd rather you didn't do that," she said.

"Why not?"

"I've shied away from parties the past few years."

"Since Jerry's death, you mean?" Diane asked bluntly.

"Well, yes."

"Shar, Jerry has been dead for three years. That's a longer than unusual mourning period."

"I'm not in mourning," Sharon said stiffly. "I just don't like parties anymore, that's all. It's… well, it's different when you're a widow."

"Is it, now?" Diane remarked skeptically. "It seems to me that I meet up with a number of very attractive widows at the parties I go to here on the Beach, as I have in many other places I've been. If you want to become a recluse, that's one thing. But I don't think you honestly do. In my opinion, Sharon, you've been in that shell of yours quite long enough. You crawled in there *before* Jerry died, and I intend to pry you out of it."

Diane smiled. "Maybe I got the genes for extroversion," she admitted, "and you got the ones for introversion. But deep down inside we're very much alike. It's not just on the surface with identical twins, you know. Our similarities are very special, Shar. I hope someday there'll be a man in your life who will know you as well as I do. Though no one will ever know you quite like I do, right?''

"Right," Sharon echoed faintly.

"Don't look so distressed. I'll just ask a few people. It won't be an enormous bash, and you'll have fun, I promise. Now, I have to shower and get out of here...."

Sharon, left alone on the patio, surveyed Diane's lovely tropical garden and sighed wistfully.

How could she explain to her twin that all she wanted during this month in Miami was peace and quiet, and the chance to spend some time with the two people she loved most—Diane and Tonette?

Her inherent honesty forced her to amend the thought. That wasn't *entirely* so, she confessed to herself. She wished, very much, that this month in Miami could include seeing Scott Williams, too. But as Sylvie might put it, that just didn't seem to be in her cards.

CHAPTER FIVE

ALTHOUGH DIANE INSISTED that the party she was throwing wasn't going to be a big bash, it seemed to Sharon she was inviting an inordinately large number of people. As the weekend approached and preparations mounted, Sylvie—who had given up her job at the souvenir shop after three hours of employment—was on the scene more and more, fashioning a delectable assortment of appetizers. And Maria was constantly busy, popping dozens of delicacies in and out of the oven, then freezing them for later reheating in the microwave.

Also, Diane hired a catering firm to handle the bar and the serving details. When the caterers arrived on Saturday morning to transform the premises with two long tables covered by red cloth, flowers, and even a couple of potted palms, Sharon was tempted to ask her sister what her idea of a large party was!

By early afternoon, she was feeling completely useless and on edge at the idea of being the center of attention later in the day. After having offered help and being refused at least a dozen times, she put on her bathing suit, a terry robe, snatched up lotion, sunglasses, a mystery novel and a towel, and headed for the beach.

There was a relatively undiscovered public beach within a few minutes' walking distance of Diane's house, and even at this time of year—the height of the Miami Beach tourist season—it was surprisingly uncrowded.

The sky was the blue of Scott Williams's eyes, punctuated with white cotton cloud puffs, magically suspended. The Atlantic, spreading all the way to Africa, was painted in tropical shades of blue green. Behind Sharon, and for miles along the beachfront in both directions, were the towering hotels and condos that created the famous Miami Beach skyline.

Stretching out on the dazzling sand, Sharon still felt as if she was living in a movie set. The contrast to the winter climate up north was staggering but totally pleasant. She liberally anointed herself with sun-blocking lotion, because the last thing she wanted was to encourage the number of freckles that sprinkled her nose. She'd have to ask Diane what she did about her freckles, though Diane didn't seem to have as many as she did. Identical twins weren't *that* identical, she reminded herself.

Despite the relaxing atmosphere of the beach and the peaceful sound of waves lapping the water's edge, Sharon was dreading the party. The only people she'd know were Diane, Sylvie and Tony, who'd enthusiastically told her that he was really looking forward to this get-together.

Tony had been great when they'd visited his club the night after her arrival. They'd been ushered to the best table in the house, presented with orchid corsages, no less, then plied with fantastic food and vintage champagne. Tony joined them several times, but mostly he left them alone. A couple of friends of Diane's had shown up, and late in the evening they'd joined forces. Remembering this, Sharon supposed they would be two more people she'd know at the party—Diane had invited them—but she couldn't even remember their names.

Finally, she'd had enough of the sun, even with the screening lotion to protect her. Reluctantly, she stood up, shook off the clinging grains of sand, then gathered her things and trudged back to Diane's house.

It was a hot day, and the walk seemed longer than it had earlier. Sharon felt sticky all over as she turned onto Pine Tree Drive then pushed open the front screen door of her sister's house. She started up the stairs immediately, heading for her shower, and was midway up the spiral stairway when Diane hailed her.

"He called!" Diane exclaimed, her eyes shining, her voice vibrating with excitement.

Sharon frowned. Obviously there was some new man in Diane's life whom she couldn't wait any longer to tell about. Right now, though, Sharon didn't want to hear about him. She wanted to feel the shower's cool water cascading over her hot skin.

She asked, with restrained patience, "Who called?"

"Scott Williams!"

At that particular instant, Sharon could not have moved an inch had her life depended on it. Her hand became welded to the stair rail as she gazed down at her twin, her green eyes as enormous as they were incredulous.

"You're making it up!" she accused.

"I am not making it up," Diane sputtered indignantly. "He called about an hour ago. I invited him to the party."

"You *what*?"

"I invited him to the party," Diane announced serenely, her momentary indignation forgotten.

"How did he find me?"

"I have no idea, but I'm sure he'll tell you."

"You mean he's coming?"

"Of course he's coming. He even asked if he could bring a friend, and I said that would be great."

A friend? Sharon watched her sister turn back to the living room, where she was supervising the final floral arrangements, and her heart sank within her with a leaden thud.

So... there *was* someone in Scott's life. As she showered, she tried to tell herself that it was ridiculous to be so upset by that fact. He was a young, virile, handsome man, after all, not a monk. She'd come to all the wrong conclusions about him. Oh, maybe not all the wrong conclusions. Maybe once there had been a Mrs. Williams, and there wasn't any longer. That didn't mean that Scott had become celibate.

"Idiot!" she chided aloud, vigorously drying herself with an enormous pink towel as if she could rub away all the silly illusions she'd begun to have about a man she'd only known for a day.

Still, for the rest of the afternoon Sharon couldn't get him off her mind, and this whipped her into a small emotional frenzy. If she had been dreading the party before, she dreaded it doubly now. She certainly didn't want to see Scott if he had another woman in tow.

On the other hand, if that was true, why had he gone to the trouble of finding her? That didn't make sense, because it must have taken effort to locate her, given what little information he had to go on. In fact, she couldn't imagine how he'd even begun to go about it.

Now she was glad she hadn't been as resourceful as Scott proved to be. Suppose she'd somehow ferreted out a way of locating him, and then called his number only to hear a cheery female voice answer his phone?

With an effort, Sharon forced herself to concentrate on getting ready for the party, because she was commit-

ted to it whether she liked it or not! Diane, after all, was
giving it in her honor. For her sister's sake, she could not
behave like the shrinking violet she felt. She'd rise to the
occasion, be sociable, mingle and all the rest of it.

The mere thought made her groan.

Nevertheless, as she descended the spiral stairway
early that evening she was, visually at least, a credit to
her twin. She and Diane had gone shopping during the
week, and Diane had convinced her to splurge on a gorgeous green Chinese silk dress that almost exactly
matched "their" eyes. It was a lovely creation that
sculpted her body in the most flattering of ways, then
flared into a full skirt that swirled around her ankles.
With it, she wore a pair of Diane's gold, strappy high-
heeled sandals, and a jade and gold necklace with
matching dangling earrings that also belonged to Diane. Her perfume was her own—Arpège—her favorite.
So was her makeup, but she'd used more of it than usual
and applied it more skillfully. The effect was tremendous.

Sharon knew she was looking her best, and she was
more determined than ever to put her best foot firmly
forward. Yet halfway down the stairs she nearly faltered, yearning to reverse direction.

She glanced out over the assembling crowd—a *small*
party?—desperately searching for a familiar face, and
quickly spotted Diane, elegant in beige satin. She smiled
as she noticed that her sister was already deep in conversation with the handsomest man in the room. Then
she froze...because the "handsomest man" was Scott
Williams.

As if she'd called his name, he turned at that precise
instant and, across the crowded room, their eyes met.

Scott quickly murmured something to Diane, and started toward her. When he reached the stairs, Sharon was at the second step, and they faced each other eye to eye. For a long moment they just stared at each other, blue eyes meeting green eyes with a vibrating intensity. Then Scott said, simply, "Whew!"

Sharon looked at him questioningly, and he added, "I can't believe I really did it. I can't believe I actually found you. I can't believe I'm here!" He smiled, a heart-flipping smile, and suggested, "Maybe you should pinch me?"

Before Sharon could respond, Scott drew her down to his side. "On the other hand," he told her, "the touch of you makes me know you're real. Come on, I want to introduce you to my friend."

Briefly, she held back. Then she fixed a smile on her face and moved with him toward Diane and another very handsome man with whom Diane was now talking avidly.

The man turned as they approached, and he didn't wait for an introduction. "So, this is Sharon," he said, grasping both of her hands in his.

She looked up into warm, very dark brown eyes that were viewing her with definite approval. This man was not as tall as Scott, but he was equally well built and almost as good looking, in a Latin way. Thick black hair waved back from his high forehead, and his nose had an aquiline cast. A full mouth, a firm chin...and a definite charisma. No wonder Diane was looking slightly befogged!

"Sharon," Scott said, "this is my good friend, Dr. Ricardo Fabrega. I'm staying with him while I'm here in Miami."

Sharon caught the rather strange glance that passed between the two men as Scott said this, before Scott added quickly, "But for Ricardo, I'm afraid I wouldn't be standing here right now."

The young surgeon smiled. "Well, yes," he agreed teasingly, "I suppose it could be said that I saved your life when I operated on you. There's an inherent danger to any surgery."

"I wasn't talking about surgery," Scott shot back. "I was talking about the way you enlisted the secretaries at your hospital to help me track Sharon down."

"Ah, yes," Ricardo said slowly, nodding.

Diane, Sharon noticed, still had her eyes on Ricardo. But now she swerved her attention to Scott to ask, "Just how did you manage to track Sharon down, Scott?"

"It wasn't easy," he said wryly. "After I lost her at the station, the only thing I had to go on was my memory of some of the things she'd told me about herself. Believe me, I wracked my brains trying to recall absolutely every word she'd said."

"And he nearly drove me crazy in the process," Ricardo reported.

"Finally, I remembered that her brother-in-law owned a nightclub in Miami Beach, and that his name was Tony."

"That's ex-brother-in-law," Diane corrected calmly.

"Oh . . . I'm sorry," Scott said, slightly taken aback.

"There's no need to be," Diane said assuredly. "Tony and I are good friends. In fact, he's around here somewhere. Anyway, please go on with your story."

Scott smiled awkwardly and continued, "Well, that was the only clue I could remember, so I followed it. With the help of Rick's girls—"

"I'm not sure they would thank you for that," Ricardo put in.

"Well, with the help of the hospital personnel, we started calling every club in Miami Beach—every hotel and restaurant with any kind of entertainment—and asking if the owner's first name was Tony." He paused. "Do you have any idea how many places like that there are out here?" he asked, looking back and forth between the sisters.

"I can imagine," Diane answered. "And I commend you, and the ladies you enlisted, for your perseverance."

"I had a lot of motivation," Scott told her.

"And I was afraid I was going to have to put him on tranquilizers for the rest of his life if he didn't find her," Ricardo teased. "When this man has a mission, nothing stands in the way of his accomplishing it. But then I suppose that's the way with—"

Ricardo Fabrega broke off abruptly, and Sharon was puzzled. Was that a *warning* look she'd just seen flash between Scott and his Cuban-American friend? Why should that be?

Scott saw the quizzical expression on Sharon's face and felt a momentary pang of guilt. He, who had been deceived on far too many occasions by his ex-wife, hated deceit more than almost anything else, yet he was being deceitful to Sharon.

True, he had what he considered a very good excuse. If he suddenly told her he was a jet pilot and not staying with Rick at all, but on limited duty at Homestead Air Force Base for the next six months, he was sure he'd jeopardize his chances of getting to know her better.

He wanted to know her better. He'd only fully realized how much after he lost her in that crazy mix-up at the railroad station. Then he'd nearly driven Rick crazy as he tried to remember something that would provide a clue to finding her. It hadn't been the hospital personnel who'd helped him out, though. Rather, he'd enlisted the secretarial pool at Homestead, but to tell Sharon that would mean giving himself away.

He wasn't good at playing games like this, Scott thought unhappily. Neither, obviously, was Rick. He'd just nearly blown Scott's cover by saying words to the effect that he'd been *trained* to complete his missions.

Scott took Sharon's arm, forcing himself back to reality. She was so lovely tonight, she made his senses swim.

"Suppose we could find a drink?" he asked.

Sharon grinned. "Aren't you afraid I'll get tipsy again?" she challenged, her voice a near whisper. She didn't want her twin's imagination to conjure up all the wrong scenarios, but she didn't have to worry. Diane and Ricardo were now deep in conversation.

"I'd love you to get tipsy," Scott murmured wickedly.

"I don't intend to, believe me," she told him softly. "But I would like a glass of champagne. Diane? Ricardo? Excuse us, will you?"

Diane and Ricardo nodded absently, and Sharon moved away, leading Scott toward the patio where a corner bar had been set up. At the moment, it was less crowded than the bar in the dining room.

They toasted each other with bubbling champagne, then Scott nodded toward the garden beyond the screen. "Want to take a stroll?" he asked.

"Yes," Sharon told him.

The garden was attractively lighted by soft yellow bulbs hidden among the bushes. The orange trees were in full fruit, and their sweet scent filled the air.

Scott asked, "Where did you disappear to, once you got off the train?"

"Where did *you* disappear to?" Sharon countered.

"I went back to look for my wallet, like I told you. When I couldn't find it, the conductor asked me to report it to the stationmaster as a theft. By then, Rick was there. We looked for you, but you'd vanished."

"I guess we somehow just missed each other," Sharon decided. "Anyway..."

"Anyway, here we are," Scott finished. He paused, then asked carefully, "Did you try to find me? In Miami, I mean?"

"I wanted to," Sharon confessed, "but I had no clues to go on. You, at least, had Tony."

She was right, of course. He'd said practically nothing about himself, especially after the story of her husband's plane crash and her hatred of flying.

"Thank God for Tony."

"I'll drink to that," Sharon agreed.

They clinked glasses. Then Scott said with a frown, "We've wasted nearly a week of your stay here. We're going to have to make up for that. Your sister won't mind if I take up a fair share of your time, will she?"

The idea of spending *any* time with Scott was an answer to her prayers, and Sharon smiled broadly. "On the contrary, she'll thank you," she told him. "She keeps apologizing for being so busy and not doing things with me."

"What does she do? I think you told me, but I've forgotten."

"She's in real estate, and she's really into it," Sharon explained. "I hadn't realized how involved she'd become until I got here. I thought she was just...well, just playing at it, to get through her divorce."

Scott cringed ever so slightly, hearing the word. He asked slowly, "Was it a rough divorce?"

"From what she's told me, no. The final decree is due in the mail any day now, and she and Tony are friendlier than they have been in years. Strictly friendship, of course, which makes it great for Tonette."

"Tonette?"

"Their seven-year-old daughter. If you happen to look toward the top of the stairs later on, I'm sure you'll find her peering through the railing."

"Is that what you used to do when your parents had parties? You and Diane?"

"My parents didn't have parties," Sharon said wistfully. "We never lived in one place very long, never knew enough people to throw a bash like this. My father was a sales rep for a big pharmaceutical company. He loved traveling. Sometimes I think he must have asked them to transfer him the way they did. Anyway, I never felt I had a home I could call my own."

"You didn't like moving around?" Scott queried.

"I hated it. I'd just get settled in a new school and begin to make some friends, and then we'd move somewhere else. Also, my mother..."

"Yes?"

"Well, please don't take this the wrong way, because I loved my mother very much, but...she tended to be sort of introverted. She didn't make friends easily. She kept to herself, she read a lot. Looking back, I think her happiest times were all vicarious, derived from the pages of the novels she read."

"Did moving around bother Diane, too?"

"Not as much as it did me. But then Diane is more...adaptable, I guess you'd say. I think I'm more like our mother and Diane is more like our father. He probably would have loved a party like this. As it was, he always seemed to find a poker club wherever we went. He spent his social nights with the boys, as they say."

Scott sipped his champagne thoughtfully, and Sharon added, "The one thing I wanted most, by the time I grew up, was to live in one place forever. I wanted a beautiful, comfortable home and lots of friends. I wanted to be part of a community."

"But that didn't happen?"

Sharon laughed mirthlessly. "No, it didn't," she said. "I married a man who needed to move around just like my dad did. We never lived anywhere for more than six months. Isn't that strange?"

"Who's to say? Did you know that about him when you married him?"

"No," she admitted. "I was young, only twenty-one when I got married. Jerry was ten years older."

"He swept you off your feet?"

"That doesn't make it sound as if I had much backbone," Sharon protested, "but yes...I guess I'd have to say he did sweep me off my feet, to a point. It was a whirlwind courtship and then we eloped. My parents didn't like him, my mother especially. They both thought he was too old for me, and I guess my mother was hoping I'd find someone like the rich, handsome heroes in her novels."

Scott smiled and said, "Perhaps this is too personal, Sharon, but...was your marriage a happy one?"

Her profile was etched in silhouette by a nearby landscape light. The effect was cameolike and made her look suddenly remote to Scott. It was disturbing. He didn't want her drawing away from him; he wanted her to be all flesh and blood. Suddenly he wished he could take back that question.

She answered simply, "How do you define happiness, Scott?"

He paused. "That's a big order," he admitted.

He was thinking—though it was crazy, considering the circumstances and how short a time they'd known each other—that Sharon was a woman he'd have a very good chance of finding happiness with. The irony was . . . she hated planes, and he was a pilot. She hated to move, and his military career made moving his way of life. He'd be transferred from base to base at least every few years until, way down the line, he retired.

The thought of retirement brought Scott up short. Suppose he didn't pass the critical physicals. The Air Force would retire him, and then what? Flying would still have to be a mainstay in his life, even if he couldn't fly for his country. Nor could he imagine living in one town—one house, no less—for his many remaining years. He'd feel hemmed in.

Sharon said softly, "Scott?"

"Yes?"

"You look so sad."

"Sorry," he replied quickly. "I don't mean to."

They were silent for a moment, then Sharon said, "We should go back inside. This party's supposed to be for me, and Diane's going to have a fit if I don't mingle."

"I suppose you're right," Scott conceded.

He followed her into the living room, into the din of party voices and catchy jazz playing on the stereo, and was sorry he'd given in so easily. He should have stolen at least a few more minutes with Sharon and steered their conversation toward safer channels. He should have made a definite date to take her around Miami.

His time, he'd discovered upon reporting in at Homestead, was pretty much his own. "Limited duty" could as well be called "convalescent leave" in his case. He was expected to put in some desk time, do a few reports now and then. But the general impression given was that everyone wanted him to take it easy until the final diagnosis was in.

He'd been extremely discontented with that, until now. Now, he saw it as a blessing in disguise. His freedom from duty would make it possible to see a lot of Sharon over the next three weeks, till she headed back north.

Making a date with her was probably the only way he'd get a chance to be alone with her again, Scott thought as Diane pounced on both of them immediately and led them through a series of introductions.

Names and faces became hopelessly jumbled in Sharon's mind, except for Diane's employer, Greg Dubrinski, who proved to be a big, hearty, white-haired man with an infectious sense of humor. Then there was Sylvie, regal tonight in a tight-fitting gown of shimmering gold metallic cloth. And Tony, who seemed as much at ease on the premises as if he were still master of the house.

Late in the evening, as she came down from a trip upstairs to freshen her makeup, Sharon was cornered by Tony who insisted she share some champagne with him. It was then that she realized her ex-brother-in-law was not as blithe as he appeared to be with everything going on in his life.

Over the rim of his champagne glass, Tony watched Diane chatting with a group of people across the room, and there was pain in his dark eyes. "Sometimes I think I was a damned fool to give her up," he muttered.

Sharon said carefully, "Diane mentioned that you both agreed it was the best thing to do. Best for each other, and for Tonette."

Tony nodded. "Yes, that's so... as I tell myself when I'm being rational. But tonight I don't feel very rational when I look at Diane. Who's that guy she's spending so much time with?"

"Ricardo Fabrega," Sharon answered, following Tony's glance. "He's a doctor—a surgeon."

"So let's hope Diane doesn't need an operation, or he'd probably give her too much tender loving care, judging from the way he's looking at her," Tony commented. He met Sharon's eyes and added apologetically, "It's the atmosphere, the drinks. I can't help it if it gets to me a little. In the sober light of day I'll realize that we did the right thing. A few years down the pike we'd have wound up hating each other," he went on, paraphrasing what Diane had told Sharon on her first night in Miami Beach. "Now, I'd say we not only love each other—in a different way, of course—but we genuinely like each other. Sometimes, Sis, liking's more important than loving."

"Yes, that's true."

"I've also got a lot of admiration for your sister's business sense," Tony volunteered.

"Oh?"

"Diane's a sharp lady," he reported. "Greg Dubrinski's delighted to have her with his outfit. Diane's beautiful, she's got class—she wows the customers the minute they see her. But she's also got an inborn ability to sell, which is something I didn't know about her."

"Neither did I," Sharon admitted.

Tony laughed. "I thought identical twins knew everything about each other."

"Not quite."

"Anyway, Diane and I are thinking about going into business together. A separate venture, aside from my nightclub and her real estate."

"Are you serious?" Sharon asked, surprised.

Tony smiled. "We really do get along, Sis. And yes, we're very serious. We've stumbled on this idea—" He broke off, then said, "Look, I'll tell you more about it another time, or I'm sure Diane will. Right now, I think we could use some more of the bubbly. Be right back."

He bestowed a brotherly kiss on Sharon's cheek and swiftly made his way through the crowd. Sharon was about to start after him—she really didn't want any more champagne—when she felt her arm gripped by a strong hand with a very familiar touch.

She swung around and looked up into Scott's handsome face, to find that his mouth was smiling, but his blue eyes weren't. In fact, they looked both perplexed and stormy.

"On rather good terms with your ex-brother-in-law, aren't you?" he observed, the tightness in his voice not escaping Sharon.

"Tony and I have always been good friends," she answered easily, watching a play of emotions cross Scott's features that would have been funny if this were anyone else but him. She didn't want to make any mistakes with Scott, she didn't want to misread him, but . . . was that a faint hint of jealousy she was seeing?

"Just friends?" he asked, before she could say anything further.

"Just friends," Sharon stated firmly.

She saw that the conviction in her voice must have re-assured Scott, because he relaxed visibly. Then he grumbled, "For the past hour I've been trying to get near you and you've been swamped. Your sister must have invited half of Miami Beach to this shindig."

Sharon chuckled. "Diane assured me this would be just a small party, not a big bash. I guess I'll have to ask her to explain her definitions more precisely in the future."

"Well whatever it is, you've certainly been the center of attention," Scott told her. He removed his hand from Sharon's arm and added, "Your sister should be pleased with you. I'd say you've made the best of impressions."

"Thank you," Sharon managed, distracted by the absence of his touch.

"I thought you weren't a party girl," Scott said suspiciously. "At least, that's not the impression you gave me."

"I'm not. But sometimes it's easier to give in than it is to fight. Temporarily, that is. Tomorrow, I'll be back in my same old shell."

A thin filament of time stretched between them before Scott said softly, "You've been in a shell for quite a while, haven't you, Sharon?"

"Yes . . . I guess I have," she admitted reluctantly.

"Then don't climb back into it. You're much too lovely to stay out of the mainstream. You belong where life's happening, not cooped up in a closet."

Sharon looked around her and whispered, "I don't think I could stand this sort of thing all the time."

"Being in the mainstream doesn't mean being in the middle of a party," Scott pointed out. "Look, let me give you an idea of what I mean during the next few days, okay?''

"I'm not sure I'm following you."

"I'd like it if you'd explore Miami and Miami Beach with me," Scott said. "After all, this area is new to me, too. Then maybe we'd get to know each other a little better."

"I'd like that, Scott."

"Do you suppose we could begin right now?" he suggested innocently. "Do you suppose we could slip out for half an hour or so? I have the keys to Rick's car, and we could drive over to the beach just to get a little space. To tell you the truth, parties sometimes give me claustrophobia."

This was especially true after his ear problem had developed. Before the corrective surgery, he'd dreaded being involved in a crowd, because he'd feared that a sudden attack of dizziness might overtake him.

His divorce, too, had contributed to his need to be alone, with space around him and room to breathe. Up in the sky there was endless space, sunlight and clouds, and a majestic sense of touching the infinite.

In a jet fighter? Thinking of the many hundreds of business hours he'd spent at the controls of sophisticated aircraft, Scott was amused at his poetic references to flight. Yet those references, he thought seriously, were valid.

He said to Sharon, "Honestly, I won't keep you away very long. Let's each get a glass of champagne and sort of walk over to the front door and just slip out, okay?"

"Okay," she agreed softly.

As she did as Scott bade, Sharon felt like a young girl testing the waters of potential love. She wanted nothing more than to share the night, and the moonlight, and feel the magic of being alone with him.

CHAPTER SIX

THEY DROVE TO THE BEACH near Diane's house where Sharon had sunned not so many hours earlier. But as she strolled toward the moonlight-sprinkled sand with Scott at her side, she felt as if she'd stumbled onto an entirely different planet. An enchanted place, full of soft sounds and sweet scents.

They walked hand in hand, not needing to speak. Suddenly Scott laughed and said, "My shoes are going to be a nuisance in the sand. What do you say we go barefoot?"

Sharon needed no second invitation. She slipped off Diane's gold sandals and secreted them in a niche in the stone wall that separated the parking lot from the beach. Scott placed his shoes by hers. Then, hand in hand again, they ran across the sand like two children released from school.

Near the water's edge they slowed to a walk, and Scott began humming the strains of "Moon Over Miami." After a minute, he stopped, looked down at Sharon and said, "Corny, huh? But I couldn't resist it."

"Keep singing," she urged. "You have a nice voice."

"I don't believe anyone's every told me *that* before."

"Well, maybe I'm tone-deaf."

"Thanks a lot!"

He gave Sharon a playful shove and, caught off balance, she collapsed onto the sand, sinking into its softness, her green silk skirt swirling around her. In an instant, Scott was beside her. In another instant, his arms were around her waist. They were laughing, tussling... then, suddenly, they were still.

The kiss was mutually spontaneous, electric yet tender. A meeting of their psyches, as well as their mouths. Sharon, remote for so long, yielded up buried emotions as she gave in to Scott's touch. And he, who'd completely sworn off women, felt himself adrift with desire... and knew he could easily drown in Sharon's sweetness.

It would have been easy, so easy, to completely lose control with her. As it was, there wasn't much he could do about his arousal... too late for that! Yet he wondered if Sharon had any idea just *how* aroused he was— not physically, but emotionally—and decided it would be better if she didn't know.

Scott would never have labeled himself chivalrous, but he felt the need to be quixotic where Sharon was concerned. Her kiss was cue enough to her feelings and, especially since she'd been sampling champagne at the party over the course of the evening, he wondered how easily she'd be influenced past the point of no return.

He didn't want that intimacy with her, not yet, though he knew that in an hour he'd probably accuse himself of being hopelessly old-fashioned. But that didn't matter. What did matter was beginning this relationship on an honest note. And that couldn't happen until she knew considerably more about him. Particularly, what he did for a living.

Scott released her gently, tumbled over onto his back, and stared at the stars. Then, abruptly, he got to his feet, and tugged Sharon up onto hers.

"Let's go wading," he suggested impulsively.

"Are you crazy?" She laughed.

"Maybe, but let's do it anyway," he insisted. "Come on, I dare you!"

Sharon responded to his challenge. Somehow, she tucked up her swirling silk skirt and flew down to the water, moving so fast Scott had to race to catch up with her, after pausing to roll up his trousers. Then, like a couple of kids, they splashed in the cool tropical water.

After a minute, Sharon turned to him and said simply, "Thanks."

"For what?"

"For stopping us back there. I...we were at the edge. And you were right. It wasn't the moment to... continue."

His eyes sparkled in the moonlight, and his smile was whimsical. "You can't expect that I'll always have such self-control, Sharon," he said gently.

"I know," she whispered.

"I...I had to yank myself to my senses," he confessed.

"I know that, too."

"Sharon, there are things I have to tell you."

"Yes, I think I know that, too."

"But not tonight."

"Not tonight," she echoed, agreeing.

"Tomorrow. What about having lunch with me tomorrow?"

"I'd like that."

"Shall I call you first?"

"You don't have to. I'll be at Diane's, so whenever you get there is fine."

"Noon?"

"Sure."

As if they'd made a pact, they clasped hands and trudged out of the water and up across the sand. When they reached the spot where they'd stashed their shoes, Scott said ruefully, "Next time I keep a late date with you I'll bring a towel. My feet are a mess."

"So are mine, but there's an outdoor faucet right over there for washing off the sand. I used it today. Come on."

Scott followed Sharon to the far end of the stone wall, then waited while she dowsed her feet. "Your turn," she said, stepping back.

"Ah, much better," he told her over his shoulder.

Sharon smiled. "We might as well stay barefoot until we get back to the house. Our feet should be dry by then."

"Should be," Scott agreed.

Back on Pine Tree Drive, he parked Rick's car as near as he could to Diane's house, about a half block away. Then they slipped their shoes back on and walked the remaining distance, entering the house with empty champagne glasses in hand.

Some of the guests had left, but there were still enough people around so that their arrival wasn't especially noticed. After a while, though, Diane caught up with Sharon and asked, "Where did you and Scott disappear to? Ricardo and I were looking everywhere for you."

"We just went outside for a breath of fresh air."

Diane surveyed her sister skeptically. "The air in Miami isn't always that exhilarating," she observed. Then she smiled and added cheerily, "Never mind, darling. He's terrific!"

Sharon made no answer to that. Knowing her twin as she did, Diane was going to leap to conclusions no matter what she said. In fact, the less she protested, the more likely Diane would be thrown off course.

She didn't want Diane's matchmaking instincts to take over, or for her to start thinking up ways to "bring her together" with Scott. If that was meant to happen, it would happen all by itself, she told herself resolutely.

To her surprise, Diane continued, quite seriously, "Ricardo Fabrega is pretty terrific, too. What hospital was he at when he did Scott's surgery, do you know?"

"No, I don't know. In fact, I didn't realize he was Scott's doctor until he made that comment tonight. How long has he lived in Miami?"

"Only about a month, but he grew up here. In the city, that is. Anyway, he's joined the staff of St. Christopher's Hospital as a neurosurgeon. Can you imagine that? He certainly must have the right stuff." Diane paused, then asked, "Speaking of the right stuff, what does Scott do for a living?"

"Would you believe, I don't know?" Sharon told her sister. "He only said he was convalescing from surgery for the next few months, and I let it go at that."

Thinking this over, Sharon's curiosity nagged her. She again realized how little she actually knew about Scott. But then he'd said as much, on the beach. He'd said there were things he needed to tell her, and he'd indicated that tomorrow, at lunch, he would.

Why, she wondered, did that give her such an uneasy feeling?

SCOTT WENT BACK with Rick that night to Rick's apartment, a high-rise condo with a view of Biscayne Bay.

Shrugging off his jacket and loosening his tie, Rick said, "Thank God I don't have any surgery scheduled in the morning. That party was good."

"As parties go," Scott agreed.

"She was worth finding, wasn't she, amigo?"

Scott grinned. "What do you think?" he kidded.

"I think they were both worth finding!"

"Very true." More soberly, Scott said, "You know, I really had a terrific time tonight. I mean, yesterday I'd almost given up hope of ever seeing Sharon again, and then all of a sudden we're escaping barefoot down the beach like a couple of kids." He paused, then added almost reluctantly, "I'm having lunch with her tomorrow, Rick."

"Yes?"

"I'm going to lay the cards on the table about myself, so who knows what might happen after that."

Rick relaxed on his living room couch. "Why do you sound so dire about it? What do you think is going to happen?"

"I have no idea. That's the problem." Scott sat down in a leather armchair and stretched his long legs out in front of him. He said flatly, "She doesn't know I'm a pilot."

"So?"

"Well, her husband was killed when his private plane crashed three years ago. She was waiting for him at the airport . . . saw the whole thing. As a result, she has an intense hatred of anything to do with flying."

"Natural enough, I suppose," Rick conceded.

"Yes, but where does that put me?"

"Why should her husband's accident relate to you?"

Scott stared at his friend. "Are you deliberately being dense?" he asked bluntly.

"No, I don't think so. Look, Scott, suppose her husband had been killed in a car crash. Would that mean she'd subsequently avoid anyone who drove a car?"

"It's not the same thing, and you know it."

"Not quite, but in many ways it is. Fear of flying is pretty common, I'd guess. Even though it's practically impossible to travel long distances without hopping on a jet."

"This is more than fear of flying, Rick."

"You're sure of that?"

Scott stirred restlessly, then he decided, "Yes, I'm sure of it. If you'd seen her face when she told me about her husband's crash, I think you'd agree with me. This is a very deep-seated trauma with Sharon. She won't consider flying herself. That's why she took the train. I don't think she can even look at an aircraft without reliving that horrible memory."

"Then she must do a lot of reliving," Rick observed coolly. "Look, Scott, I'm not trying to be insensitive, but Sharon struck me as a very rational young woman. Sure, she has a terrible memory of something that happened in her past. But who doesn't have a few bad memories by the time they get into adulthood? Maybe hers is more dramatic, I'll grant you that. But maybe she never liked flying to begin with. Did that occur to you?"

"I don't know," Scott said dully.

"Look," Rick advised, "don't let this get to you. What I'm saying is, don't presuppose it's going to ruin your relationship. What do you think she's going to do? Write you out of her life when she learns you're a pilot?"

Scott posed the question that constantly haunted him. "*Am* I a pilot, Rick?"

Ricardo Fabrega sat up. "I won't pretend I don't know what you're asking me. You want me to make an accurate prognosis about your future in flying, right?"

"Yes."

"I can't, Scott. Believe me, I would if I could, but I can't."

"You did the operation, for God's sake."

"Yes. And as I told you at the time, the surgery was successful."

Scott smiled wryly. "That always sounds like such a cop-out," he said frankly. "The operation was successful, but the patient died...."

"Dios!" Rick exclaimed, shaking his head. "I know the state you're in, so I won't get on my Latin high horse and permit myself to become insulted over that statement. I do ask, though, that you consider the consequences if you hadn't had the operation. You'd be in pretty sorry shape by now, I assure you. Definitely washed up, as far as the service is concerned, with a strong chance of permanent deafness in the bargain."

"You don't have to tell me how lucky I am," Scott said wearily. "I know it. And I'll always be grateful that you were my surgeon. But you must understand it's plain hell to be living in limbo like this—not knowing whether or not I'll ever be fit for anything again."

"I presume by that you mean whether or not you'll be fit for flying," Rick interpreted dryly.

"Correct."

"Scott... suppose you can't fly again? It wouldn't be the end of the world," Rick pointed out. "You're thirty-four and in peak physical condition except for this single problem."

"Quite a problem!"

"It could have been considerably worse," Ricardo Fabrega reminded his patient soberly. "The tumor in your inner ear was especially deep-seated. That's why it wasn't diagnosed in England—it couldn't be found by routine otiscopic examination. It took a CAT scan to reveal it."

"Yes, I know."

"Then you also know that the surgical procedure in your case went beyond ear surgery and into the realm of brain surgery, technically speaking." Rick smiled, then said, "Hell, man...I did such a good job with my incision that you have almost no scar. There's just that small curve behind your ear, which your hair covers anyway."

"So, cosmetically I'm fine. But otherwise?"

"As I've said, you were lucky," Rick reported. "Such neuromas can be either malignant or benign. Yours was benign. Had it been otherwise, you would have had a lot more to worry about than whether or not you'd be flying again."

Scott knew that. It was something he'd thought of many times since his surgery, and he'd given profound thanks for things turning out as they had. Even so...living without flying, he thought grimly, would be only half a life for him. Ever since he'd gone up in his brother Hugh's small plane, he'd known he'd found his niche, his career. The first time he'd piloted a jet, he'd felt that no matter what happened with his life on earth, he had his own inviolate space in the sky.

Was that because his life on earth hadn't been all that great and had become increasingly miserable as his marriage disintegrated? For the first time, those thoughts crossed Scott's mind.

Rick said suddenly, "I understand how you feel about flying, perhaps better than you think. I feel the same way about surgery. On the other hand, a colleague of mine— a man in his early sixties, one of the most distinguished surgeons in the country in his field—recently had to give up that aspect of his career because of failing eyesight.''

"How did he manage?''

"He has gone into family practice, where he can put his expertise to full use in other ways and still be of great service to people.''

"Nevertheless, he must be very bitter.''

"He was…until he realized that what he was doing was feeling sorry for himself. When he stopped indulging in self-pity, his world changed. Much to the better, I might add.''

"Do I detect a message in what you're saying, Doctor?''

"I'm not much of a preacher,'' Rick said wryly, "but yes, I suppose I am trying to give you a message. Don't jump to the conclusion that you won't be able to fly again when I say this, but…even if you did have to give up flying—being an Air Force jet pilot, that is—it wouldn't be the end of the world, Scott. You're not that limited a person. You would find other outlets for your talents and energies, believe me.''

"Perhaps,'' Scott said moodily. "Perhaps.'' After a moment, he added, "I suppose part of the agony is not knowing. Especially now that I've met Sharon.''

"Why do you say that?''

Scott smiled ruefully. "If flying were not an issue, it might make a difference.''

"In other words, there'd be one less obstacle to surmount?''

"Yes.'' He managed a laugh and added, "I'm rushing my guns a little, wouldn't you say? God knows, I'm still not ready to be involved with a woman. In fact, I would have sworn I'd never want to be serious again.''

"That's not the way I saw it when I looked at you and Sharon together tonight," Rick interrupted, grinning.

The memory of that intense moment on the beach swept over Scott. In a way, he wished he could put it down to an outburst of pure physical passion between two people who were undeniably attracted to each other. It certainly had been *that*, and yet it had been so much more. He had sensed something beyond the physical. And, by Sharon's responses, he guessed—he hoped—that she had, too.

Their kiss transcended every other kiss he'd ever experienced. The sensitivity of her touch, the tantalizing depth of her passion....

Scott said uneasily, "When you get right down to it, Sharon and I scarcely know each other."

"Knowing is a relative perception," Rick observed sagely. "Whatever happened between the two of you on the train must have been pretty special, if you ask me!"

Memories flooded Scott's mind. Memories of Penn Station, of Thomas Chalmers the Third, of Sharon staring down at him from the doorway of bedroom four, her wondrous green eyes full of questions, of Sharon sipping her whiskey sour in the club car, of Sharon tucked into her berth, her lacy satin nightgown and creamy skin a fantasy, beckoning...

He became aware that Rick was looking at him with a certain intentness, and remembered the many occasions when the skillful surgeon had bent over his hospital bed at Walter Reed, checking up on him.

"What?" Scott asked.

"Nothing specific. You look bushed, that's all."

"I *am* tired," Scott admitted uncomfortably. "I seem to tire awfully easily these days. It sort of worries me."

"No need for it to," Rick assured him. "It'll be a while before you can entirely shake off that feeling of fatigue. Matter of fact, you're doing very well. But I'd rather you didn't drive back to Homestead tonight. No need to...especially since you have a lunch date with Sharon tomorrow. I will yield the twin bed in my room to you."

Scott didn't argue. And, once he was stretched out on Rick's extra bed, he was glad that his friend had made the suggestion. Traffic through Miami and South Miami, heading toward the Keys, was apt to be heavy even this late at night, and not something Scott relished dealing with.

Still, tired though he was, sleep did not come easily. He felt so ambivalent about his lunch date with Sharon. He wanted to see her again, wanted this badly. Yet he fervently wished that he could skip telling her his life story.

SHARON SLEPT RESTLESSLY that night, too. The party had stretched into the small hours, and she'd begun to think that some of the people were never going to leave. Finally, though, they departed.

Diane took one look at the chaos created by glasses and napkins and ashtrays and leftover food, and said, "We'll deal with this tomorrow."

Sylvie was spending the night, and she languidly agreed. "In the morning, it will be nothing," she assured the twins.

Sharon felt, privately, that getting the house back into a semblance of order would be a long and tedious job, whenever they tackled it. But that wasn't what made her toss and turn after she'd collapsed on her rose velvet bed. Rather, it was the thought of her luncheon date with Scott. She kept having this strange feeling that whatever he was going to tell her about himself would put a damper on this friendship between them that was starting out so magically.

Friendship? Yes, there was friendship. And there was romance . . . and a physical attraction so potent it scared Sharon more than a little. Once, in the night, she dreamed that Scott was making love to her, and she woke up with a start, at first feeling oddly ashamed of herself, then feeling a sharp sense of loss. It had been a very long time since she'd had a dream like that!

Finally, with daylight, she drifted into a deeper sleep, and then overslept. By the time she got downstairs, she discovered, to her astonishment, that Diane had already gone off to keep an appointment with a real estate client, and Maria and Sylvie had the house restored to remarkable order.

Maria produced Cuban coffee *con leche* and some flaky breakfast pastries, and Sylvie joined Sharon at the round table out on the patio where Diane usually had her light morning meal.

It was a beautiful day. Bright blue sky and golden sunlight bathed the house and its tropical garden in colorful contrasts, and Sharon said, "I'm beginning to think the weather's always perfect around here."

"Not always," Sylvie disagreed mildly. She shrugged slightly and added, "But it is enough of the time so there is no cause for complaint. Later, it becomes quite hot. But then, one can always find an air-conditioned spot to relax or a pool to cool off in." She stirred sugar into her coffee and stated, "At the moment, I feel I have found my paradise."

"I can imagine."

"And you? Do you think you would like to stay here?"

Sylvie had a habit of asking unexpected questions, but this one was easy to answer. "I only have a month off," Sharon reminded her.

"Suppose you decided you did not want to go back to New England, or your job?"

Sharon had given thought to not going back to her job, but it hadn't occurred to her not to return to New England. She frowned slightly, then said, "I don't know, Sylvie. I admit I came down here needing to think things out . . . about myself, my job and my future. But I never really expected to reach any conclusions while I'm here. I just want to . . . well, sort out my priorities, if you know what I mean."

"I know exactly what you mean," Sylvie assured her. She reached for the gold cigarette case she always carried with her, extracted a cigarette and lit it. "You do not mind if I smoke?" she asked as something of an afterthought.

"No. I used to smoke myself."

"But you wisely gave it up?"

"Yes. Although I guess I wasn't that addicted."

"I am," Sylvie said firmly. "At least, until something—or someone—comes along to take its place. But back to this subject of your future. I am not telling tales out of school, I am sure, when I say I think Diane would like very much for you to stay here with her."

"You mean to *live* here?" The thought had never occurred to Sharon.

"Yes, to live here. To share her home, now that Tony will no longer be doing so."

Sharon shook her head. "I don't think it would work, Sylvie. I mean, we get along very well . . . but we lead such different lives. I don't think I could happily fit into Diane's life-style, and I'm sure she wouldn't want to fit into mine. She'd find it very dull."

"Could you not each be yourselves in a house this large?" Sylvie asked practically.

"I doubt it. Diane tends to be the leader when the two of us get together. She'd want me to follow her footsteps."

"She leads because you assign her that role, I suspect," Sylvie murmured. "Basically, Diane is not as aggressive as she seems. A lot of this brilliance she displays hides insecurity. This divorce has not been easy for her, you must realize."

"I know."

"I thought so. As you say, the two of you are very much in tune, despite your differences. In Diane's case, I would say her motivation for wanting you to follow her footsteps is that she wants only the best for you."

"Yes, I'm sure that's so."

With that, they fell silent. Since Tonette was at a friend's house and Diane was working, the only sound to be heard was that of Maria washing the more fragile glasses and dishes by hand. Diane's patio was, on this morning, a small oasis of peace in the heart of throbbing Miami Beach. Sharon welcomed that peace, as she did the empathy she felt with Sylvie Grenda.

What had Diane said about Sylvie—that she'd survived revolutions and three divorces and a welter of other things, and had come to terms with herself?

Sharon rather envied this fascinating "older woman." She had such a long way to go before she could say she'd come to terms with *herself*. Thinking this, she decided that it wouldn't be a bad idea to take a few lessons from Sylvie!

As if reading her mind, her companion said, "Diane tells me that you paint."

"I did paint. It's pretty much past tense. I've had very little time for it over the past few years."

"There have been many moments in my life when I have had to put away my paints and my easel and my brushes," Sylvie said, nodding. "In fact, it is a while since I have painted, myself. But now I suddenly feel the stirring to go back to it, which will please your sister. It would please her even more if you would go back with me! Shall we arrange for a painting expedition soon, and see if we can still translate what we see out there onto canvas?"

It was an invitation Sharon had subconsciously hoped to hear, and she said sincerely, "I'd really like that."

"Today would be a good time," Sylvie suggested, further surprising her. "If you are free, that is."

Sharon suddenly became aware of the time. "Actually, I have a lunch date with Scott Williams. You met him last night."

"Ah yes," Sylvie said. Her topaz eyes were shaded by large sunglasses, but Sharon imagined there was a smile in them that matched the smile curving her mouth. "That is a much better thing for you to do today," she stated. "But we will paint together soon, okay?"

"I promise," Sharon answered.

"Too bad Diane does not also have a luncheon engagement...with Scott's surgeon friend," Sylvie mused. "I would say that they should see more of each other, no?"

CHAPTER SEVEN

SCOTT PULLED UP in Diane's driveway at exactly noon, driving the bright red sports car he'd rented shortly after his arrival in Miami. Maria answered the door and welcomed him effusively—they'd met in the kitchen the previous night and talked for a while—then ushered him into the living room.

"Sharon will be down in just a minute," she told him.

Scott took a seat and decided that, as interesting as Diane's striking living room was, he doubted he could live with it. The houses he'd been brought up in—military homes around the world—all had a characteristic simplicity about them. Once, a cousin of his mother's, visiting them in Germany, had remarked that an American military base was an American military base, no matter what country it was in.

"I could as well be in Abilene, Kansas," she'd stated.

His mother had been a bit miffed, but the observation was essentially true. As his father had progressed in rank, their accommodations had kept pace with the promotions. By the time Elliott Williams was a major general, they were living in veritable mansions. His parents were living in veritable mansions, Scott corrected. He and Hugh had both departed the nest by then, he for the Air Force and Hugh to pursue a career in architecture.

Hugh, as far as Scott knew, was the first male in five generations of their father's family not to have followed an Army career. Well, he'd chosen the Air Force, not the Army, but thus far his living quarters had been just as bland. In England, he'd sidestepped base housing for a charming apartment in a nearby town. He'd lived there alone—Claudia had stayed in the States—and that had been his favorite "home" to date.

Surveying Diane's bold Deco decor, he supposed that his conservative taste stemmed directly from his early surroundings and the fact that he'd never been exposed to much variation in interior design. His mother, a traditionalist, had decorated each home she'd been assigned to with practical upholstered pieces in practical colors, interspersed with family heirloom tables, beds, dressers, bric-a-brac and the like. There'd been a formality to the rooms in their houses, which Scott had gotten away from only in his own bedroom. His father had deplored the condition in which he'd kept his bedroom, and had repeatedly assured him that once he was in "the Academy" he would quickly have to straighten up.

His father had been thinking of West Point, not the Air Force Academy at Colorado Springs. Nevertheless, General Williams had been satisfied with Scott's career choice. Still, on those rare occasions when they had been together, he could seldom resist pointing out that the infantry won the wars, not the advanced technology favored by the Air Force and Navy.

Scott smiled at this memory. It was a point he'd never been able to win with his father—not that he'd tried very hard. Funny, when you were part of a military family there was always a certain sense of rank, even in the privacy of your own home. He'd rarely called his father anything but "Sir."

He wondered, if he ever had a son, if his kid would be calling him "Sir." Somehow, he didn't think he'd like that. Anyway, much though he loved the military life himself, he'd never inflict it on any child of his. If he ever had a son— "Hello," Sharon called, behind him.

Scott swerved around to see her stepping down into the living room, and was glad to be relieved of the burden of his thoughts.

She looked lovely in a sleeveless, peach-colored shift, her coppery hair framed by a headband of the same color. Scott yearned to take her in his arms and kiss her by way of greeting. But there was a subtle reserve about Sharon today that made him settled for a simple, "Hi."

As they left the house, he said, "Rick suggested we try a place called Sunday's. It's at the Haulover Marina, a few miles north of here, and looks out over Biscayne Bay."

He felt oddly nervous, like an adolescent on his first date. Hoping he sounded reasonably urbane, he asked, "How does that strike you?"

"Fine," Sharon replied agreeably.

The traffic was heavy along Collins Avenue, and Scott was forced to concentrate on his driving, which was just as well. As they passed hotels and business centers, high-rises, homes and parks, he was appalled to discover that he didn't know what to say to Sharon, how to break into conversation with her. He could hardly stare straight ahead and blurt out, "Look, I'm a jet fighter pilot. So if you don't think you can deal with that, maybe I'd better take you home!"

After a while, they passed over an inlet and saw the Haulover Marina to their left. Scott parked in the large lot that served both Sunday's and the adjacent marina, then strolled with Sharon, as casually as possible, toward the side of the restaurant and the waterfront entrance.

They were led through a low-ceilinged, open-air dining area, and given a table at the water's edge. Pleasure boats—including several snazzy "cigarettes"—were tied up right alongside the tables, and it was fun to watch the owners and guests climb out of their boats and saunter directly across to the bar for a drink, or linger at a table for lunch. Nearby, at the marina, a series of charter boats were busy with customers and catches, while pelicans swooped overhead, adding the perfect whimsical touch.

"Have you recouped from the party?" Scott asked, after they'd placed their order.

Sharon smiled. "I think so. I went downstairs this morning to help with the cleanup, but Sylvie and Maria already had the house restored to normal."

"I noticed," Scott commented. "It looked like it was ready to be photographed by a decorator magazine."

"Very true. Say, have you had any word on your wallet?"

"None," he told her. "It wasn't too bad, though. I had my credit cards stashed in my carryon."

They were making idle chatter, Scott realized, and they kept on chatting as they ate: about the party, about Diane's career, a little bit about Tony, a little bit about Sylvie, a lot about nothing in particular. By the time they left Sunday's, Scott was feeling annoyed with himself, because he hadn't had the courage to tell Sharon what he'd intended to.

As they started back along Collins Avenue, he made a sudden decision. He saw a sign for Bal Harbour Beach, and pulled into the parking lot.

"Let's get a little sun," he announced abruptly.

Sharon, glancing at him, knew at once that he had a lot more on his mind than revitalizing his tan. He already had a terrific tan...and that suddenly posed a new question in her mind. He'd been traveling from north to south, as she'd been. Where, she wondered, had he acquired such terrific color?

She'd assumed he was not long out of the hospital. But people recovering from surgery usually looked pallid, not like bronzed lifeguards.

"You tan easily, don't you?" she commented as they walked out onto the beach.

"Yes, I suppose so."

"Were you someplace warm before New York?"

"Huh?"

"Where did you get such a great tan, Scott, at this time of year?"

He grinned. "Believe it or not, at Walter Reed Hospital," he told her. "Once I was ambulatory I spent most of my time in the solarium. You'd be surprised how much sun filters through glass, even in winter. Also, I put in a few hours under a sun lamp, simply because it felt good. I was your typical pale post-op patient."

Sharon was taking in the pretty tropical scene around them, but now she frowned. "Walter Reed Hospital?" she repeated. "That's a military hospital, isn't it?"

Scott swallowed hard, knowing the die was cast. "Yes." He paused, then added reluctantly, "Actually, it's the Army Medical Center, located in Washington."

"That's what I thought." She looked up at him and laughed rather weakly. "You know, I don't have the faintest idea what you do for a living," she admitted. "Do you work for the government or something?"

He said hesitantly, "Well, I guess you'd say I work for the government. Strange as it may seem, though, I don't usually think of it that way."

"What do you mean?"

"I'm in the service, Sharon. I guess we think of ourselves as being somewhat separate from government, Washington-style. I'm...a career officer."

"You're in the Army?"

"No, not the Army."

Sharon looked as him quizzically, and Scott imagined a dark cloud passing across her beautiful green eyes. It was the moment of truth, and the uncertainty of her response was causing him to actually feel cold, though the air was unquestionably warm.

"I'm in the Air Force," he told her levelly. "I'm a pilot. I fly jet fighters."

Sharon reeled as if he'd struck her. And when he instinctively reached out to grasp her arm, she shook him off. Her face went white, and she stared at him as if he'd suddenly become a total, horrible stranger.

He sympathized with her feelings—for a moment. But then he found himself resenting the way she was staring at him. She was overreacting, damn it! He could understand why, but even so, she wasn't a child.

She said, in little more than a whisper, "Why didn't you tell me?"

"There hasn't really been a chance."

"On the train, when I told you about Jerry, why didn't you tell me you were a flier?"

Scott tried to smile, but it was a sorry attempt. He said wryly, "It seemed like the worst of moments to tell you something like that."

"I disagree, Scott. I made it plain how I felt about flying—how I *feel* about flying." She gathered her breath, then stated, "The flying Jerry was involved with must be utter child's play compared with what you do..."

Her words dwindled off, but Sharon didn't have to finish the sentence. She could as well have said aloud, *And look what happened to Jerry!*

Scott exhaled heavily and looked away from her. He spotted a rustic bench in the shade of a nearby coconut palm and started toward it, nodding to Sharon to follow him. Then, when he'd motioned her to sit beside him and she'd done so, he said, "It wasn't my intention to hold anything back from you. But when I found out how you felt about flying, I decided that if I ever wanted to get to know you, I'd better keep quiet for a while. We seemed to be getting along, and I was afraid that if I told you, you'd refuse to see me again."

To his surprise, she nodded. "I would have."

She was staring out at the turquoise Atlantic as she spoke, and her profile again had that cameolike quality that Scott had noticed in Diane's garden the night before. He felt as if she'd gone miles away from him, as if her inner self was entirely somewhere else. It was disconcerting, sitting next to a flesh and blood woman who wasn't really *there*.

"Neither of us knows much about the other, Sharon, which makes this . . . feeling between us all the more unusual. Please don't deny that there is a special feeling between us."

"No," she said softly, still staring out to sea. "No, I won't deny that."

"All right, then, suppose we start from square one and learn a little about each other. That was the reason

I asked you to lunch today. I thought that maybe if you knew more about me you'd understand why I do what I do."

Sharon faced Scott slowly, her green eyes mirrors of doubt. "You first," she told him.

"Okay."

Scott again attempted to smile, and again his effort came up short. "My full name," he began, "is Scott Elliott Williams. I come from a military family. My father was the fourth generation of Williams males to graduate from West Point and rise to the rank of general."

"Where is your father now?"

"He passed away seven years ago."

Sharon was visibly startled. Still, she persisted, "And your mother?"

"My mother moved back to Chicago soon after my father died. She has family there. In fact, she grew up there."

"That's right," Sharon recalled. "You mentioned your mother was in Chicago. Remember, on the train, when we were giving character references to each other?"

Despite himself, Scott chuckled. "Yes," he told her, "I remember. At the same time, you told me about your sister. Then, the next morning in the breakfast car, you told me about Tony. We wouldn't be sitting here if it wasn't for that."

Now Sharon smiled, a wistful smile that brought the light back to her features. "Did your mother visit you while you were in the hospital?"

"She doesn't even know I've had surgery," Scott admitted quietly. "I decided not to tell her anything until I know what the results of my...convalescence bring. You see, my father died of cancer, so it would only cause her unnecessary worry.''

"I don't understand, Scott. What does cancer have to do with what you had? I thought whatever you had was corrected by the operation Ricardo performed.''

"It was," Scott agreed, his mind racing. "But . . . let me back up a little, okay?" Before Sharon could frame any of the questions that were flickering across her face, he continued, "My problem, as it was, started in England, after I returned from a mission. I was home in my apartment, and all of a sudden I had a dizzy spell that was pretty scary. It just came out of the blue, for seemingly no reason at all.''

"How long did it last?''

"Fifteen minutes or so. I managed to crawl into bed without getting sick, and buried my head in the pillows until it passed. Then I tried to put it down to something I ate, even to something in the air. Remember—and I say this without conceit—I was in top physical shape.''

"I'm sure you were," Sharon murmured.

"Anyway, a couple of weeks later, I had another spell, and I realized that I shouldn't be flying. The next day I checked myself in at the base hospital and from there on it was one test after another. I wound up with a bunch of British medicos in London, but no one could find anything wrong with me. That's when they shipped me back to Walter Reed and Rick Fabrega took over.''

"And Ricardo made the diagnosis?''

"Using a CAT scan, yes. I had a tumor deep in the inner ear. Rick did the operation, and got it all.''

"I see.''

Scott noted the uncertainty in Sharon's tone, but went on. "Meantime, I was going through another pretty rough experience on the personal front. My wife and I had separated long before any of this happened, but at about the time I became ill we started thrashing out all the details that go with divorce. With one thing and another, I . . . well, I didn't want my mother in on it. I love her, but she sometimes doesn't see things quite my way.''

Sharon smiled at that. "I kind of thought there was, or had been, a Mrs. Williams,'' she admitted. "And I know what you mean about parents. My mother was understanding enough, but my father, extroverted as he was, was very strict with Diane and me. If I had been in your position, I might have done things the same way.''

Scott felt the faintest ray of hope. At least they'd reached a few grains of common ground. "Well, now that I'm done here on the way to full recovery, I'll call her soon.''

"Is Ricardo Fabrega in the Air Force, too?'' Sharon asked unexpectedly.

"Rick *was* in the Army,'' Scott corrected. "He was paying back a military scholarship he received for medical school expenses. Matter of fact, I was his last patient as an Army doctor, though the Air Force still wants him to keep an eye on me here in Miami.''

"He must be very good,'' Sharon commented.

"Very,'' Scott agreed.

He and Sharon were sitting only a few feet apart, yet there was a larger separation, not physical, that Scott felt keenly. He wished he could become so much closer to Sharon . . . in every way. He wished that this fear of losing her would disappear. This lovely, copper-haired twin had woven herself into his life in a quiet manner that astonished him. He wasn't pretending that there was any permanence to it—that would be too much to hope for. But at this particular moment in his life, Sharon filled a very deep need, a void that he hadn't recognized until, suddenly, being with her brought him to life again.

She said, "How long have you been divorced, Scott?"

He wished he had another answer to that, because his divorce was too recent. She'd certainly think his interest in her was of the rebound variety.

He said, his mouth tightening, "My divorce became final just before I made this trip to Miami. I was in New York to work out a few last-minute details."

"And Ricardo... is he married?"

Again, her question was unexpected, but Scott managed to camouflage his surprise. "No," he answered steadily. Then he added, "He told me once that he was engaged when he was quite young. The girl died, and he was shattered. It was a long while before he could even look at another woman, but by then he was in medical school and totally dedicated to his career. I must say, though, that since I've touched bases again with Rick here in Miami, I do detect a certain change in him. Witness the way he was looking at your sister last night."

"Yes, I noticed."

Sharon was silent for a moment, then she said, almost blurting the words, "Diane doesn't need another unhappy involvement, Scott. She was crazy about Tony in the beginning—as I'm sure he was about her—but after the honeymoon was over, their marriage went right downhill. Then Tonette came along and kept them together, but that still didn't cancel the fact that their marriage couldn't work."

"It's amazing that they're friends," Scott remarked.

"Yes, it is."

"So... what makes you so sure that an involvement with Rick would end in unhappiness?" Scott asked.

"Well, he's that same romantic type, wouldn't you say? I mean, Tony's Italian, and Ricardo is Cuban."

"Isn't that stereotyping people, Sharon? It seems to me that aside from any romantic proclivities he has, Tony DeLuca must be a pretty astute business man. And Rick is certainly a damned good doctor. Which means that they must both have their feet on the ground a good deal of the time."

"Perhaps I'm unduly apprehensive," Sharon admitted. "After all, I sort of feel like I'm protecting myself. If there's going to be another man in Diane's life, or even another marriage, I only wish I could be sure that this time she'll be happy. Consistently happy."

"Is anyone ever consistently happy?"

"Come on, Scott. You're making me feel foolish," Sharon protested mildly. "There has to be a truly mutual understanding for a serious relationship to work, that's all I'm saying."

"Did you have that kind of understanding in your marriage?"

For a moment, Sharon felt like not answering that question. Then she said, carefully, "No, as a matter of fact Jerry and I didn't have that. We were happy, most of the time. Very happy, in fact. But I think I told you that having a home, a permanent home, was one of the most important things to me, and Jerry never wanted that. We traveled from pillar to post and never lived long enough anywhere to even establish residence so I could vote. I'm twenty-nine years old, and it's only within the past couple of years that I've voted in elections. Maybe that's not important to a lot of people, but it's made me feel like a second class citizen."

"I haven't voted very often either, Sharon," Scott told her. "People in the military move around a lot, too. I don't know when I've ever spent more than two years of my life in the same place." He spoke slowly and deliberately, wondering what her reaction might be. But she disappointed him. She didn't visibly react at all.

Another question occurred, and Scott asked abruptly, "You and Jerry never had any children, did you?"

"No," Sharon answered, looking rather shocked. "If I had kids, they'd be with me now." After a moment, she asked, "What about you?"

"What about me?"

"Did you and your wife have children?"

"My wife's name is Claudia," Scott said, "and no, we didn't have any children."

"Oh."

Scott studied Sharon for a moment, his blue eyes intense. "Look, I don't normally go around telling this to people, but I want you to know that Claudia's an alcoholic who refuses to face up to her problem."

Sharon had a sudden memory of the way he'd reacted when the drinks had made her tipsy on the train. No wonder he'd looked the way he had! Stirred by empathy for him, she murmured softly, "Scott, I'm sorry."

"It was one of the reasons why our marriage broke up," he said tensely. "We were married for eleven years before we finally separated, about a year ago. We gave it more than a fair try, really. In retrospect, I can't help but wish that we'd given up sooner. I'm only thirty-four, but I feel that somewhere along the way I lost a large chunk out of my life."

"You wanted a divorce?"

"I filed for the divorce, yes. In fact, I fought for it." He paused, putting the memories of pain behind him and added calmly, "Claudia's already dating a wealthy banker in New York. I hope she hooks him, if that's what she wants, though I know that's not a very nice way of putting it. But she's beautiful, and she's still young. Maybe, with the right man, she could find the strength to give up drinking and turn her life around. I," he finished definitively, "was not the right man."

"I wasn't the right woman for Jerry, either," Sharon responded, hoping this admission would let Scott know that he wasn't alone.

"Did he want children?"

"No."

"Did you?"

"Yes."

"That creates a pretty difficult hurdle to get over."

"Yes, it does."

Sharon fell silent and gazed out to sea again, her hands clasped in her lap. Outwardly she seemed serene, but inside she was churning. *Why, given all the occupations he could have become involved with, did Scott have to choose flying?*

Sharon tried not to shudder visibly, tried to keep her eyes open. She knew if she shut them she'd see that crippled plane careering earthward, hear the crash, see the flash that had seemed to light up the world, see the billowing black smoke and terrible orange flames leaping skyward...

"Sharon?" Scott called gently.

"Yes?"

"I can feel you turning away from me. Please don't do that. We've only begun to know each other, but please...let's not stop now. I enjoy being with you, I enjoy *you*. I've sensed that you feel the same way about me. Am I wrong?"

"No, you're right."

"Then don't shut me out like this," Scott implored. "I can imagine how you must feel about what I do. Why do you think I hedged as much as I did about telling you? I wanted you to give me a chance as a person, not a pilot. The last thing I wanted was for you to put me in a mold."

She smiled faintly. "I can't imagine anyone putting you in a mold, Scott."

"Thank you. That's one of the better things I've heard you say today." Seriously, he added, "I'd really like to see you as much as possible while you're in Miami."

Sharon hesitated, then asked, "Are you on vacation, Scott?"

"No, I'm assigned to Homestead Air Force Base, just south of the city. Sharon...don't look like that! I'm not flying, nor will I be for quite a while. In fact, my future as a pilot is questionable until I've passed some very tough physical exams. Meantime...believe me, I'm grounded! Does that satisfy you?"

She turned toward him, her green eyes hinting at reproach. "I'm not that selfish, Scott," she said. Glancing toward the sky, she added, "If you went to all the trouble to learn how to fly sophisticated jets, then you must love it up there."

"Yes," he told her quietly. "Yes, that's true."

"Then I respect that. It's...well, it's just not something I can share in, that's all. Still, it doesn't mean that we can't go out with each other while I'm in Miami."

Her words came out cautiously, even bravely, but Scott felt like letting out an exultant whoop. Sharon was at least giving him this much of a chance, something he'd seriously doubted would happen.

Later, after he took her home, Sharon did her own share of doubting and decided that she'd been very foolish. The way she already felt about Scott, seeing more of him could only lead to a deepening attraction. And, in the final analysis, there was no place for them to go—not together.

His career and his life-style represented the ultimate things she didn't want any part of. She wanted a home, a permanent home. A place where she belonged, a place she could truly call her own. It would be nice—it would be wonderful—if there was a man to share that home with. But if that wasn't to be, she was willing to go it alone.

Perhaps, at some point, she could adopt a child. She'd heard of single people adopting children. Maybe she could even adopt two kids—a boy and a girl.

Later that afternoon, lying on the chaise lounge in the screened room outside her bedroom, Sharon thought about those things... then realized how ridiculous she was being when it struck her that she'd wanted the boy to have blue eyes exactly like Scott's.

CHAPTER EIGHT

SYLVIE AND SHARON SET OUT on a painting expedition early Monday morning, after the customary Cuban coffee and pastries on the screened patio. Diane had not been exaggerating when she'd called Sylvie's used car a jalopy. It was a shambles of an automobile, all rusted dents and torn upholstery. About all one could say for it was that it ran—after a bit of initial coaxing.

As they started out, Sylvie said, "In my wanderings, I have found an area that I think would be good for us to begin with. It is at the very end of the Beach, not far from where the MacArthur Causeway crosses over Biscayne Bay. There are flat rocks, where I sometimes go to sun. They overlook the Port of Miami. I think we might find something there."

They talked idly as they drove south along Collins Avenue. Then Sylvie wove her way through several colorful neighborhood streets, passing any number of paintable scenes along the way. Finally, she found a parking space, and they went the rest of the way on foot.

Sharon was enthralled by the spectacular aquatic view and became so fascinated with the ship activities going on in the channel leading to the bustling Port of Miami that it was a while before she set up the easel and painting supplies she had borrowed from Sylvie.

Opening the paint box, the familiar odors of turpentine and linseed oil filled the air, and she realized how much she'd missed doing this over the past few years. Longer than that, really. Somehow, she'd rarely been motivated to paint during the span of her marriage to Jerry.

Watching Sylvie get to work, Sharon suddenly wondered if she'd really been any good to begin with. Or if her parents—and Diane, as well—had deluded her about her talents, as families sometimes tend to do. It felt wonderful, though, to position her canvas and squeeze dabs of oil paints in rich colors onto a fresh palette.

In earlier years, she'd been somewhat photographic in her renditions of the scenes she painted. Now, her brush was guided by the magical tropical hues of her surroundings and the Deco architecture and ambience that asserted itself across the entire city. It didn't take long before Sharon once again knew she was a natural at painting. Whether her artwork was good or bad, it was *her*. She was expressing herself, and felt a marvelous freedom in doing so.

She lost all track of time, and was surprised when Sylvie, standing nearby at her own easel, said, "I am hungry. How about you? I brought us a picnic. Shall we eat?"

So saying, Sylvie put down her brush and stretched lazily. Then she approached Sharon's easel, silently studied the work in progress, backed off a few paces and looked again.

"Eh, now," she commented. "Diane said you were good, but you know how it is. She is your sister, so I took her opinion with grains of salt. But you are very good, *cherie*. Very good, indeed. What an atmosphere you create! It is exactly right, and yet so different."

"Thank you," Sharon said, honestly pleased at the flattery. She stepped back to assess the work herself, and added, "It's funny, Sylvie, but I've never painted this . . . freely before. I think your example has inspired me to let myself go."

Sylvie chuckled. "Me? Do not, for heaven's sake, follow my example in anything. Most of what I do leads to disaster! Of course, if you feel I have this effect upon your painting, I will not argue with you." She smiled eloquently, then added, shyly for her, "Would you like to see what I have been doing?"

Sharon eagerly approached Sylvie's easel, took one look and exclaimed, "Oh, that's tremendous!"

"You are just being polite, no?" Sylvie queried quite seriously.

"Not at all," Sharon assured her. "Diane had high marks for the paintings she'd seen in your studio, and if they're even half as good as this, well . . ."

Their styles were totally different, Sharon realized appreciatively. Sylvie, certainly, was the more uninhibited artist. She was doing a view of two docked freighters that bordered on surrealistic, her colors and textures as bold as they were innovative.

"I love the way you've discovered the hidden drama within such . . . well, mundane colors. The rust stains on that freighter's hull, those gray boulders in the jetty, the muted peach tone of that fuel tank—" She broke off and laughed delightedly. "You'd almost think I know what I'm talking about!" she said, mocking herself.

"Ah, but you do," Sylvie observed. "And you are obviously no slouch at using color yourself." Her accent gave the slang word a special flavor of its own, and Sharon felt a great respect for her individuality.

Sylvie had concentrated on a small segment of the scene before them, while Sharon was doing a panoramic view of Biscayne Bay with the Miami skyline in the distance. But both women had recognized the essence of what they were seeing, and transferred that essence onto canvas.

As they munched on the chicken sandwiches and iced tea Sylvie had brought, Sharon said, "Why don't we consider ourselves charter members of a mutual admiration society?"

Sylvie laughed. Then, soberly, she mused, "This day is being very good for me, Sharon. For you, too, I think. I think we have both been suffering from emptiness."

It was an accurate diagnosis. Hearing it, the knowledge of just how much she'd been suffering from "emptiness" swept over Sharon. And with it came the realization that Scott Williams, in only the short time she'd known him, had started to fill that emptiness— until yesterday.

Since yesterday, she'd tried very hard to put her thoughts about Scott and any possible relationship with him on a different level. She didn't want to lose his friendship over the bombshell he'd dropped. Nor did she not want to see him because he'd been forthright in telling her about both his career and his life-style.

Her problem, she'd told herself sternly in the small hours of last night as she lay staring at the moon-streaked ceiling in her bedroom, was that she'd plunged too quickly with Scott. She'd let her emotions take over... and she should have known better.

From that first moment when she'd spotted him in the train, sitting next to the window in bedroom four, car 714, he'd had such an *effect* on her. She tried to tell herself it was natural, because he was an extremely attractive man. She tried to rationalize how long it had been since anyone had managed to pry that shell of hers even the slightest bit open. She had been receptive, she could see that now. Receptive, and ready to consider letting someone into her life. Though until now, she would have firmly denied this.

Scott, so kind and gentle and wonderful, had been the person to open that shell. He hadn't pushed or pried. He'd simply let her be herself. For that, Sharon reasoned, she should be grateful to him. And she was. Nevertheless, she could not let him open the shell any further. If that were to happen, there would be pain and possible grief, and a despair far worse than the emptiness he'd started to fill.

At her side, Sylvie said reflectively, "Strange, when I look back on my life, there have been so many people in it—so many men, I should say. And yet few of them, so few of them, have counted for very much. I am not a cynic, but I did learn a long time ago that there is nothing more valuable than true friendship, whether with a man or woman. It is a very rare commodity."

She paused to sip her tea, then went on, "I have learned to separate the different things, you know? The sex, the love, the friendship. Sometimes they all go together, sometimes they are alone. If one is fortunate enough to find someone in whom they all go together, then...I think that is as close to paradise on earth as one can come."

"Did you ever find such a person, Sylvie?" Sharon dared to ask softly.

"Yes, I did." Sylvie nodded. She smiled wistfully and continued, "It was a long time ago, Sharon, in Italy. He was one of the ones I did not marry. He was killed. I think, if he had lived, we would have married and he would have been the only one. And you, Sharon...was your husband such a person?"

Not too surprisingly, Sharon found herself shaking her head. "No," she said quietly. "No, Jerry wasn't like the man you mean. I loved him, I really did, but . . ."

"I know," Sylvie said, touching a slender finger to her lips. "I know."

AFTER LUNCH, the two women went back to their painting. But their introspective conversation had cast a brooding shadow over both of them. Although they tried, they didn't work with quite the same verve and, after a time, Sylvie said, "I think we should call it a day."

At the house on Pine Tree Drive, Sharon invited Sylvie to come in, but she declined.

"Thank you, but I have a date for cocktails," she explained. There was an impish quality to her grin. "A wealthy hotel man I met when I was with Diane at Tony's club one night," she admitted. "An entertaining person, at first acquaintance. So, who knows?"

Did anyone ever really *know*?

Sharon pondered that question without reaching a satisfactory conclusion as she took her paints, easel and her partially completed canvas upstairs with her. Then, as she set up the painting in the screened sun room to dry, the answers started coming.

Sometimes, a person could know. Sometimes it could be so right a person couldn't fail to know.

She suspected it might have become that way between Scott and herself, if not for his Air Force career. A career that involved constant flying and regular transfers between faraway places that equalled if not exceeded the moving around she'd done first with her family, then with Jerry.

Worst of all, from Sharon's viewpoint...Scott gave every indication of loving his life. She could well imagine that his greatest fear, at present, must be that he might not be able to fly again as a professional jet pilot.

Sharon rubbed a few lingering traces of paint off her hands with turpentine, then showered and slipped into a flowing caftan she'd bought with Diane in a fashionable North Miami boutique. It was made of sheer, filmy cotton, buttoning fairly low in front, and was in a gorgeous shade of lilac. Feeling cool and comfortable, she stretched out on her bed and, after her day in the fresh air and sunshine doing something she loved to do, promptly fell asleep.

It was dusk when she awakened. Diane had mentioned at breakfast that she had no plans to go anywhere that evening, so Sharon didn't bother to change. She slipped on a pair of silver sandals and pattered downstairs.

The spiral stairway was covered with thick white carpeting, so her descent was noiseless. As the full length of Diane's Deco living room came into view, she saw the two people sharing cocktails before they saw her. Diane...and Scott!

Diane was ensconced in her favorite white armchair. Scott was sitting in a corner of the black velvet couch. They were talking earnestly but in such soft tones Sharon couldn't hear what they were saying. Then Diane leaned forward, looking very intent, as if she were in the process of making an important point. And Sharon had the uncomfortable feeling that the subject of that point was her!

As at the party, Scott suddenly looked up, then promptly got to his feet. "Well, there you are!" he commented easily.

"Scott called hours ago," Diane reported blithely. "I invited him over to take potluck with us tonight, since it'll be just the two of us. Tonette's spending the night with a school friend." To Scott, she added, "Pajama parties start at much younger ages, these days, than they did when Sharon and I were growing up."

Sharon could remember only one pajama party in her entire life. That had been when she and Diane were about twelve, and it had been at Diane's instigation. She'd gotten their mother on her side, and she'd interceded with their father, who wasn't much for such things. But her father had monitored the few girls who'd come to stay overnight so closely that it hadn't been much fun.

Scott, Sharon noted now, was looking at her anxiously, as if waiting for her approval of Diane's invitation. But before she could say anything, Diane said, "Scott made piña coladas, and they're terrific. Is there enough left in the blender for Sharon, Scott?"

"Sure," he said quickly. "And for our second round, too."

He took his glass and Diane's and headed for the kitchen. Once he was out of earshot, Diane hissed, "You might have shown a bit more enthusiasm, Sharon. You came on as if he was the last person in the world you wanted to see."

Had she looked like that?

Sharon said, rather vaguely, "It was unexpected, that's all."

"Well, you didn't have to look so absolutely *blank*," Diane muttered. "I'd hate to have you on a welcoming committee if it involved any of my clients!"

"Aren't you mixing business with pleasure, Di?"

"I'm just saying—" Diane began with some asperity, then had to break off, because Scott was on his way back bearing a tray and three frosty piña coladas.

After a time, Diane said, "Maria made a marvelous Cuban dish called Picadillo. You put it over rice and have black beans and fried plantains with it. I think I'll go check things out so it'll be ready when we're hungry."

Sharon groaned inwardly. Diane obviously wanted to give her time alone with Scott. But if he thought so, too, he didn't show it. He looked very much at ease, very sure of himself.

He leaned back, drink in hand. "I hear you were out painting today."

"Yes, with Sylvie."

"How did it go?"

"It went very well. Sylvie's tied up tomorrow, but we plan to go back to the same place on Wednesday."

Scott muttered something not quite audible, then said, "My bad luck! I'd hoped you'd go to Vizcaya with me."

"Vizcaya?"

"Some people say it rivals Fontainebleau. I mean the real Fontainebleau, not the Miami Beach hotel," Scott told her. "Vizcaya is a magnificent mansion in South Miami—a palace, really—that was built at the turn of the century by James Deering, the magnate who founded International Harvester. Rick says it's really worth seeing. A glimpse of an opulence unknown to most of us these days. But," he finished philosophically, "we can go another time."

"Scott, if you want to go on Wednesday by all means go," Sharon said quickly.

His look was very direct, and there was a stubborn thrust to his chin as he said, "Thanks, but I wanted to go with you. I have to put in some time at the base tomorrow, or I'd suggest we go in the morning. I should be able to get away by late afternoon, though, so how about having dinner with me? Rick tells me that both Miami and Miami Beach abound with marvelous restaurants. He's given me a list of potentials it would take at least a year to cover, if you went out with consistent regularity...."

Why was she being so hesitant? Scott wondered.

She said awkwardly, "I more or less promised Tonette I'd do something with her after school tomorrow." This was not entirely an untruth. She'd promised Tonette they'd do as much as possible together during her stay in Miami Beach. So far, they'd walked to the beach, and that was it.

"Does that include a late dinner?" Scott inquired stiffly, his eyebrows arched.

"No."

"Sharon...if you don't want to see me, tell me so. Maybe, since yesterday, you've mulled things over, and that's the decision you've come to. If so, I'd rather know now."

Sharon said slowly, "I think you know I want to see you, Scott. It's just that..."

She hesitated, wishing she had Diane's talent for being forthright. If this were Diane, she'd come right out and say what was on her mind. She'd say, "I want to see you more than anything in the world, but I'm afraid. I don't see how we can keep from becoming involved if we go on seeing each other. And I just can't risk involvement with you, Scott, not deep involvement, anyway. So the question is, could we keep things between us close to the surface? That's what I'm afraid of, that we won't be able to...."

Scott seemed to be waiting politely for her to complete her sentence, but Sharon could feel his impatience. She couldn't blame him, because he had no idea what she was thinking.

She said, carefully, "I think we should see each other, but not too much of each other. Does that make sense to you?"

His expression was hard to read. Certainly, he wasn't pleased, yet at the same time he seemed relieved. He said, "I suppose it makes sense to me." He managed a slight smile. "It's just that we have less than three weeks left, if you're heading back to the frozen north on schedule. Is that still your plan?"

"Yes," she said, surprised. "It is."

"I have the impression Diane might like you to stay here," Scott admitted, his voice low. "That's why I asked."

Sylvie also thought Diane wanted her to stay. Knowing her twin as she did, Sharon marveled that Diane hadn't come out and told her, herself. Well, Diane hadn't, and until she did, that was something she didn't have to deal with, Sharon decided.

"Will you have dinner with me tomorrow night?" Scott asked again.

An inner voice whispered to Sharon, *Why torture yourself? You know how much you want to have dinner with him tomorrow, or any night!*

"I'd like that very much," she said abruptly.

"Terrific," Scott told her, his blue eyes sparkling with delight. "I'll check out a few places and try to find one that's special. I think Rick wants to take us over to Calle Ocho one night. That's the heart of Miami's Cuban district. Maybe this weekend—"

Scott was interrupted by the sudden peal of the door-bell. From the kitchen, Diane called, "Get that, will you, someone? I think it's Tony."

It was Tony, looking especially debonair in a raw silk charcoal suit with a deep yellow shirt. He greeted Scott warmly and, after kissing Sharon on the cheek, settled into a chair as if he still lived there.

Glancing at their half-empty glasses, he asked, "What's everyone drinking?"

"Piña coladas," Scott answered. "How about my whipping up another batch?"

"Sounds good to me," Tony approved.

With Scott gone from the room, Tony grinned at Sharon and asked, "Having a good time in Miami Beach, little sister?"

"Definitely, yes."

"What have you been doing with yourself? Going out with Scott?"

"Not today. Today, Sylvie and I went on a painting excursion."

"Good." Tony nodded. "I agree with Diane, that woman's got real talent. What she needs is to put some of the stuff she does out where people can see it. A while back, I wanted to hang some of her paintings in the lobby of the club, but she turned me down flat."

"I wonder why?"

"I don't know. Maybe she's afraid of rejection. Sometimes that keeps people from sticking their neck out, or putting a painting on display, or letting anyone else in on what matters most to them." Tony took a pack of slim, black cigarillos out of his coat pocket and lit one. "Didn't know I was such a philosopher, did you?" he joked.

Sharon laughed. "Nothing I found out about you would surprise me, Tony," she teased. "You're a man of many talents."

"Let's not investigate *that* remark too deeply," he warned lightly. He looked around the room. "How do you like this place?"

"I keep feeling as though I've dropped in on a thirties movie set," Sharon confessed.

"Me, too. I've been living in a small apartment above the club these past few months. Sort of a makeshift arrangement. But I told Diane I think when I get a place of my own I'll go traditional and decorate it in Colonial," Tony quipped. "On the other hand, I'd say this place suits Diane. Sort of expresses her personality."

Sharon could find no quick answer to that. If anything, she would have thought that the decor in the Pine Tree Drive house expressed Tony's personality more than it did Diane's. It was a surprise, actually, to get the message that evidently Tony hadn't had much to do with the choice of colors and furnishings.

Maybe she didn't know her twin as well as she thought she did! Maybe, in these years apart, Diane had changed on some really deep levels. It was a strange thought, because Sharon had always felt that, in Diane, she had her counterpart in the world. Someone so like herself they'd always be in tune. But more and more since being in Miami Beach, she'd picked up on their differences.

She noticed these differences anew as she, Diane, Scott and Tony feasted on the delicious Cuban meal Maria had prepared. They ate by candlelight out on the patio, and the setting could hardly have been more romantic. Tony put some Latin-American music on the stereo, "to go with the food," he said. Flickering candles, the sensuous pulse of the music, the scent of the oranges...all these combined to make a very heady mixture.

Sharon tried to repress her awareness of Scott, but found this impossible. He was sitting beside her, so close she could literally feel his warmth. As an exercise in distracting herself, she unobtrusively studied her twin. She watched the way she moved, listened to the things she said, noted her general demeanor.

Suddenly, she realized that Diane really *had* changed. There was a new brittleness about her, a little too much laughter that didn't go very deep, a little too much energy, a fragile quickness.

She's not happy, Sharon thought, *and neither is Tony. Was this divorce a mistake after all?*

They finished the meal with flaky tarts filled with guava paste, complemented by demitasse cups of steaming Cuban espresso laced with sugar. They sat around the table, talking casually about a variety of things, until finally Tony said, "Di, I meant to tell you this sooner. I think the permissions we need to record most of the music will be in the bag before long."

Diane had left the table and was stretched out on a nearby lounge. Now she sat up straight and exclaimed enthusiastically, "Really? That's fantastic!"

"I've found a lawyer up in Lauderdale who's really into this. He's worked with some of the big music corporations in New York—he'll know how to shortcut the red tape. Meanwhile, I've got another man scouting for a studio where we can begin production. He told me just this afternoon that he thinks he's on to something."

Catching Sharon's puzzled expression, Tony asked, "Has Diane told you anything about this business the two of us are getting into together?"

"I haven't been specific," Diane interjected.

"Okay, Sharon. Do you know what a compact disk is?" Tony queried eagerly.

"I've seen them in music stores, but I don't really know what they are," she admitted.

"Well, I think they're going to be the recording medium of the future," Tony stated. "Hell, they're already proving themselves, and they haven't been around that long. The first ones were produced in 1983, and it's estimated that by 1990 they will account for fifty percent of the retail sales in music stores. They'll be way ahead of cassettes and LPs, that's almost a certainty."

"Aren't the CD players rather expensive?" Scott asked.

"Not really," Tony said. "They were up around a thousand dollars when they first hit the market in '83, but you can get a good one now for a couple of hundred bucks. As the market increases and technology improves, the prices will probably drop even more."

"What about the disks themselves?" Sharon queried, her interest piqued.

"The disks were pricey in the beginning—around eighteen dollars. Now, though, they're selling for between twelve and fourteen bucks. Within a few more years, they'll be under ten. At least, that's what my research into the matter strongly predicts.

"You see," Tony went on, warming to his subject, "the thing about compact disks is…they never wear out. You never have to replace them. They never scratch or warp, like albums. And the sound they produce is fantastic. A much broader range, superior to anything else. The disk itself carries a digital code that is activated by a laser in the player, so nothing mechanical like a needle ever touches the surface. Am I going too fast on this?"

"Not for Scott, I'm sure," Sharon said, smiling. "But for me, well . . . I'm not exactly a wizard when it comes to electronics."

"You don't have to be to enjoy CDs," Tony promised her. "They've really caught on, and *before* the companies that produce them were ready, actually. I talked with the general manager of Miami's largest music store the other day, and he told me they're having a hard time getting enough stock from their suppliers to keep their customers happy. From the feelers I have out, that's about what you hear everywhere."

"So, what are you and Diane going to do?" Sharon asked curiously. "Start manufacturing your own disks?"

"Precisely," Tony announced happily. "You see, a problem has been that the variety of stuff available on CDs has been fairly limited. Mostly top rock bands and the big-name symphony orchestras. So, Di and I were saying one day that the way Deco seems to be more popular than ever, we thought CDs featuring music of the Twenties and Thirties might be big sellers, too.

"I've got a lot of music world connections because of the club," Tony went on, "and Di and I kept kicking around the ideas we had. It's taken a while to get our act together, but now it's starting to jell."

"We're going to incorporate as Di-Tone, Inc.," Diane announced excitedly. "What do you think of that?"

It was Scott who answered. "I think it's pretty fantastic," he said, "and you count me in as one of your first customers when you get into production. I've always liked the kind of music you two are talking about. And now whenever I hear a song like that, it'll remind me of being here, in Miami.

"That's the kind of memory," he added significantly, "that I'd like to fall back on quite often."

CHAPTER NINE

SCOTT TOOK SHARON to the Forge for dinner the next evening. The restaurant was a popular Miami nightspot on Arthur Godfrey Road, famous not only for its food, but for the grandeur of its decor.

As they were following the maître d' to their table, Scott said, "I see what Rick meant about this place. He called their collection of art nouveau staggering and, from my first glimpse, I'd say he used the right adjective—to say nothing of all the genuine antiques and art objects. Sometimes I wish I were more culturally knowledgeable, shall we say?"

Sharon looked exquisite in a shell-pink chiffon dress she'd borrowed from Diane—as she had quickly admitted to Scott when he complimented her on it. She'd basked in the sun at the beach in the early afternoon, and her cheeks had a healthy blush. Later, she'd picked Tonette up at school and taken her for an ice-cream cone. Then, she'd treated herself to a nap and a fragrant bubble bath, with the result that she felt great.

She, too, was impressed with the setting, but she laughed and said, "I imagine you probably know more about art and culture than a lot of people. Certainly you have an appreciative eye, and that's half the battle."

"I have an appreciative eye for *you*," Scott murmured huskily. His blue eyes were glowing with warmth, and the cream-colored suit he was wearing appeared to have been designed specifically for him. He looked fantastic, and Sharon could feel herself melting long before she should be thinking about melting at all!

The Forge had its own popular lounge, which, according to the report Scott had garnered from Rick, swung with some of the best live disco music around, until three in the morning, no less. Still, after dinner Scott suggested they move on to Tony's club, since Tony had promptly invited them to stop by when he'd heard they were planning to go out.

There was an appealing intimacy to Tony's place. As Sharon and Scott entered there was a vocalist perched on top of the grand piano, singing, "As Time Goes By." She was a stunning blonde wearing a short, flapper-type blue satin dress banded with a long silk fringe. The outfit was straight out of the Twenties.

"She wasn't here the other night," Sharon mused, after they'd been seated and the waiter had taken their drink orders.

"She's good," Scott observed. "There's a unique quality to her voice. It's husky and provocative, like a lot of nightclub singers, but it has something of its own, too."

"She's also pretty great to look at," Sharon decided.

"Yes, I guess she is, now that you mention it."

"Come on, Scott. You don't have to pretend you're blind when you're out with me!"

"On the contrary, I'm all eyes...for you," he quipped, giving his words an exaggerated emphasis that made Sharon chuckle.

The blonde finished singing, and there was an enthusiastic round of applause. The bandleader took the mike to say, "Thank you, ladies and gentlemen. Genevieve will be back with us a little later. But there's plenty of music left in these guys, so don't go away!'' With that intro, he led his eight-piece jazz combo into a sultry rendition of "Sophisticated Lady."

"Now I know I've bitten into a time capsule and I'm back in the thirties," Sharon told Scott, leaning toward him and speaking into his ear.

Couples were drifting onto the small dance floor. Scott turned to Sharon, dangerously close, and asked, "Shall we?"

It was so natural to move into his arms and dance "swing style," cheek to cheek. Sharon's forehead brushed Scott's chin. His after-shave was subtle and provocative, and its musky scent went straight to her libido. She felt herself gripped, way down deep, by an extremely basic sensation. And she was just a little shocked at the explicitness of her desire.

Maybe it was the wine she'd had at dinner, or the sip of Chartreuse she'd tested just before heading out onto the dance floor. But all of a sudden, Sharon felt oddly free. She pressed closer to Scott, humming the refrain softly, swaying in time with his every move. She felt his lips press lightly against her temple, combining promises of passion and tenderness. Wonderful sensations shimmered through Sharon, little silvery ribbons of anticipation and delight.

Then the music stopped. And, unfortunately, the next number the band swung into was an old-time jitterbug rendition of "Chattanooga Choo Choo." A great song, Sharon thought ruefully, but completely out of tempo with her mood.

Scott guided her by the arm back to their table, his touch burning Sharon's skin with erotic fire. The excitement that washed over her was a magic potion she wished she could distill and carry around with her in a little bottle, to be released and absorbed whenever he was away.

There was no sense in pretending that this man at her side wasn't someone very special, Sharon knew. No way to deny that he would be very easy to fall in love with.

Scott was right. They had less than three weeks left in Miami, barely a handful of days to enjoy being together before she'd be traveling back north.

And during that time I want to be with him whenever I can, Sharon found herself thinking recklessly. *I'll go wherever he wants to go, do whatever he wants to do....*

Dangerous words. She recognized the danger, and her heart beat faster.

She wanted so much to be alone with Scott. She wanted to whisk him away to a more intimate setting and begin exchanging a new kind of confidence with him. She wanted to leave this club and discover romance under the stars. And then she saw Tony bearing down on them.

He reached their table just as they did, snatched a nearby vacant chair and sat down. Surveying them both benevolently, he asked, "Well, children, are you enjoying yourselves?"

Sharon saw a hint of amusement in Tony's dark eyes, and more than a little knowing. She'd never had a poker face. She knew she must looked flushed, at this point . . . and also radiant. And those were telltale signs.

Scott said, sincerely, "This is a terrific place you've got here, Tony. And your singer is tremendous."

Tony's smile faded. "I want you to meet her," he said solemnly, mostly to Sharon. "Her name's Genevieve Landry, and she's quite a person. She came to the Beach about six months ago. The band was advertising for a vocalist at the time, and none of us could believe it when we auditioned her and heard her sing. I told her then, as I do now, she could write her own ticket. All she needs is the right kind of promotion.''

Tony drew one of his thin black cigars out of his pocket. ''Do you mind?'' he asked Sharon.

She shook her head, but Tony was already lighting up.

He said, ''She likes it here, though. And I like having her here. I was thinking maybe after she finishes her next set, the four of us could sneak off for a late supper someplace.''

Scott shook his head reluctantly. ''I'd like to, Tony,'' he said, ''but I have a long drive back to Homestead.'' At Tony's puzzled expression, he went on, ''I'm on temporary duty at the Air Force base there.''

''You're in the Air Force?''

Scott nodded. ''Yes ... sort of a combination of limited duty and convalescent leave, at the moment. It's a long story. Anyway, I cut out rather early this afternoon, and I have some work I'll have to finish up first thing in the morning. Could we have a rain check?''

''Anytime,'' Tony said expansively. ''Maybe I can get Genevieve to come over and meet the two of you before she goes on again.''

Tony headed toward the rear of the club. Watching him, Sharon commented, ''I'd say Tony has more than an employer-employee interest in his singer.''

''Has Diane mentioned Genevieve?''

''No, she hasn't, though I imagine she's heard her sing. I don't know how often Diane comes here, but she does come now and then. Sylvie mentioned that they've been here several times together.''

Sharon continued thoughtfully, ''Tony says he's known her for six months, so I don't suppose I should be having this feeling that she might be the straw that broke the camel's back, in regard to Diane's marriage.''

"From the little I've heard, I'd say their marriage was on the rocks for a long time," Scott opined. "Marriages don't just snap, Sharon. It's more a question of erosion."

As he listened to the sound of his voice, Scott recognized that a certain quality—something that reared its ugly head every time the subject of divorce came up—had disappeared. That quality was bitterness. For many long months, he'd been unable to speak of divorce, or marriage, without his own bitterness coming through. Suddenly, he viewed the whole subject in a new perspective.

I think I've finally washed Claudia out of my hair, he found himself thinking.

He looked at Sharon, and a funny feeling came over him. On the dance floor he'd felt that sudden spiraling of desire on her part—they were so incredibly in tune with each other. Never in his life had he been so totally in step with another person. It was one of life's mysteries that he'd known her for such a short time, and curiously ironic that they had several profound differences that would test the validity of their feelings.

While dancing, it had taken very little prompting for his own desire to meet and match hers. Now Scott wished he could play caveman and swoop Sharon into his arms, carry her out into the tropical night and lower her into some sensuous secret lair where he could make her his!

He wanted her. He wanted her with a tender yet passionate desire such as he'd never felt for any woman. And the combination, Scott knew, was potentially devastating!

He saw Tony returning, the blond singer at his side. She was shorter than she'd appeared in the spotlight, and maybe a shade older than he'd thought, too. But she was very pretty, with dazzling gold hair and eyes that had an open, almost ingenuous look about them.

Tony, as he introduced her, looked slightly be-mused...or maybe the word was bewitched, Scott thought whimsically. Genevieve Landry sat down at their table in another chair their attentive waiter managed to find, and Tony promptly ordered a bottle of champagne.

Scott sighed. He was beginning to feel a dull headache coming on, and he really didn't want any champagne. He knew that his energy was waning fast, and felt a flash of resentment at this persistent, physical weakness of his. Rick insisted that he was doing extremely well and, given time, would do better. But Scott wasn't used to feeling other than completely first-rate, and he had little patience with lingering malaises.

He accepted the champagne and sipped in response to the toast Tony proposed, which included all four of them. Afterward, though, he nursed the glass along, and let Tony carry the conversation.

Sharon, he noticed, was nursing her wine, too. But she'd also begun to watch him rather anxiously. Was the oncoming headache and his general feeling of fatigue so obvious?

The answer came when he and Sharon left the club shortly after Genevieve excused herself to get ready for her next set. They were walking toward Scott's car when Sharon said abruptly, "I can drive, you know."

"I'm sure you can," Scott conceded.

"Well?"

"Are you trying to tell me something, Sharon?"

"Why don't you let me drive back to Diane's."

He stopped in the light of a streetlamp and stared down at her. "If you think I've had too much to drink, I assure you that's not so. I don't like mixing drinking and driving, so I was pretty careful."

"I believe you, Scott. But all of a sudden, back in Tony's place, you looked so *strained*. You . . . well, you look pretty tired. Are you sure you're all right?"

"I'm fine," he said tersely, though the headache was getting worse. He carried a prescription analgesic with him at Rick Fabrega's insistence, but he couldn't down the pills without water and he was damned if he was going back to Tony's place and request a glass.

Sharon said softly, "Don't fight it so. Ricardo told Diane that you're doing marvelously, but that you do need to take it easy for a while longer."

"He did, did he?" Scott growled.

"Yes, he did," Sharon said steadily. "He called her up the day after the party to tell her what a good time he'd had, and mentioned it then. Also, he wants her to have dinner with him some night."

"Is she going to?"

"I don't know. Anyway, right now what I'm interested in is seeing you stop pushing yourself and get a little rest."

"Sharon, I don't need a nurse!"

Scott snapped the words at her and promptly wished he could retract them. She looked up as if he'd slapped her. Nevertheless, when they reached the car, she said briskly, "Keys, please?"

"I can drive, Sharon."

"I'm sure you can. But let me right now, okay?"

Scott gritted his teeth and handed her the keys. His head was throbbing, he felt lousy. And he swore at himself for not telling Tony, politely, that he'd have to take a rain check on the champagne, too.

So much for pride, he thought wryly, as he slid into the passenger seat and let Sharon take the wheel.

It was a muggy night. Scott leaned his head against the headrest and closed his eyes, wishing that it was about twenty degrees cooler. The humidity didn't make him feel any better.

It was only a short ride to Diane's and, as far as Scott was concerned, it ended much too quickly. He wearily lumbered out of the car, then followed Sharon to the front door where he intended to say good-night and quickly get on his way. When she opened the door and invited, over her shoulder, "Come on in," he groaned.

"I'd like to," he said wearily, "but I've got to get on the road. I really do need to get back and collapse for a while."

"That black couch of Diane's can double as a bed," Sharon reported.

"What?"

"I'll get a pillow and some sheets and blankets—"

"It must be over eighty, Sharon. Who needs a blanket?" Scott demanded, then added quickly, "Look, it's nice of you, but I can't. I really have to get some stuff done on the base in the morning."

"Can't it wait? Or is it something top secret, or classified, or whatever you call it?"

He smiled. "It's not a top priority, no," he admitted. "I'd just like to finish with it, that's all. Frankly, it's an extremely boring report on a lot of very boring material I was asked to read."

"Then you can do it when you feel better," Sharon stated firmly. "Look, Scott, there are towels in the powder room. You know where that is, don't you?"

"Yes."

"Then I'll go get some sheets and pillows," Sharon compromised, and ran lightly up the spiral stairway before he could frame another protest.

At this point, Scott didn't care. He sat down wearily on the edge of the couch, hating himself for feeling not only very weak, but completely inept. He was used to handling a situation, to being in control, to commanding. This was a strange role reversal for him.

By the time Sharon hurried back downstairs, though, he was feeling as if little shrieking demons had taken possession of his head and were pounding it with red-hot hammers.

"Sit over there while I fix this up, okay?" she asked, quickly shaking out a sheet.

Scott was past the point of arguing, and collapsed into a chair. Watching him out of the corner of her eye, Sharon said bluntly, "You look terrible, Scott. Do you want me to call Ricardo?"

"Good Lord, no!" He fumbled in his pocket for the vial of pills. "What I would appreciate," he managed, "is a glass of water."

She got the water. But seeing the pills, she demanded, "Are you sure it's safe to take those on top of alcohol?"

Scott glared at her over the rim of his glass. "Yes, Sharon, I'm sure. Enough time has passed, I didn't have that much to drink, and I'm not leaving this room, okay?"

"Okay."

It would take a while for the pills to take effect, Scott knew. Yet in another way he already felt better, and he knew the reason why. Sharon was a comfort, a panacea. Though he was appalled at himself for giving in to her, he had to admit that he loved the element of TLC in having Sharon hand him the glass of water, then watch him take the pills as if she were his private Florence Nightingale.

Scott couldn't remember a woman caring for him like this. Claudia certainly hadn't. He supposed that his mother had lavished a required measure of maternal care on Hugh and him, but he didn't really remember. Because ever since he'd been old enough to fend for himself—and the same applied to Hugh—they'd received no special cuddling from their mother. She'd been too busy being an Army wife, doing the right things to help her husband's career move up the ladder.

When he thought back to childhood and his mother, the picture that came to mind was of a strong, good-looking woman dressed elegantly but conservatively, about to leave the house for an officers' wives luncheon, or tea at someone's home, or one of her seemingly eternal bridge parties.

Then, at night, there were the receptions and various other Army affairs that had been requisite for both General Williams and his wife. Scott could remember his father in Army blues, and his mother with her hair arranged in carefully stylized waves. . . .

At his side, Sharon suddenly spoke. She'd taken the water glass back out to the kitchen and had returned without making a sound. He looked down and saw she'd kicked off the silver slippers she'd been wearing, and was barefoot.

"Scott," she urged gently, "the couch is all set. I think you'll be comfortable, but I'll come back down in a few minutes to check on you. Okay?"

He watched Sharon climb the curving stairs and yearned to follow her. Yearned? Scott suddenly realized that the pills *were* having an effect. In place of a throbbing headache, he'd taken off on a sensuous flight of fancy. In his own self-interest, he decided to reverse directions!

He slowly got his feet, used the guest bathroom off the foyer, then returned to the living room. Flicking off the remaining lights, he sat down on the couch, pulled off his shoes and undressed down to his briefs. He made a neat pile of his clothing on the closest chair, then slid between the sheets.

It felt strange to be spending the night in the home of Sharon's sister. More than strange, really, yet Scott had made his decision and was too tired to argue himself out of it. The half-hour-plus drive to Homestead would not be easy. It rarely was.

The air-conditioning was on in the house, keeping the heat and humidity at tolerable levels, and the couch was surprisingly comfortable. Scott stretched to his full length, and gradually drifted off toward sleep.

When he felt warm lips touch his forehead, he thought he was dreaming. Without opening his eyes, he reached out his hand, and it promptly was taken into Sharon's clasp.

"Feel better?" she whispered, her voice a lovely, melodious chime in the muted darkness.

"Yes," he murmured, his throat thickening. Then, to Scott's chagrin—to his *horror*—tears came to sting his eyes.

He hadn't cried since he was ten years old. He'd been skateboarding with his brother at the Presidio in San Francisco, where his father was then stationed. He'd taken a nasty fall and suffered a deep cut requiring several stitches. The doctor in the Army hospital's emergency room hadn't given him enough anesthetic to dull the pain, or hadn't allowed it to work before he'd started suturing. The tears had come, and as hard as Scott tried to hold them back, they'd still spilled over.

He'd felt foolish and embarrassed then. Now...he wasn't sure what he felt. He only knew that he'd been brought up within the doctrine that men didn't cry. Especially military men.

Sharon said, "I left my door open in case you need me in the night. My room's right in the corner, upstairs. If you call, I'm sure I'll hear you. So call me if you don't feel better soon, will you?"

"I will," Scott promised huskily. "And...thank you."

By way of answer, she kissed him again. And it was only actual physical exhaustion that kept Scott from clutching her and easing her down beside him, to let Nature's forces take charge.

As Sharon slipped away, it shocked Scott to realize that he'd become emotionally unstrung to the point of tears. He, Scott Elliott Williams, a man who'd made a reputation in the Air Force as one of the most cool-headed of all the veteran jet pilots.

She had said to call her if he needed her in the night. As Scott drifted back to sleep again, he wondered if he would.

UPSTAIRS, SHARON LAY AWAKE for a long time, listening. She was worried about Scott. At Tony's, he'd become so pale that she'd really been frightened, and though he'd tried to disguise it she'd known there was something wrong.

Had Ricardo Fabrega kept something to himself? she wondered. Was there more to Scott's illness than his brilliant surgeon friend wished to tell?

Sharon shuddered as her vivid imagination plunged forward. Then she sat up in bed and told herself sternly that she was being an absolute fool! They weren't living in the dark ages. Today's doctors believed in laying it on the line. They no longer kept dire secrets from their patients. Like most patients themselves, they believed in a person's right to know the medical truth.

Sharon suspected that Scott had been through more with the dizzy spells and the subsequent surgery than he'd let on. At the same time, he'd had the added trauma of an unpleasant divorce. No wonder he was finding it hard to get fully back on his feet again, both physically and emotionally.

Beside him on the couch, in the dim light that filtered in from Pine Tree Drive, she'd seen those tears shimmering on Scott's long eyelashes. It had taken a selfless effort not to lean over and kiss them away. She had had to fight her desire to lie down alongside him. The consolation she intended to give would have soon led to something much more perilous, Sharon knew, than the touching encounter she and Scott had shared on the beach....

Sharon had visions of Diane's party, of her and Scott talking in the garden, of the two of them escaping into the night. She knew what his kiss was like, she knew how quickly she aroused him. And...she knew why he'd stopped.

What would it be like to make love with him? she wondered, getting back under her covers. She could only imagine. And the more she imagined, the more she knew she wanted Scott to be her lover

CHAPTER TEN

WHEN SHARON WENT DOWNSTAIRS the next morning and walked into the living room, she began to think she'd been hallucinating the night before. The couch certainly didn't look like anyone had slept on it; there were no sheets or pillows in evidence, and everything was in order.

She found Diane out on the patio, scanning a local real estate journal as she sipped her coffee. Her twin was wearing reading glasses these days. And even though she whipped them off when she saw Sharon, the glasses added one more little difference between them. Sharon thought wryly that in a number of ways these "differences" were mounting up.

"Well!" Diane greeted her. "There's nothing like coming downstairs in the morning and finding a man asleep in my living room. I won't say a strange man, because he wasn't." She giggled and added, "I must admit, Shar, you pick handsome specimens to bring home with you."

Maria appeared with coffee *con leche*. Sharon thanked her, then sat down opposite Diane, feeling faintly resentful. "When did Scott leave?"

"About an hour ago. You were sound asleep. I checked."

That was no surprise. After making sure that Scott was settled comfortably on the couch, Sharon had reluctantly padded upstairs to her room. Then she'd stayed awake most of the night in case he called her—a fact she wasn't about to confide to Diane.

After a moment, Diane continued, "Scott said to tell you he was feeling fine, and he'll call you around noon. What happened last night, anyway?"

"Scott still gets headaches occasionally, an expected reaction to the surgery Ricardo performed," Sharon explained. "One came on last night while we were at Tony's club. I didn't think he should drive back to Homestead by himself."

"Good thinking," Diane applauded. "However...I must admit that had I been in your shoes, I probably would have coaxed him upstairs and into my bed!"

"Fine," Sharon retorted shortly, "that's what *you* would have done. I did what I thought I should do."

"You don't need to get defensive, Sharon," Diane countered. She paused, and there was something about the quality of the pause that made Sharon look at her twin more acutely than she might have otherwise. She saw that Diane had put on her "casual face," which meant that she had something on her mind she wanted to express, but wasn't quite sure how to do so.

Sharon's suspicions were verified when Diane said, too offhandedly, "Did you meet the new singer at Tony's place?"

"Genevieve Landry?"

"Ah, so you must have been introduced to her."

"As a matter of fact, we were."

"Gorgeous, isn't she?"

"She's very pretty, yes."

"Tony's crazy about her," Diane stated rather testily, her "casual face" fading into a grimace.

"Must you always leap to conclusions, Diane?" Sharon asked sharply. "I think Tony's glad to have her there because she's quite an attraction."

"Isn't she, though!"

"What I mean is...she has an unusual voice, and she's drawing customers into the club."

"I'm not talking about her professional attributes, Shar," Diane announced. "I'm saying that Tony has fallen head over heels for her."

"What makes you so sure of that?"

"He told me so."

"Well, then..." Sharon floundered.

"I think it's mostly because he's on the rebound," Diane decided coolly. "There's this lost feeling you get after a divorce. Even when divorce is the most *right* action in the world, it involves separation. And separation from the things and people that have been your life always has a degree of pain to it. Do you know what I'm saying?"

"Yes, I know what you're saying."

Diane nodded. "Well, Tony and I were together a long time. In some ways, it's harder to get used to the separation when we still see so much of each other. I mean, there's Tonette to consider, and our business venture, and . . . well, we *do* like each other."

"I'm glad you do," Sharon said honestly.

Diane managed a weak smile. "It's a long time, though, since Tony's been a bachelor," she said dully.

"I don't mean to sound cold, Di, but so what?"

Diane took an introspective sip of coffee, then said, "Well, I sense he's sort of at odds with himself. I know the feeling. There are those nights when I go to bed, or those mornings when I get up, feeling exactly the same way. Lonely, that is."

Sharon sat silently for a minute, mulling over what Diane was saying. Then she posed the question that had quietly plagued her since her first night in this house.

"Are you sure you two should have gotten a divorce?"

"Definitely," Diane stated, without hesitation. "I've told you that, and Tony would totally agree. Still, that doesn't alter the trauma that goes along with the whole thing."

"Yes," Sharon said slowly. "Yes, I know you're right." She was thinking that Scott Williams had alluded to the fact that divorce was traumatic, no matter what.

"Anyway, I just don't want Tony to get hurt, that's all."

"And you think Genevieve might hurt him?"

"Looking at her, I'd say there's an excellent chance of it."

"Sure that's not sour grapes, Di?"

Diane's eyes narrowed. "If anyone but you said that to me, Sharon—"

"No one but me is saying it to you," Sharon prodded gently. She chuckled and added, "I think you're suffering from a brush with the green-eyed monster."

"What?" Diane demanded, incredulous.

"Before you get furious, think about that. I think it's probably as natural to be somewhat jealous of your ex—for a time, anyway—as it is to feel the sense of separation and loss you've been talking about. As for Tony...he is a grown man, Di. He moves in a very sophisticated world. If he becomes infatuated with a new singer and even has a fling with her...I'd say it's nothing for *you* to worry about. If she burns Tony in the process, he'll get over it."

Diane glanced up at the bright blue sky. The sun was blazing. She said, "Two hours till noon, and you're already waxing philosophical. Is this really my twin I'm hearing?"

"Yes, it's really me," Sharon assured her. "I guess I'm just getting older and wiser," she quipped.

"Wiser is okay, but go easy on the older!" Diane advised, sounding her normal self once again.

At that, Sharon chuckled, and her twin returned to her perusal of her real estate journal. Sharon picked up the morning paper and began scanning the news section. After a while, Diane announced that she had an appointment to show a prospective client a house, and she headed inside to get ready.

Left alone, Sharon stretched out on a lounge chair, closed her eyes, and found that the only thing she could think about was Scott Williams.

Perhaps it was mental telepathy, but a few minutes later the phone rang, and Maria called out that it was Scott on the line.

Sharon discovered that she loved the sound of his voice over the phone. It had a mellow richness to it, combined with a certain crispness—an offshoot of being so involved with the military, she decided.

Scott said, "I've got sort of a crazy idea for this afternoon, if you're free."

"I'm all ears."

"Good. Then let's go for an airboat ride in the Everglades."

"The Everglades!"

"They're not that far away," Scott informed her cheerily. "Actually, they begin only a few miles past the outskirts of Miami. Suppose I pick you up in about an hour and a half. Okay?"

It was more than okay...until Sharon remembered she'd made a painting date with Sylvie. Still, she was sure Sylvie wouldn't mind a change of plans just this once. A quick phone call confirmed this.

Scott and Sharon drove west from Miami following Highway 41, also known as the Tamiami Trail, and within thirty minutes found themselves in the middle of a seemingly endless expanse of flat wetlands. Coming from the glamorous, high-rise world of Miami Beach made the transition especially fascinating, because they'd so quickly plunged into a different world.

They spent the next two hours touring the swampy glades in a large noisy airboat, spotting alligators in the wilderness and glimpsing the thatched-roofed huts of an occasional Miccosukee Indian village.

"I especially liked the birds," Sharon commented as they started back toward Miami. "Those white herons look so exotic, and those crazy things drying out their wings...what were they called?"

"Anhingas," Scott told her.

"Right, anhingas."

They were driving beside a wide canal along which people were fishing, often with very long bamboo poles. Out of the blue, Scott asked, "How about going to the greyhound races in Hollywood tonight?"

"No way," Sharon stated firmly. "I have other plans."

Scott glanced across at her, obviously disappointed.

"Oh?" he muttered.

Sharon couldn't help but smile as she said, "They include you, Scott. Believe it or not, I'd like you to come back to Diane's house with me and spend a quiet evening at home. Just you and me and Diane and Tonette. I left word with Maria that I wanted to cook dinner tonight. My famous linguini with white clam sauce. Maria offered to pick up the ingredients for me this afternoon, so it's all set.''

There was an odd catch in Scott's voice as he said, ''You're going to cook dinner? I've never pictured you doing anything . . . domestic.''

Sharon didn't know quite how to take that, so she said only, ''Yes, I can cook. I don't too often, because I live alone and it's difficult cooking gourmet meals for one person. But both Diane and I learned how to cook when we were growing up, despite our peripatetic life-style. My mother was very creative in the kitchen, and she always encouraged us—wherever that kitchen happened to be.''

''You really did hate not having a permanent home base, didn't you?'' Scott queried softly.

''Well, let's just say that I sensed there was something missing. It took me a while to realize that the missing ingredient was never having a real home of our own. Anyway, Diane and I can hold our own in the kitchen, I assure you.''

''I can't wait to find out,'' Scott said honestly. ''And I surely don't object in the least to spending a quiet evening with you and Diane and Tonette. It's just that you sort of made it sound like some kind of a prescription.''

''Well, I don't think you should push so much,'' Sharon ventured. ''You're not completely well yet, you know. I think last night proved that.''

Scott sighed. He detested the invalid role, and tended to react very negatively if anyone suggested he play it— even temporarily. At Walter Reed, his nurses had often battled him back to his room, just syllables short of swearing at him.

Now . .

He looked at Sharon's lovely face, and the concern he saw there did something to him.

She cared about him. Regardless of anything else, she deeply, honestly cared. He saw that written on her face and in her beautiful green eyes, and nothing else mattered.

He said huskily, "Sweetheart, I admit I don't have my usual stamina. How can I not admit that, after the way I conked out on you last night? But I'm okay now. Honestly, I'm okay."

Sharon said, a bit shakily, "I want you to stay okay, that's all."

AN HOUR LATER, Scott found himself sitting cross-legged on the floor in Diane's living room, playing Tonette's favorite board game with her. He'd never had much experience with children, and was quite surprised that he and Tonette got along famously. Next, they watched a TV show together, during which Tonette ate her dinner: a peanut butter and jelly sandwich, carrots and a glass of milk. Then she was off to her room, solemnly reminding Scott to come up later and make sure she was asleep.

For the adults' repast, Diane cleared off her dining room table, which was littered with newspapers, brochures, legal pads, two telephone books, a phone and a potted plant. As she placed everything on the floor in the corner of the room, she said, over her shoulder, "One of these days I'm going to buy a computer, and that will probably end up here, too!"

Sharon's dinner was an unqualified success. Along with her linguini, she made garlic bread and a tossed green salad vinaigrette. Diane produced candles, linen napkins and a bottle of Valpolicella, and even pulled out Scott's chair for him.

"A simple evening at home?" Scott queried skeptically.

"Absolutely," Sharon and Diane answered in chorus, then turned toward each other and laughed.

The evening was relaxing and pleasurable and exactly what Scott needed to regain his strength. When, a couple of days later, he was called into conference with a superior officer at Homestead who asked him how he'd like to head up a special training program while still on limited duty, he began to feel that things were going a lot better than he had expected.

Sharon was painting almost every day with Sylvie, but she also saved lots of time for him. Still, their time was running out, and Scott fervently wished that there was some way he could persuade her to stay in Miami Beach a while longer.

EVERY TIME SHE AND SYLVIE ventured somewhere to paint, Sharon felt a new sense of release. Inspired tremendously by Sylvie, she let her creativity run loose, gained confidence in her artistic ability, and wondered more and more if her work was good enough to sell.

One afternoon, as they were heading back toward Pine Tree Drive in Sylvie's battered old car, Sylvie suddenly asked, "Would you care to stop by my studio for a glass of wine?"

Sharon knew from Diane that invitations to Sylvie's studio were a rarity. Despite her growing friendship with this unusual woman, she'd often wondered if she'd ever get one.

"I'd like that very much," she said.

Sylvie's studio was a fairly large room with a high ceiling and three skylights. She had a small bathroom and a tiny kitchenette, and had converted every inch of space into something uniquely her own. Each wall was a crazy pastel color, and hung all across them, in no particular order, were her remarkable paintings.

Sharon, moving from one to the next, murmured, "I honestly think you're a genius!"

"Not even close, I assure you," Sylvie said with a laugh, as she poured wine from a beautiful crystal decanter. "I am merely uninhibited, *cherie*. When I paint, I let it all out. As you are learning to do, no?"

"Well..."

"It is true, Sharon. Every day your work becomes stronger."

"Maybe so," Sharon allowed, "but I'm not even close to your league, Sylvie. You *must* exhibit these, you really must."

"Perhaps some day, if the wolf really comes to howl at my door," she decided. "But then who knows if anyone would buy one of them, anyway? One can never tell, with art."

"I can tell with this art," Sharon insisted stubbornly. "If you'd let these paintings out of your studio I guarantee you'd become famous."

Sylvie sank back on a daybed piled with pillows and eyed Sharon speculatively. "I am not sure I want to be famous," she admitted. "Perhaps you have not noticed, because most of the time I appear so much the extrovert, but I am really a very private person, Sharon. I think I would shrink away from fame."

"Why don't you try it and see?"

"Maybe, maybe sometime." Sylvie nodded vaguely. "As for you...do not sell yourself short. You will be ready for an exhibition soon, the way you are going."

"No way," Sharon objected. "For one thing, when I get back to Providence I won't have much time for painting. Also...a lot of the fun of this has been having you to paint with, Sylvie. You really have brought me out of myself. I'm very grateful to you for that."

Sylvie smiled. "I have not brought you enough out of yourself," she contradicted.

"What's that supposed to mean?"

"I sense that you are holding back where your handsome flier is concerned. Ah, I know it is none of my business. But now and then when I have been at Diane's and I have seen the two of you together, what is between you has been so obvious to me. It is not an ordinary attraction, *cherie*."

Sharon took a sip of her wine, then she said, soberly, "Yes, I know that."

"If you go back north and put him out of your life, I think you will come to regret it very deeply," Sylvie pronounced, her voice husky, almost hypnotic.

Sharon looked at her and asked carefully, "Do you consider yourself psychic, Sylvie?"

"Oh, people have said now and then that I seem to have this ability to see a little way into the future. But no, I do not consider myself possessed of any rare powers. What I do have is a voice of experience. I have made my own mistakes and lived to regret them. So when I care for someone—as I have come to care for you—I hate to see them heading in the wrong direction. My theory, you see, is that love is a very precious thing. It should be cherished, not abandoned."

SYLVIE'S WORDS HAUNTED SHARON that night as she lay awake in Diane's lovely pink and rose guest room.

Love is a very precious thing. It should be cherished, not abandoned.

She'd been trying to thrust the word love out of her consciousness. But it kept persisting ... and suddenly it stuck. And though she wasn't ready to say it yet, even to herself, Sharon was very afraid that love was becoming synonymous, for her, with another word: Scott.

The next morning, after a restless night's sleep filled with dreams of Scott, Sharon set up her easel on the screened patio. She intended to put the finishing touches on her latest canvas, a moody rendition of a Deco-style building at night. She hoped it would help to place her feelings for Scott in perspective, if only for a few hours.

But then another diversion presented itself. A not so welcome diversion, really. The mail brought Diane's final divorce decree from Tony.

Diane, home for lunch, read it aloud then sighed deeply. "Crazy, but this is taking all the starch out of my sails," she said.

"What do you mean?" Sharon asked, putting down her brush and walking over to peruse the legal document her sister was holding.

"I don't really know," Diane muttered.

"Di, I'm not suggesting a drink's the cure—it's usually anything but for me—but why don't you go in and make us each a mild Blood Mary?" Sharon told her. "I'll be along as soon as I stash my paints away."

Sharon did a quick putaway job, then headed for the kitchen. She discovered Diane leaning motionlessly against the counter, the drinks beside her.

"Are you all right?" Sharon asked.

Diane looked up. "I will be," she reported, a note of resignation in her voice. "Maria's going to fix us omelets for lunch," she added, "but she says she'll wait till we're almost through with these before she starts."

Diane moved into the dining room and sat down at her table, which was again littered with her "research," as she accurately termed it. Restlessly, she asked, "Do you have anything on for tonight?"

"Nothing definite," Sharon answered. "Scott said he'll call me as soon as he get through at the base, but I imagine that won't be for a few more hours."

"Do you suppose maybe we could go out somewhere?" Diane queried. "Maybe Scott has a friend at the base, and we could double date?"

"What about Ricardo?" Sharon suggested automatically.

"I don't know. I'm not sure it would be the wisest thing for me to go out with Ricardo just now."

"Why not, for heaven's sake?"

"Because I'm too attracted to him, that's why."

Sharon smiled. "You do, sometimes, bewilder me," she told her twin. "I should think you'd prefer going out with a man to whom you're attracted."

"You're a fine one to say that!" Diane scoffed. "You approach each date with Scott as if you're putting on a dozen pairs of kid gloves. Have you even let him kiss you yet, sister mine?"

Sharon flushed. "Honestly, Diane!"

"Honestly, Diane!" Diane mocked. "Look, I'm making my point, that's all. There's an element of danger in going around with someone to whom you're intensely attracted. In short, you let yourself in for something, and I don't think I'm in a state to let myself in for much of anything."

"You've been going around with him?" Sharon
prodded.

"That's not funny, Sharon. You know the answer is
no. But he has called a couple of times and . . . I've sidestepped his invitations."

Diane sighed. "The moment he walked in with Scott
I could . . . well, I could just feel the vibes," she admitted. "I wasn't looking for anything like that and, to tell
you the truth, I found it highly disconcerting. Fortunately, I still have a supply of little emotional warning
flags in working order. They popped up quickly where
Ricardo was concerned, and I've been trying to heed
them. The last thing I want is to fall in love again."

"You're sure about that?"

"Very sure," Diane insisted.

"Well then, I *would* like to see Ricardo," Sharon shot
back. "So if you want to go out with me, you'll have to
put up with him and Scott. It's as simple as that."

Diane turned away. "He's probably tied up at the
hospital," she decided moodily. But then she gave Sharon a look that let her know she'd won this battle.

Ricardo wasn't tied up that night. Sharon discovered
this after she tried tracking down Scott at Homestead
and, to her surprise, succeeded.

"Actually, he's been wanting very much to get the
four of us together for dinner," Scott reported. "There's
a place called the Malaga over on Calle Ocho he wants
to take us to. I know he's working till around seven, so
I'll ask him to make a reservation there for nine o'clock,
unless that's too late?"

"Not at all," Sharon said. "We could drive over and
meet you there, if you like. I mean, there's no reason for
you to come all the way out to the Beach if—"

"Enough of that," Scott interrupted. "I'll be at your house at eight. That'll give us time for a drink, and then we can head back downtown and meet Rick at the restaurant."

The Malaga was in the heart of Miami's Cuban district, and had a delightfully Latin, romantic ambience. Spanish conversation flowed around the four as they dined, prompting Sharon to say, "I envy you for being bilingual, Ricardo. You have the advantage over the rest of us. This makes me want to start taking Spanish lessons."

"You should, Sharon. And please, call me Rick. Only my grandmother calls me Ricardo these days!"

Scott laughed, and Diane said unexpectedly, "I plan to start taking Spanish lessons very shortly."

"Really?" Rick queried, favoring her with a dazzling smile.

"Well, if I'm going to be conducting business in this area, it won't hurt," Diane said practically. She changed pace abruptly and added, "Listen, people...I have something I want you to celebrate with me tonight."

Sharon looked up curiously at that. Was Diane speaking of receiving her final divorce decree? If so, a desire to "celebrate" certainly reflected a quick mood change.

Instead, Diane said, "As I told Sharon when she first came down here, I've been negotiating for the purchase of a small apartment complex on the Beach. The sale went through today. So, I'm now a bona fide landlord!"

"That's terrific, Di!" Sharon exclaimed.

"Very definitely, it calls for champagne," Rick announced, promptly beckoning to their waiter and placing an order with him in rapid Spanish.

Sharon was happy to toast her twin, but she went easy on the champagne thereafter. Scott, she noticed, was doing the same thing.

They finished their dinner with flan, a popular custard dessert, and small cups of strong black coffee. Then Rick suggested, "Shall we adjourn to the lounge for a little while? A combo's playing there, if anyone wishes to dance."

They sat at a small corner table and sipped liqueur by candlelight. When Rick led Diane onto the dance floor, Scott leaned close to Sharon and said, "I think Rick is totally smitten with your twin, and has been, ever since he first laid eyes on her at the party."

"Diane has feelings for Rick, too. But I've got to tell you, Scott, it frightens her. She received her divorce decree in the mail today, and she was pretty depressed about it."

"It's a hard thing to get through," Scott said, nodding knowingly. "And I'm very glad the two of you decided to come out." He paused, then asked, "Will you dance with me?"

"I'd love to," Sharon told him.

She felt her heart swell as Scott took her into his arms. As they swayed slowly to the melody of a sensuous Latin love song, all the emotions she had locked inside surfaced anew.

Sharon pressed her cheek against his, and let the knowledge she'd been holding back flood over her.

She loved Scott. She loved him very much.

He felt her shudder ever so slightly, and looked deeply into her eyes.

"I know, darling," he whispered huskily. "And I don't see how I can possibly last another night without you."

CHAPTER ELEVEN

THE EVENING came to an end that was considerably more abrupt than expected when Rick, accustomed to listening to anyone paging anyone, caught a passing waiter stating, in Spanish, that there was a telephone call for "Señora DeLuca."

Diane became distraught at once. "Sylvie's with Tonette and I told her where I'd be! Oh dear God, something's happened to Tonette."

Rick said quickly, "I will go to the telephone with you."

Diane didn't protest. She and Rick left the lounge, and Scott called for the check. A few minutes later, the two couples reunited in the vestibule.

"Let's all drive back to the house in my car," Rick said decisively. "Tonette has some abdominal pain and, after hearing what her baby-sitter had to say, I'd like to look her over myself before we leap to any conclusions. Scott, you can leave your car parked where it is. The owner is a friend of mine, and I have spoken to him so there will be no danger of the police towing it. We'll pick it up later."

"Yes, Doctor," Scott replied dutifully.

That forced a grin out of Rick, but as they hurried out of the restaurant and climbed into his car, no one said a word. Rick knew the roads as well as a native of Miami, but even moving at a good clip, the trip took almost twenty minutes. By the time they pulled up in front of the house on Pine Tree Drive, Diane was fighting back tears.

As she whisked through the front door, Rick admonished, "Get control of yourself, *linda*. You don't want your little daughter to see that you are upset."

Diane's chin tilted a bit defiantly, but she only said, "You're right."

Following Rick's instructions, Sharon and Scott waited downstairs. "We don't want Tonette to think the adults are all panicking and rushing to her bedside," he pointed out correctly.

For the first time in a long while, Sharon wished she had a cigarette. But she'd given up smoking years ago, and she had no intention of rekindling that habit now. Still, she complained, "Rick's taking forever!"

"It hasn't even been ten minutes," Scott told her gently. "Look, Sharon, try to relax a little. Tonette couldn't be in better hands."

Shortly thereafter, Diane came down the stairs looking a bit pinched around the nostrils, but nonetheless relieved. Sylvie, decidedly harried, followed her.

"Rick asked us to leave Tonette to him for a while," Diane reported. "He doesn't think there's any cause for alarm. No indication of appendicitis or any other emergency like that."

About half an hour later, Rick joined them. He flashed a reassuring smile at Diane, then said, "I think it may be a while before your daughter craves chocolate candy again."

"Chocolate candy?"

"Evidently you had a big box of chocolates on your dresser. Full, I believe?"

Diane nodded, "That's right. A client gave them to me yesterday after I found her the house of her dreams."

"Well, it is a nearly empty box now. Tonette confessed to me that after Sylvie tucked her in and went back downstairs, she got to thinking about those chocolates. So...she sneaked into your room and had a feast for herself. Not an unusual thing for a seven-year-old to do."

"Wait till I get my hands on her!" Diane threatened.

"*Linda*, I think she has paid for her mistake. She woke up with severe stomach pains—"

"She was screaming," Sylvie stated calmly.

"Yes, I imagine she was. She had strong cramps, and subsequently she has been sick to her stomach. At the moment, there is not much chocolate or anything else left in it!"

"What can I do to make her feel better?" Diane asked.

"You can see that she drinks some fluids from time to time tonight. Plain water or carbonated soda would be better than fruit juice."

Diane smiled. "I think I can handle that, Dr. Fabrega," she told him, and added sincerely, "Thank you."

"*De nada,*" Rick replied, his eyes aglow. For a moment, his attention seemed concentrated solely on Diane. Then he remarked, "Oh yes, I found a fresh nightgown in her dresser, and she is cozy in her bed again. She asked that we all come say good-night to her...and one at a time, that is fine. In the morning, Diane, she may still feel seedy from an empty stomach and lack of sleep, so it would be a good idea to keep her home from school. With a little food and rest, her energy quotient should be back to normal by the afternoon.''

Rick was exactly right in his prognosis. By the time Sharon and Diane were finishing their patio lunch of shrimp salad and iced tea, Tonette was her old self again, proclaiming that she must be ''allergic'' to chocolate candy in a very serious way that made the twins smile.

Watching her daughter take up residence in front of the TV, Diane prophesized, ''She'll dramatize this experience to the max when she sees her classmates tomorrow!''

THE WEEKEND approached. For some time, Diane had been planning to fly to the Bahamas with friends, and Sharon had already volunteered to stay with Tonette.

''It will give me a chance to have my niece to myself,'' she'd said enthusiastically, and Diane had concurred.

But now Diane began to have qualms about leaving her daughter, just in case the stomach malady should somehow reassert itself.

Hearing this, Sharon looked at her twin sternly and said, ''How can you imply such a thing? Don't you have any faith in Rick's diagnosis?''

''Of course I do,'' Diane said quickly. ''It's just that—''

''It's just that you're having an attack of mommyism,'' Sharon decided. ''I think you need to get away from the Miami Beach scene for a couple of days, so take advantage . . . okay?''

Diane, who'd been about to call her friends and cancel the trip, nodded meekly.

Sharon privately wished that Diane was going to the Bahamas with Rick Fabrega. Still, she was glad to see her twin pack her overnight bag and head off. In small, often unexpected ways, Diane had been showing that her nerves were more than a little frayed. Then she'd been genuinely upset over Tonette's "chocolate candy attack." This two-day escape from the responsibilities of her home and business could only help her, Sharon reasoned. As for herself...

She and Scott had been playing things pretty much day-to-day since the night at the Malaga. He was involved with planning the special training program at Homestead, and she continued to go painting with Sylvie. They did manage to get together for a movie one rainy afternoon, but aside from that, most of their exchanges had been on the phone.

It wasn't until Scott called her Saturday afternoon and asked if she'd like to visit Vizcaya that Sharon realized she hadn't told him she'd be tied up over the weekend, baby-sitting her niece.

"Miami's Metrozoo is supposed to be fantastic," he responded promptly. "They claim they've duplicated the plains of Africa, the jungles of Borneo and the forests of Europe. They've even built an Asian temple for their tigers and a replica of a Malaysian village where people can touch and feed a variety of exotic animals. I think Tonette would go wild over that."

"I'm sure she would, but—"

"They have elephant rides," Scott persisted. "And there aren't any cages. The wild animals appear just as free as they do in nature. The only thing separating you from them is a few feet of open space."

"You've really done your homework," Sharon observed.

"I've had it on my agenda to ask you about visiting the zoo with Tonette," Scott admitted. "With your sister away, it's the perfect opportunity."

"Scott, there's no reason why you should involve yourself with entertaining a seven-year-old child," Sharon told him directly. "I feel sure there are things you'd rather do."

"Didn't I just tell you this is something I've been wanting to do?" he demanded, tossing the question back at Sharon and sounding more than a little affronted.

"All right," she relented. "Tonette will be absolutely ecstatic at the whole idea."

"Then let's go for it," Scott said, mollified. "I've got a surprise idea for tonight that includes Tonette, too."

"Remember, she's only seven," Sharon warned.

"I'll remember."

The Metrozoo was all Scott promised it would be, and more. On their way back to Pine Tree Drive, Tonette—as happy as any little girl could possibly be—fell asleep in the back of the car, temporarily done in.

Glancing at her in the rearview mirror, Scott said in a low voice, "She's really a doll. Funny, she looks so much like you and Diane, but there's a lot of Tony in her, too. Anyway, she's a total delight." He paused, then ventured lightly, "I believe you mentioned that you wanted children?"

"I used to wish that more than anything else," she confessed. "A home and children. I wanted both, more than I can say. But neither were in Jerry's scheme of things. Which was just as well, I guess, considering the way things turned out. What about you?"

Scott smiled ruefully and said, "Claudia and I never really discussed having children in any depth. I was right out of the Academy when we got married—all young

and ambitious. And Claudia . . . had other things on her
mind." He paused, then asked suddenly, "How old are
you, Sharon? I don't think you've ever told me."

"I don't think you've ever asked. I'm twenty-nine."

"Then you still have many years to have kids," Scott
observed.

"Well, so do you."

They fell silent, each absorbed in their own thoughts.
Then, to Sharon's surprise, Scott drove past the Pine
Tree Drive house and swung over to Collins Avenue.

"I want to run into a market and get a couple of
things," he informed her. When she looked at him
questioningly, he explained, "This time it's my turn to
make dinner."

That night, Scott grilled some fantastic barbecued
chicken and tossed together an equally fantastic salad
combining spinach, sunflower seeds, mandarin orange
slices, water chestnuts and a tangy dressing like nothing
Sharon had ever tasted.

As she munched she said, "You're an extremely
imaginative cook, Scott. I'm rather surprised."

"Why's that?"

"Well, I guess I didn't expect a jet pilot could have,
uh . . . the time for imagination."

"Oh?" He would have considered that a real dig had
it come from anyone but Sharon. As it was, the fact that
she'd mentioned his profession was a plus—perhaps
even a step in the right direction, Scott decided. This was
fragile turf she was testing, and he made a mental note
not to push her too hard.

Carefully, he asked, "What do you imagine the average jet pilot to be like?"

"Anything but average."

"Seriously, Sharon, I'm curious to know what you think."

She considered this, then said, "Well, you'd have to be tremendously coordinated, of course, and in top physical shape. That goes without saying. Also, I'd say you'd have to be proficient in all the higher forms of mathematics. I mean, you'd have to do calculations very quickly, though I suppose there are computers..."

Her voice trailed off, and Scott prompted, "Yes? What else?"

"Well, you'd have to be a natural with machines, and have lightning-fast reflexes. But at the same time you'd have to have nerves of steel, and be able to function almost, uh..."

"Mechanically?" he suggested.

"Yes, I suppose so."

"With flashing lights and programmed voices?" he persisted.

"Scott!"

"Well, what you're describing sounds more like a robot than a man," he told her. "Pilots do have all those attributes you just mentioned, but we're still warm-blooded individuals, Sharon. Human beings, you know? That's why, unfortunately, we sometimes make some pretty terrible mistakes in the course of our work. On the other hand, I'd hate to think I could ever be so programmed I'd begin to confuse myself with a robot!"

Tonette had been sitting quietly on the floor, totally absorbed in the coloring book Scott had bought her at the zoo. Now she looked up and asked, "Do you have a robot, Scott?" Like a lot of children her age, she easily adopted calling her elders by their first names when she saw they didn't object.

"No, I don't, Tonette. Do you?"

"No, but I thought I might like to get one for my birthday," she confided. "Maybe a white one, with bright red eyes and blue lights flashing on his chest when he walked."

"I'll tell the Birthday Present Person to keep that in mind," Scott promised her solemnly.

Later, Sharon took Tonette upstairs and gave her a bath before tucking her into bed. But it was Scott who read her a *Winnie the Pooh* bedtime story, then turned off her table lamp when she'd finally fallen asleep.

Sharon was curled up on the living room couch reading a magazine. She looked up as Scott came down the curving stairway. When their eyes met, her heart melted. She'd never seen Scott look so vulnerable.

"She's quite a kid," he murmured huskily, sinking into one of the white armchairs.

"Yes, she is," Sharon agreed.

"I'll never forget tonight, you know. It's sort of been like this was our home and Tonette was our kid. As if we've been playing house, I guess." He smiled wistfully. "Whatever you want to call it," he finished quietly, "it's been a very special day for me."

Sharon's throat began to choke up as she stared across at Scott's intensely blue eyes. "It's been a very special day for me, too," she said softly. "When we were having dinner together, and talking, and Tonette was sitting there on the floor with her crayons..." Sharon swallowed hard, and barely finished, "I'm being silly, aren't I?"

Scott moved out of his chair and came to sit by Sharon's side. "No," he told her gently, "you're not being silly. Did you know there are tears in your eyes?"

"Yes, I suppose there are," Sharon managed. "I...I think you and I both have our weak spots, Scott."

"Who doesn't?"

"No one, I suppose. Though a lot of people, most people, go to great lengths to camouflage them."

"We cover up because we're afraid to do otherwise," Scott said simply. "There's too much risk in letting other people know everything there is to know about you. But with you and me..."

Scott looked deeply into Sharon's lovely green eyes and whispered, "I want to know all there is to know about you, Sharon. And I want you to know all there is to know about me. In another week, you'll be going away. The mere thought of that does something to me that I can't explain in words. I don't see how I'm possibly going to let you go."

"Scott..."

"Please don't stop me, darling. I've been stopping *myself* until I think I'll surely go crazy if I... if I don't have you, sweetheart. I've never wanted anyone in my life as I do you. You believe that, don't you?"

Sharon believed him. And her pulse began to pound steadily harder as desire became a potent injection, filling her veins with fire. Scott reached out to caress her, almost cautiously at first, then with growing assuredness as she began to yield herself to him like a slowly opening tropical flower.

It felt so natural, so right, as his hands explored her body with tender messages of their own. And after a few timeless moments, Sharon was helping Scott undress her, shrugging off her clothes, wanting only to feel her naked flesh next to his. She fumbled a little helping Scott pull first his shirt off, then his trousers. Then they visually consumed their full share of each other before Scott reached over to turn out the light.

"I want to see you, but I want our privacy more," he whispered. "Not that there's apt to be anyone peeping in the windows, but you never know."

Dimly, Sharon realized they were in Diane's house, in Diane's living room, on Diane's couch. Yet her normal sense of precaution didn't assert itself. She felt free with Scott, just as she'd felt more and more free in her painting. She was totally herself with a man for the first time in her life. Because it had never been like this with Jerry, the only other man in her life. Now she knew she'd never want anyone else but Scott.

He made love to her patiently, tenderly, passionately. And as her desire for him mounted, Sharon knew Scott wanted her equally as much. In the muted shadows his excitement was evident as he gently pressed her back against the cushions. And even as she began to whirl out of control, even as he concentrated on satisfying her passion first, she marveled at his self-restraint.

"I want it first for you, my love," he whispered in her ear. "Then again, for both of us...."

His hot breath caressed her cheeks, his moist mouth claimed hers, his burning fingers touched the very essence of her sexuality. And as a cascading onrush of incredible sensations washed over Sharon in wave after sensuous wave, she felt herself explode among the stars and melt into the far crevices of the universe.

"Darling, darling Scott," she moaned. "I...I want to know all of you."

Moments later, Scott moved himself within her, thrusting deeper...and deeper. Until finally, blissfully, he let his own passion give way.

His excitement brought Sharon to yet another crest of love. She surged over the edge just as Scott could move no more. And together they were spent, floating in wonderful peace toward calmer, cooler seas.

In the quiet of the night, Sharon finally managed, "I think my heart's beginning to slip into place again."

"I'm not so sure about mine," Scott confessed softly. "I'm not really sure where it's been."

"Don't say too much, darling," she cautioned. "Not now. Let's just let it be. Let's just be with each other."

He drew her close against him, she pillowed her head on his shoulder. They were quiet for a long time. Then passion stirred again, and once more they began their voyage through space to the stars and beyond.

Much later, Scott got up off the couch and slipped into his clothes, even though Sharon urged him to stay.

"I'd rather not have Tonette find me here in the morning," he told her. "Maybe I'm crazy, but I think it might confuse her. Anyway, let's not take that chance, okay? Lord knows, she's had enough mix-up in her life for a seven-year-old."

Sharon pulled aside the sheer white curtain behind the couch and, in the light of a streetlamp, watched Scott get into his car and drive off, taking her heart with him.

LATE SUNDAY NIGHT, Diane returned from her trip to the Bahamas. Scott had spent the afternoon at the beach with Sharon and Tonette, then had taken them to a Chinese restaurant where he taught Tonette how to use chopsticks.

He'd left early this evening. A little later, when Sharon was tucking Tonette into bed, her young niece looked up at her and stated, "When I grow up, I'm going to marry Scott."

It was a child's whimsy, of course, but it gave Sharon a funny feeling.

What would it be like to marry Scott? What would it *really* be like?

She tried to imagine life with a man whose profession was soaring through the stratosphere in sophisticated jet aircraft. She tried to imagine them moving from base to base, from country to country, with a predictable frequency. And she knew she lacked the courage to settle for a life like that, if indeed Scott were to ask her someday to be his wife.

They'd talked a little about their marriages. Scott had suffered more, Sharon knew, though he managed to speak of Claudia with an admirable lack of bitterness. She was certain that the flames of hurt had long died out, but the ashes of disillusionment were still there. Maybe the winds of time would someday blow them away, and Scott would again be free. Until then...

As she sat in the living room after putting Tonette to bed, Sharon all but convinced herself that marriage to Claudia had done such a job on Scott it was unlikely he'd ever want to marry again.

She was trying, and failing, to concentrate on a mystery novel when she heard a car door close outside. A minute later, Diane was regaling her with descriptions of the Bahamas so exuberantly that Sharon finally looked her right in the eye and told her, "You didn't have such a great time, did you?"

"No, I didn't," Diane admitted. "So what are you, a mind reader?" she accused.

"Just a twin," Sharon corrected.

"Hmm." Quickly changing tacks, Diane asked, "Did you manage to keep Tonette in line?"

"There was no need to," Sharon reported. "Tonette was in paradise the whole time. Yesterday Scott took us to the Metrozoo, and today we went to the beach and he built sand castles with her. Then he took us to dinner at a Chinese restaurant. From now on, Tonette will be demanding chopsticks with any food that even remotely resembles chow mein!''

"Well," Diane commented, looking at her twin more closely. "Didn't that cramp your style somewhat? Having Tonette around, I mean?''

"Not at all," Sharon said. "The only problem," she added, "is that Tonette has fallen in love with Scott and intends to marry him when she grows up. I didn't have the heart to tell her he may not wait that long.''

"She won't mind too much if you beat her to the altar," Diane observed lightly. Noting Sharon's reaction, she quipped, "Why that *look*, sister mine? If I were in your shoes, I'd be counting the days you have left down here and praying Scott will ask you the billion-dollar question before it's time for you to leave!''

"Don't be ridiculous!" Sharon snapped.

"How can you say it's ridiculous?" Diane inquired reasonably. "At that restaurant over on Calle Ocho the other night both Rick and I were noticing the way the two of you were dancing with each other. You stepped right out of this world.''

"What about Rick and yourself?''

"We did just fine," Diane informed her. "Now stop trying to change the subject. I mean...I know you, Sharon. And I'd bet my new apartment complex that you're in love with Scott and he's in love with you.''

"Diane!''

"What?''

"You're way off base.''

"Really? About what, may I ask?''

"About inferring that there could ever be anything in the way of a permanent relationship between Scott and myself."

"Why not, for heaven's sake? You're a widow, he's divorced. I must be missing some vital point somewhere."

"I could never involve myself with a pilot," Sharon said steadily. "A man who loves flying more than anything else in the world."

Diane stared at her sister disbelievingly, then her expression softened. She said, almost gently, "Darling, I wasn't there with you when Jerry died, and I can only imagine the horror you went through. I remember telling Tony I would have done anything in this world to spare you that experience."

"I know," Sharon murmured.

"Nor have I blamed you because you've refused to fly since then. As I remember it, you never really liked flying to begin with."

"That's true, I never did."

"Well...I can understand the way you feel, then. But don't you think the time has come to examine yourself and your feelings without flinching from them?"

"Stop playing amateur psychologist!" Sharon exploded. "I *have* examined myself and my feelings— dozens and dozens of times. It's still practically impossible for me to watch a plane in the sky without wincing. Call me a coward, say whatever you want to say about me... but that's simply the way it is."

"And you're saying you can't possibly change?"

"Yes, that's what I'm saying."

"Have you ever considered consulting a professional about this?"

"I saw a psychologist nearly two years ago," Sharon said to her twin's surprise. "My motivation wasn't to get over my fear of flying, though. It was to stop my recurring nightmares of Jerry's plane...exploding." She faltered briefly, then her voice steadied. "We had a series of sessions, we talked it all out. And finally the dreams stopped. Still, the person I was seeing didn't offer any false hopes. He admitted it would take a great deal of therapy, maybe even years, for me to accept flying as a fact of life. Aside from that one...neurosis, he considered me a normal, well-integrated individual. I accepted that, and we agreed upon a parting of the ways."

"Why didn't you tell me?" Diane asked softly.

"I'm not really sure," Sharon admitted slowly. "Anyway, except for annoying you a couple of times when I've refused to fly out to the West Coast to visit Dad and his wife, I've done very well. As I would have continued to do...if I hadn't met Scott."

A single tear rolled down Sharon's cheek as Diane reached out and took her in her arms. For a moment, they held each other quietly. Then Sharon managed, "It's ironic, isn't it? It's so terribly unfair."

CHAPTER TWELVE

SHARON AWAKENED Monday morning, stretched lazily as she stared up at the pink ceiling above her, and tried not to focus on the fact that this was the beginning of her last week in Miami Beach. Come Saturday afternoon, she would be boarding a northbound train for her return trip to Providence, her holiday over.

She showered, then slipped on white shorts and a short-sleeved green and white shirt. All the while she had the crazy feeling that the most important days of her life were literally slipping away from her.

There was something else to be reckoned with, too. She'd come down here determined to do some in-depth thinking about her future. She needed to seriously mull over the changes she might make that would lead to a happier, more productive life. Leaving her job was practically a necessity, she knew. She was truly fond of Gary Freeman, her employer, but she'd come to the end of the road at his printing firm, as far as career advancement was concerned. The job simply wasn't challenging. At least, not often enough.

She'd been thinking of leaving Providence entirely. Maybe moving to Boston, where there would most likely be more opportunity in her field. Or perhaps taking up residence in some small, peaceful New England community where, Sharon thought whimsically, she might have a chance of becoming the biggest frog in the littlest pond! Someplace where she could make the kind of real home for herself she envisioned.

Since arriving in Miami Beach, she hadn't thought about much of anything except Scott. Scott, and her painting. Her treks with Sylvie had rekindled her buried artistic desires, and brought home to Sharon how much she truly loved to paint, how painting was her best and most natural mode of expression.

Unfortunately, she couldn't think of any jobs where she'd be given the free rein to simply sit back and let herself go, doing nothing but challenging, creative designs for some well-paying employer, then having ample time and energy left over to seriously pursue her painting.

As she headed downstairs, Sharon's mood bordered on melancholy. She couldn't block out the realization that, at this time next Monday, she'd be back working in Gary's office. Then, before too much time passed, she'd have to decide whether to give notice—which Gary would not accept lightly—or let herself sink deeper into the same old rut.

Maria was bustling around the kitchen with that air of importance she assumed when something out of the ordinary was coming up. Spotting Sharon over her shoulder, she verified this by happily announcing, "Tonight we will have a fantastic Cuban dinner!"

"Is it a special occasion?" Sharon asked, while Maria took time out from her bustling to prepare a fresh pot of coffee and heat a plate full of apricot tarts in the microwave.

"Oh, yes. Diane has invited her Cuban doctor friend to dinner."

"Rick?"

"Dr. Fabrega, yes. And also your friend Scott."

Sharon frowned. Precisely when had Diane decided to do *that*? she wondered.

She found her twin out on the patio, busily making notations on a yellow legal pad. Hearing Sharon approach, Diane looked up and said, "Ah, there you are." Paper and pen were set aside and replaced with a cigarette. "Don't scowl at me like that," she cautioned.

"You shouldn't smoke."

"I know I shouldn't, but right now I'm edgy."

"About anything in particular?"

"No, about everything in general."

Sharon looked at Diane more closely, and her vibes went into action. She was certain her sister was up to something, and that the "something" involved her.

She said casually, "Maria tells me you've invited Rick and Scott to dinner tonight."

Diane nodded.

"How come?"

"I was in the mood for company, that's all. Fortunately, they were both free."

"When did you call them?"

"My, aren't *we* inquisitive?" Diane responded lightly. Seeing Sharon's impatience mounting, she answered, "I called them both this morning—Rick at the hospital, and Scott at Homestead. They'll drive out together," Diane added. "Scott will pick up Rick at the hospital around seven, so they'll be here some time after that, depending on the traffic."

"I see."

"You don't sound especially enthusiastic, Sharon."

"Well, isn't Monday sort of a funny night to entertain?" Sharon countered.

"Why?"

"Oh, I don't know. Most people tend to gear their entertaining more toward weekends, that's all."

"I'm not most people."

Sharon couldn't repress a smile. "I'll second that," she agreed.

Diane stood up abruptly and said, "I'm going to get another cup of coffee. Want anything?"

Sharon shook her head and sat down. Left alone, she found herself staring at the huge golden oranges on the trees in Diane's garden as if she'd never seen an orange tree before.

Last night, Scott had said he'd call her today. They hadn't made any definite plans, though she was certain he was every bit as aware of her imminent departure as she was, certain that he wanted to spend as much time with her as possible this last week. She realized this would make it even harder to say goodbye to him, come Saturday, but...

Sharon felt a tremor shake her. She couldn't imagine saying goodbye to Scott, couldn't imagine watching him standing on the platform by himself as the train moved out of the station, putting an irreversible physical distance between them.

Inches...feet...yards...miles...hundreds of miles...

Sharon didn't doubt that they'd stay in touch with letters and long-distance calls late at night. But once she left Miami, it would be a very long way to Providence—in many more ways than miles.

How could the ensuing gap between Scott and her do anything but widen? she thought dismally.

Considering the obstacles that loomed like giant pyramids in their path, she wondered how she would feel—wondered what she might do—if Scott asked her to stay in Miami. Not on any permanent basis, of course. She wasn't thinking of anything like marriage. But just to stay...perhaps until he got the word as to whether or not he'd be able to fly again.

If he asked her, would she stay?

It was not a question easily answered. In fact, even considering it caused Sharon to run the full gamut of ambivalence, and she was glad for the diversion when Diane returned with her coffee and the apricot pastries.

Diane resumed her seat and tapped the legal pad on which she'd been jotting notes and figures. "This concerns you, Shar," she said unexpectedly.

"Me?" Sharon asked, surprised. She'd assumed Diane was making notes involving real estate of some sort.

"Just a few facts and figures," she said. "Things are swinging into place for Di-Tone."

It took a second for Sharon to realize that Diane was talking about the compact disk company she and Tony were planning on running.

"Tony's cinched the lease on the building he was talking about," Diane reported. "His lawyer in Fort Lauderdale is ironing out copyrights and the various other legal angles. Tony plans to make the first couple of disks using the band from his club, with Genevieve Landry as vocalist." She spoke the singer's name calmly enough, then continued, "They've been doing a lot of the old Thirties songs like 'Don't Blame Me,' 'Penthouse Serenade' and 'Dancing in the Dark'—there are dozens of good ones. His patrons have been raving about the music, and Tony has some backers who are very much interested in our venture. We intend to keep control of the company ourselves, and it looks like we're going to have all the capital we need to get started without scraping the bottoms of our own financial barrels."

"That's terrific!" Sharon responded, truly enthused.

"Yes, it is," Diane agreed. She paused, sipped coffee, then said, "So...we're now at the stage where we'll soon be launching our initial promotion. Tony has contacts with everyone in the local media. I'd say we'll get quite a send-off, which is where you come in."

"Where I come in?" Sharon asked doubtfully.

"We need an artist," Diane said, getting right to the point. "Someone who's had design experience and can put together a package for us."

"What kind of package?" Sharon asked weakly.

"The cover for our first disk, to begin with. It has to be really smashing, Shar. Not just so it will stand out on store shelves, but so it will stand up on its own when it's reproduced in ads for the papers and TV." Into the silence that followed, Diane stated, "I want you to do it for us."

"Do the cover for your first disk?"

"That's what I said, ninny," Diane retorted, using the not too complimentary nickname that evoked a swift memory of childhood times when Diane so often had been the instigator, urging Sharon on.

"But I've never done anything like that." It was an honest protest.

"You've done a lot of terrific design work for your printing firm in Providence. I've seen some of it, remember?"

"Yes." Sharon well remembered sending Diane a few samples of her work one time, after Diane had asked, in a letter, just precisely what it was she was doing.

"All I saw were black and white Xeroxes, of course," Diane continued. "But I have no doubts when it comes to your use of color. I've been peeking at those paintings you've been stashing away upstairs."

"Those are just...exercises," Sharon said uncon-
vincingly.

"Come on." Diane scoffed. "Sylvie's been saying
some very complimentary things about your paintings.
She's convinced they're good enough to sell, should you
ever want to start a gallery."

"She's the one who should be starting a gallery!"
Sharon shot back. "To tell you the truth, she's the person you should be approaching to do your artwork.

"No, she isn't," Diane stated frankly. "And believe
me, this isn't because you're my sister. Tony and I spoke
about hiring Sylvie before you came down here. This
isn't something we've just conjured up, Shar. It's been
in the planning stage for a long while. Anyway, Tony and
I thought of Sylvie, but we both agreed she's not the
right person for the job. This isn't going to be a one-shot
deal. We plan to follow up our initial disk with a slow
but steady production until we are firmly established, as
I honestly believe we will be."

"So why not Sylvie?" Sharon asked stubbornly.

"Because, though she's a fantastic artist, she's totally
undisciplined," Diane answered. "We need a fantastic
artist who also has the discipline of a person who's been
making their living doing graphic design."

Sharon started to speak, but Diane cut her off. "Before you say anything...I know what's been happening
with you, spending so much time with Sylvie. I fully realize that you've begun to learn to let yourself go, sister
mine, and I applaud you for it. But that doesn't mean
you should let yourself go in the same totally abandoned way that Sylvie does. It works for her, but—"

"Sylvie and I are two very different people, Diane."

"Yes, I know you are. But that's not the point. The
point is, you have a downright Deco quality in the

paintings I've peeked at. There was one of the Collins Avenue skyline, done from the beach, that bowled me over. I mean, that's exactly the type of thing we're looking for."

"You really liked it?" Sharon asked modestly.

"It's great," Diane told her. "They're all great. If you did something like that and worked in a bunch of guys blowing on trumpets and saxophones..."

"Incorporate a musical theme, you mean?"

"That's precisely what I mean. It would be perfect! You could capture that spirit the Beach has—part Deco, part jet age. All the nostalgia of the Twenties and Thirties, plus all the promise of the twenty-first century, with terrific colors for emphasis..."

"Di, hasn't it occurred to you or Tony that you should be hiring someone really well-known to do something so spectacular?"

"It occurred, and it was ruled out."

"Why?"

"Number one, money. Number two, Tony has also seen your work and—"

"He what?"

"You heard me, Sharon. I spirited him in here to have a look at your paintings while you were out with Scott one afternoon," Diane confessed.

"Di!"

"Don't look so outraged, Shar. I know you. And I knew you'd go into a modest funk if I suggested you show Tony your paintings. Anyway, I wanted him to have the chance to be really objective. With you peering over his shoulder, well..."

"What did he say?" Sharon queried coolly.

"He was even crazier about what you're doing than I am," Diane reported. "And that's the truth. Believe me,

Tony is far too intense about Di-Tone being successful right from the start to indulge me in wanting my twin sister to do our artwork. If he had any doubts whatsoever about your talent, he would have come right out and said, 'No way.'"

There was something to be said for Diane's bluntness. Nevertheless, Sharon replied carefully, "That has to work both ways, Di."

"What do you mean?"

"I'm flattered that you and Tony think I might be capable of doing your cover for you. But I'm not yet that confident in myself."

"Oh, come on," Diane protested. "You're a professional graphic designer."

"I've been doing layout and design for a relatively small printing firm," Sharon allowed. "And the majority of what I've done has been quite straightforward, actually boring, per the wishes of our customers."

"Then this is a chance for you to do something that's really you," Diane decided practically.

Sharon sat back and sighed. "I don't know," she mused. "I just don't know." She felt like wringing her hands and moaning. "You've really thrown me a curve, Di."

"I should think you might be honest enough to say that I've presented you with an opportunity to make more of your considerable talents."

"I *am* scheduled to go back to Providence this Saturday, remember? And to be at work next Monday?"

"I'm well aware of that," Diane answered, then sputtered, "and I think it's absolute damned foolishness! Even if it weren't for Di-Tone, it would be idiotic of you to leave town now. Scott needs you, damn it!"

"Scott *needs* me?" There were needs and needs. Sharon stared at her twin, wondering just what kind of a need Diane was talking about.

"Rick and I talked for quite a while this morning," Diane confessed. "He thinks Scott needs some moral support right now from the people he cares about. His upcoming physical examinations are going to be incredibly tough. Rick's concerned that Scott is slumping somewhat on the psychological front. He told me that Scott doesn't seem as sure of himself as he used to. And Rick should know."

"Is that to be wondered at?"

"Yes and no. And I'm sure I don't have to remind you that Rick was telling me this in confidence. It would only make matters worse if any of this got back to Scott. Evidently, he has enough fears of his own."

"They're certainly not apparent," Sharon hedged.

"Well, Scott's a strong person, so I don't suppose they would be. But I gather from Rick that he's going through a lot, deep inside. His divorce took a toll. And, believe me, I know what that is," Diane stated grimly.

She shrugged and continued. "Anyway, that's neither here nor there. Scott's where he is right now, with his personal life to get in order again and some big question marks hovering over his career. The thing is, Rick seems to think that in just three weeks you've become very special to Scott. And *I* think that Scott has become very special to you. So why cut it off now, Shar?"

Sharon stirred impatiently. "I think you know the answer to that, Di. We've been through it."

"Are you listening to me, Sharon? There's a strong chance Scott might never be able to fly again."

Sharon was speechless. Did Rick Fabrega know something about Scott's condition that Scott himself didn't know? If so, had Rick actually confided something of that magnitude to her twin?

"I said a chance," Diane put in quickly. "I'm basing that on...oh, a number of things. Rick isn't breaking any confidentialities, believe me."

"I don't imagine he would."

"He isn't," Diane repeated. "He's much too fine a doctor, much too fine a person for that. And Scott has become a very close friend of his. Rick thinks the world of him."

There was a softness to Diane's voice as she spoke of the young Cuban doctor. Sharon decided she'd have to be more observant than usual as to how Rick and Diane behaved with each other at dinner tonight.

Diane said, "To get back to the cover. How long do you think it would take you to do it, Shar?"

Sharon shrugged helplessly. "I have absolutely no idea."

"Just to give us a preliminary sketch?"

"A few days, at least. I mean, I would have to talk with both you and Tony, and get an idea of the kind of concept you have in mind."

"Why don't you call Gary Freeman and tell him something's come up down here and you need two more weeks," Diane suggested quickly. "That way, you can cover all the bases. You can try your hand at a design. If it doesn't work, or if you discover that this sort of thing just isn't for you, then you can go back to Providence and your job will still be there."

It made sense. It made such good sense that Sharon found herself putting in a call to Providence in the middle of the afternoon.

Gary Freeman was at the edge of a deadline, and he was not in the best of moods. When Sharon told him she wanted to extend her stay in Miami Beach for two weeks, he snapped irritably, "No way!"

Sharon knew her employer. She knew his moods could be mercurial and, once this latest deadline had been met successfully, he'd probably be a different person. She wished her sense of timing had been better, but that couldn't be helped.

"Gary, I wouldn't be asking this if it weren't important," she persisted.

"It's important to me to have you back here at your desk," he retorted.

Sharon felt herself bristling. She'd never asked any favors of Gary during her employment with him, nor given him any reason to be angry with her. The only thing she'd ever done was sidestep most of his invitations to dinner. She suspected that it was loneliness in the wake of losing his wife, rather than any real interest in her that precipitated those invitations. Nevertheless, she didn't want to risk encouraging Gary any more than she already had.

When it came to work, she'd been totally faithful. She'd put in many overtime hours without pay, and had more than earned the occasional bonuses Gary had given her. Her job had literally become the focal point of her entire life, and she'd given it just about her all. As a result, she'd succeeded in making herself more valuable to Gary than she'd realized.

"Gary," she said levelly, "I really want these two weeks. In fact, I must have them."

"Are you giving me an ultimatum?" Gary growled.

"I don't like that choice of words. I am saying that I must stay down here this additional time. I...I'm needed here."

"Who needs you?" Gary asked suspiciously.

"My sister needs me. You know she's just been divorced." This was the truth, though Sharon was leaning on it more than a little. Because she was normally so totally honest, she began to feel a guilt complex stirring.

Partially mollified, Gary subsided somewhat. "All right," he said grudgingly. "Take the two weeks. But no longer, okay?"

"No longer," Sharon promised.

As she hung up, she wondered what would happen if her design for Di-Tone went really well, and Tony and Diane offered her the job of doing their artwork on a regular basis.

It would be tempting—very tempting. Especially during these next few months while Scott was in South Florida awaiting word of his future flying status.

EARLY THAT EVENING, when the twins were alone briefly in Diane's pantry searching for toothpicks to use with Maria's hors d'oeuvres, Diane whispered, "I think we must be dating the two handsomest men in all of Miami."

Sharon couldn't help but concur. Scott was wearing light charcoal slacks and a pale gray, open-necked shirt. Rick was wearing ivory slacks and a burnt-orange sweater that set off his dramatic coloring.

They had arrived with flowers and candy. "Like swains of old," Rick had announced, grinning.

"'Swains of old had come a-courting,'" Sharon remembered aloud, meeting Scott's deep blue eyes. He was smiling at her so tenderly she felt herself beginning to melt in some very treacherous places.

Maria had made a delicious roast pork dish that Rick informed them was "one hundred percent authentic Cuban cuisine." They ate by candlelight out on the patio, with Miami once again providing its famous hovering moon. The moonlight, the swaying palms, the scent of the oranges and a flower that Diane identified as jasmine, were none-too-subtle aphrodisiacs. As Sharon looked across the table at Scott, she was very much aware that her desire for him was showing.

Unfortunately, Rick was scheduled to be on call at his hospital early in the morning, so the evening had to be brought to an end before anyone wanted it to. Then, almost at the last moment, Diane exclaimed, "Can you believe it? I almost forgot...I have an announcement to make."

Rick looked at her quizzically. "An announcement?"

"We really should open a bottle of champagne for this," Diane went on, "but I don't want you to wake up tomorrow with a headache, Doctor!"

"Maybe I should," Rick decided. "What is it?"

Diane paused dramatically. "Sharon is going to stay in Miami Beach and do the cover for the first compact disk Tony and I are producing!"

"For two more weeks," Sharon put in hastily.

"For two weeks as a starter," Diane followed quickly.

As the foursome walked toward the front door shortly after that, Sharon felt Scott's fingers on her arm. Tugging her to a stop, he nodded toward Rick and Diane and said, "Let them go on. I think they'd like to be alone for a couple of minutes. Anyway, Sharon..."

"Yes?"

"You can't believe how I feel about your extending your stay."

Sharon felt her heart pounding. "It really is only for two weeks, Scott," she told him huskily. "I definitely have to go back to Providence after that."

"Suppose your design is a big success?" he queried reasonably. "Suppose Tony and Diane offer you a job as their art director?"

"I've been thinking about that," Sharon admitted. "I mean, it's not out of the realm of possibility, but I . . . I honestly don't know."

"Your employer . . . what's his name?"

"Gary Freeman."

"Is there . . . well, is there more than just a business relationship between the two of you?"

"Honestly, Scott," Sharon protested. "I'm sure I've told you about Gary. His wife was sick for a long time, and he was very broken up after she died. It's been difficult for him to put his personal life back together again, so I've had dinner with him a couple of times, and we've gone to a few movies, but that's been it!"

"I hope so," Scott said solemnly. "Maybe it's selfish of me, but I'd hate to share you with anyone."

Sharon couldn't read the expression on his face. He seemed almost . . . perplexed, by what he'd just said. Then, slowly, he drew her into his arms.

She smelled his wonderful scent, felt his wonderful warmth. And as their lips meshed in a kiss that said what neither of them could say aloud, Sharon knew it would be a long and lonely night without Scott by her side.

CHAPTER THIRTEEN

"FABULOUS!" TONY ENTHUSED. "Absolutely fantastic." He was standing in front of Sharon's easel, and for a full minute he'd been silently surveying the preliminary sketch she'd done for the disk cover, while she held her breath.

He turned, caught his ex-sister-in-law in his arms, and gave her an exuberant hug. "If Diane and I are as right about everything connected with this business as we were when we persuaded you to do the covers for us, we're in to make a million before we know it!"

Sharon caught his use of the plural in "covers," but let it pass. Tony turned back to her design, and she looked at it appraisingly herself. She was singularly without conceit where her work was concerned, but she had to admit this was good.

Already, in this preliminary rendition, she'd captured the spirit of Miami that Diane had talked about: the nostalgia of the Deco past plus the promise of a streamlined, hi-tech future. It was all there in what she'd done—silhouettes, mostly, of buildings, palms and people. She'd decided to use a lot of black and white and silver—Di-Tone would be using that spectrum trio in their merchandising logo—and had added splashes of vivid color to further stimulate the eye.

Now, Sharon was literally itching to get her fingers on her paints and begin work on the real thing.

She'd spent the past week and a half getting this far. First, she'd contacted Tony at the club and listened to what he had in mind. Then, brooding on her own in something approaching solitary confinement, she had tried and rejected a number of concepts. Finally, suddenly, the perfect concept struck. She'd been guided by the Collins Avenue skyline painting that Diane had liked, but she'd gone far beyond that. It was as if her imagination had been given wings.

Wings. Flying. Scott.

Scott was not very pleased with her at the moment. This morning, when he'd called to say that he had a free day tomorrow and wanted to drive down to Islamorada, in the Keys, she'd had to refuse him.

"I'm meeting with Tony this afternoon," she'd told him. "Tomorrow I'll really need to get started on the painting they'll be using for the cover design. Tony's anxious to get into production as soon as possible, and that hinges, at least in part, on my having the artwork ready."

"When I heard you'd extended your stay here, I didn't think it was going to be anything like this," Scott complained. "I've scarcely seen you since the night Rick and I were over there to dinner. Rick's doing a lot better with your twin sister, in fact. They've been out to dinner, and even went to the races at Hialeah the other night."

"Scott, please . . . be a little bit patient about this, will you? It's important to Tony and Di that the cover I come up with do the best job of promoting their product. It just has to be visually right. You can understand that, can't you?"

"Of course I can. And if I thought you might consider staying in Miami and working for Di-Tone—assuming they are successful—I'd understand it even more.''

''I haven't come to that yet,'' Sharon evaded.

To her relief, Scott didn't pursue the subject. But he did pursue the idea of her having dinner with him the following evening, after she'd finished work for the day.

''We can make it an early night,'' he conceded reluctantly. ''I'll even take you to the Twenties, out in Bal Harbour. The blurb in my guide book says that they feature an elegant art Deco motif amidst the exciting atmosphere of the Twenties. That should only inspire you further.''

''All right, all right.'' Sharon gave in, laughing.

For the next thirty hours, though, she missed Scott dreadfully. All the time she was painting, she was aware of him. Fortunately, this didn't affect the quality of her work. Thinking of Scott, actually, was an inspiration. Without realizing it, she was using him as the model for the striking male figure who would dominate part of the cover.

It was Diane who caught her up on that, as Sharon was getting ready for her date with Scott. She stood in Sharon's sun room, examining the progress of the painting, while Sharon brushed her hair and put on her makeup.

''So, Scott's going to make his debut as a model along with Di-Tone's debut as a company!'' she observed cleverly.

Depicting Scott had been such an unconscious act on Sharon's part that for a moment she thought her twin was merely teasing her. Then she looked closer and saw that Diane was right. She *had* captured Scott on her canvas. The essence of Scott, anyway.

"I think your subconscious is telling you something," Diane suggested knowingly.

Flustered, Sharon rejoined, "Well, you have to admit he makes a terrific subject!"

"So he does," Diane agreed. She surveyed the painting again. "This is really terrific, sister mine," she approved. "Tony was thrilled with the preliminary, but
he'll go out of his mind when he sees this finished. Do
you intend to capture Genevieve as the female figure in
the same way you've captured Scott?"

"That's a good idea, though honestly, Di...I wasn't
aware I was painting Scott. But yes, I think I should try
to get the essence of Genevieve into the female figure."

"Tony will like that," Diane decided.

Sharon slanted a glance at her twin. "What happened to the green-eyed monster?" she asked, with a
touch of Diane's bluntness.

"He became benevolent," Diane announced calmly.
"It's hard to let go all the way, Shar, even when there's
no longer any valid reason for clutching on to a person.
Anyway, it's so much better now, because Tony and I
actually adore being business partners. We're having
such a marvelous time with Di-Tone I don't see how the
company can fail to be successful."

"You were so worried about the possibility of Tony's
being hurt," Sharon remembered.

"Yes, I was. But Tony's a big boy," Diane said enigmatically, repeating what Sharon had tried to tell her
when the subject of Genevieve Landry had first arisen
between them.

Sharon, taking a long last look at herself in the mirror, asked, "Are you going out tonight?"

Diane shook her head. "I'm going to be a good
mommy," she reported. "I'm going to stay home with

Tonette and watch a couple of children's videos I rented for her. Rick's on call, but he said to page him at the hospital after I get Tonette to bed. By then, hopefully, things will have quieted down for him.''

Sharon thought whimsically that had she said something like that about Scott to Diane, a number of questions would have followed. Admittedly, she was curious, but she suppressed the questions. She only hoped that Diane's interest in Rick wasn't just a rebound response. Rick deserved more than that.

That night, Sharon was waiting outside the front door as her date pulled into the driveway. She was wearing a new dress that she'd intended to save for the open house Diane planned to have on Easter Sunday, only a week away. But at the nth hour, she decided to wear it for Scott.

The dress was soft lilac, and Sharon had cinched it at the waist with a deep purple sash. Antique amethyst earrings and a matching pendant completed her outfit.

Scott, gazing down at her, said huskily, ''Darling, you've never looked more beautiful.''

Suddenly Sharon realized why that might be. She was happy. Genuinely happy. She loved the work she was doing for Diane and Tony. She loved being here in Miami. And... she loved this tall, handsome man standing before her with adoration in his vivid blue eyes.

It was a perfect moment in time. Sharon only wished she could encapsulate it and keep it forever, like a tiny, suspended crystal.

They enjoyed the Twenties, but Sharon was aware that by the time they were having espressos, little patches of silence were falling between them.

As they left the restaurant, Scott said, "That beach we went to once...remember? It isn't far from here. Are you up for a short moonlight stroll?"

"After all that food, definitely," Sharon told him, trying to keep the atmosphere between them on a light note.

She and Scott left their shoes in the car and walked barefoot across the sand, still warm from the heat of the day. The moon was obscured behind clouds, and Scott's silhouette, at her side, was like something from one of her paintings. Suddenly, she wished she could read his expression.

"Sharon," he said without preamble, "about flying..."

That was the last thing she expected him to say, and she didn't know how to respond.

"Look," he said. "Let's sit down on that bench over there, like we did the other time, okay?"

He led her by the hand, and it puzzled Sharon when Scott deliberately kept a distance between them once they were seated.

Flying. Only one thing occurred to Sharon. Somehow, Scott had prematurely learned about his future as a pilot.

She said tentatively, "You haven't had that interim physical you spoke about, have you, Scott?"

"No, that won't be coming up for several more weeks," he answered. "I...well, I wasn't talking about *me* flying, Sharon. I was thinking about you."

Automatically, she stiffened. "Me?"

"I was biding some time the other afternoon waiting to see my commanding officer," Scott said. "I picked up a magazine I don't usually read—a sports magazine. As it happens, there was an article in it about professional athletes and their feelings toward flying."

"Yes?"

"Sharon, most pro athletes are pretty macho guys, you have to admit. But did you know that quite a few of them are scared to death of flying? Think about that, for a moment. With their schedules it's absolutely necessary for them to fly all the time. How else could you get from Boston to Los Angeles, for example, and back to Philadelphia two days later?

"Anyway," Scott went on, "In more than one instance, fear of flying has literally wrecked a guy's career. One baseball player, in particular, who was considered the golden boy of sports not many years ago, had such a fear of flying that it just about ruined his life. Whenever he could, he'd drive to the next game, even if it involved hundreds of miles and meant he had to be on the road an entire night to meet up with his team.

"When he had absolutely no choice but to fly, his teammates said he was so terrified he'd just sit there, white as a ghost, clutching the armrests of his seat. Yet he was actually named Most Valuable Player in his league one year. A few years later, his career was over. People who knew him said that his fear of flying literally drove him out of baseball."

Sharon was rigid. "Why are you telling me this, Scott?" she demanded coldly.

"Please, Sharon, hear me out," he urged. "One hockey star has tried therapists—and just about everything else—to get him over his fear of flying. His teammates say the minute he gets on a plane he starts sweating and shaking. Sometimes they can calm him down, but when it's time to land he begins all over again. It affects not only him, but everyone around him.

"Other professional athletes have confessed that it was fear of flying that started them on the path to becoming alcoholics. They'd hit the bar at the airport before departure, knowing just how much to drink so they'd literally pass out the moment they sat down in the plane. One famous pro football coach admitted he was so afraid of flying that if anyone even touched him when he was in a plane, he'd break out from head to toe in a cold sweat—"

"Scott!" Sharon interrupted, her voice like ice. "*Why* are you telling me this?"

"Because it's not unusual. Being afraid to fly, that is," Scott said gently. "Most of these men I read about got over it. But, to be honest, some did not. They got to the point of either learning to live with flying, or quitting their professions." He took a deep breath and added, almost in a whisper, "I suppose I'm saying that your fear isn't anything to be ashamed of."

"I've never said I was ashamed of it," Sharon managed.

"No, you haven't. But sometimes I've had that feeling. Basically, I can understand the way you feel—I really can. What I wish is that you'd try to understand the way I feel." He managed a wry laugh. "That doesn't mean that I'm attempting to convert you to my way of thinking."

Sharon looked across at him and realized he was waiting for her to say something. Slowly, she started, "Diane and I got into a discussion not long ago about my feelings toward flying. My father and my stepmother live on the West Coast, and Diane has been quite irked with me because I won't fly out to California with her to visit them. That came up when we were talking about you . . . and flying," she went on steadily. "I don't think

Diane has a great deal of sympathy for my feelings, though she can appreciate the horror I felt seeing Jerry's plane crash.''

"I can, too," Scott told her carefully.

"Yes, but I didn't like flying even before . . . Jerry's accident. Whenever I went up in that tiny plane of his, I'd inevitably get sick. Eventually he stopped asking me to tag along. I've tried therapy . . .''

"You never told me that."

"Well, I'm telling you now. As you pointed out, fear of flying isn't an abnormal affliction—if it can be considered an affliction at all," Sharon said, rather defiantly. "Man wasn't born with wings, you know."

"True. But he wasn't born with fins, either. And a lot of people like to swim and snorkel and scuba—" Scott broke off. "I'm not trying to make a case for anything," he said. "All I'm asking is that you try to understand, just a little. Believe me, I'll never ask you to put foot in a plane, knowing how you feel. But I wish you'd try to appreciate how I feel. There'd be a large empty area in my life if I could no longer fly."

"I believe you, Scott."

"It's a part of me, Sharon. Like it or not, it's a part of me. And though it's true man was born without wings, man also had the intelligence to study the birds and to figure out how to get up there himself. Once the first flight was made, once those first pioneers got their crazy-looking machines off the ground, all future generations were hooked. Myself included.

"When I was a kid," he went on, "my brother Hugh, who is several years older than I am, took flying lessons. Army brats don't always have the opportunity to make money after school, or sometimes even on vacations, like civilian kids. Most of the time, we lived on a military post somewhere, so we had to make do with the allowance Dad gave us.

"Then, when Hugh was eighteen, a great aunt of ours died. Hugh had been named after her husband, and she left Hugh some money—enough so he was able to take flying lessons and buy a small plane. They don't even make them like that anymore," Scott recalled.

"Anyway, I used to go up with him," he said, "and he pretty much taught me to fly. From day one, I loved the feel of flying more than I can possibly express to you. It seemed to me the ultimate freedom. It still does.

"By the time I was in high school, I knew that I wanted to fly for the rest of my life. I wanted to make a career of it. If I'd been a civilian kid, I probably would have considered being an airline pilot. As an Army brat, I was used to the military life, and I liked every new place we lived, though the bases were pretty much the same.

"I have friends all over the world who I keep in touch with. Germany, England, Hawaii, Italy, and many other countries, as well."

"I must admit, that is a plus," Sharon managed.

"Yes, it is. And so it was quite natural for me to apply to the Air Force Academy. The day I learned I was accepted was one of the highlights of my life. One of those few zenith experiences we ever get. I entered pilot training, and from there you might say that my life was increasingly involved with aircraft . . . and with that sky up there. Believe me, it's a real challenge to fly a modern jet bomber."

"You fly bombers?"

"Yes. And like a lot of other career officers, I've done a few things I didn't want to do."

"Because you were ordered to?"

"Don't sound so disapproving, Sharon," Scott requested gently. "Most of us have to follow orders, one way or another. There are few of us who just push our way through life without adhering to certain criteria."

"What kind of plane do you fly, Scott?"

"Well, of late I've been flying F-111's," he said hesitantly. "Actually, the F-111 has been functional since the late 1960s, but it remains an extremely sophisticated aircraft. It has a range of more than three thousand miles, depending upon the kind of mission it's used for. If a mission requires carrying external fuel tanks under the wings, for example, then we can't carry certain types of missiles. So range and firepower go hand in hand. Of course, the plane does have the capacity of being refueled in midair—" He broke off, then said, "This must be boring you."

It was not boring Sharon. It was, perhaps, horrifying her, but it certainly was not boring her.

She asked faintly, "How many people are there in such a plane?"

"Two," Scott told her. "A pilot and a weapons officer. Look, Sharon, I didn't mean to get into this so... well, so specifically."

"Are you telling me anything I shouldn't know?"

"Military secrets?" he asked wryly. "No. Everything I'm telling you has been published in newspapers all over the country at one time or another. It's no secret that the F-111 is considered a workhorse attack aircraft. It can fly at supersonic speeds, and it has an extremely precise radar bombing system which permits delivery of weapons on targets in bad weather, or at night. Further, the radar system has an automatic terrain-following device that allows us to fly at a fixed height, following the actual contours of the earth. This system guides us over mountains, or into valleys, regardless of weather conditions, either day or night. Those are extremely important safety features.''

''I can't say that flying in what sounds like an airborne bomb seems very safe to me,'' Sharon commented, her voice so tight she felt as if it had been knotted in sections.

''The F-111 is not an airborne bomb,'' Scott reproved.

''If...if there was danger of it crashing, would you simply...explode?'' It was a hard question for her to ask.

''No,'' he said gravely. ''We have a cockpit module that is both pressurized and air-conditioned. The crew of two sit side-by-side. In extreme emergencies, the module serves as an escape vehicle. Later, it can be a survival shelter on either land or water. It can be jettisoned at any speed or altitude, or even released under water.''

''My, my,'' Sharon managed. ''They've thought of everything, haven't they?''

Scott reached over and grasped her hand. He was not surprised to find it icy cold. He really hadn't intended to get so technical. All he was asking was for Sharon to try to look at his career as exactly that—his career. He didn't expect her to change in an instant. He only hoped that she might begin to soften.

If he'd known that she'd sought counseling...

He realized he was treading on potentially dangerous territory, and that she might even resent his next question. So he very cautiously asked, ''What conclusion did you reach with the therapist, Sharon?''

''That perhaps it would be best to let sleeping dogs lie,'' she stated bluntly. ''As I've said, it was nothing new, this fear of mine. Jerry's death only intensified it and added an element of horror that I don't think I'll ever get over. But even when I was a child, the sky daunted me. I used to look up at the stars, and when I learned how far away they were, that remoteness was overwhelming to me. Just as space and infinity remain overwhelming to me. I don't suppose you can understand that?"

"Yes, I can understand that," Scott said. "Because space and the stars are overwhelming to me, too, sweetheart. I really think we humans are all made of the same clay, in that respect. Maybe some of us are more visionary than others, but we all have our boundaries."

"Mine are more limited than most people's."

"I don't agree with you," he told her sincerely. "Everyone's different, Sharon. That's a platitude, but I think we sometimes forget how true it is. Anyway..."

"Yes?"

As if on cue, the moon peeped out from behind the clouds and cast a silver glow across Scott's face. Sharon saw he was smiling. He said, tenderly, "Anyway, I'd hate to have you as my weapons officer. I'd be so rattled I'd forget where the controls were."

Finally, he abandoned the space between them. He slid toward her and drew her close. "Ah, Sharon, Sharon, Sharon," he murmured. "Look, I'm sorry I brought this up. It's just that sometimes I get so frustrated about so many things. And I need so much to have your understanding. I love you, do you know that?"

Hearing those three eternally poignant words, Sharon felt herself swept by an emotional wave of tidal proportions. She didn't answer Scott. She merely reached her arms around him and embraced him tightly.

As he held her, caressing her hair, her face, her arms, he murmured, "We're in a bind, you and I—no place to go. That's crazy, isn't it? But I can't see checking in at some motel with you, or even at a posh hotel. And I can hardly take you back to the BOQ at Homestead—that's the bachelor officers' quarters, for which I now qualify. Nor should we stage a repeat performance at Diane's. There'd be too much risk of Tonette walking in on us.''

"Mmm," Sharon murmured.

She nestled her head against Scott's shoulder, and for a while they sat silently, watching the moon and the palms and listening to the waves break against the shore.

At last, Scott said, not too steadily, "I guess maybe I'd better take you home, lady. Or we're apt to find the Miami vice squad on the scene, shining their lights in our recumbent faces!"

"Scott!" Sharon protested.

Yet ... he was right. They had no place to go where they could be alone. Two people in this big, sophisticated city, with no personal oasis of their own.

"I'm going to have to do some thinking," Scott said. "If you decide to stay around and work for Diane and Tony, I think maybe I'll get an apartment somewhere. I don't have to stay on the base."

He tugged Sharon to her feet and confessed, "Come on, this proximity is getting to me. Maybe we should take a swim."

"Scott! This is my best dress."

"Who said anything about keeping your dress on?"

"Scott!"

"I love the way you say that. Somehow, despite the note of chastisement, I get the feeling you want me as much as I do you, Sharon, my love."

Sharon, my love. She liked the sound of it. And he was right, so right. Definitely, she wanted him every bit as much as he wanted her. And if she did decide to stay in Miami, she and Scott would have to do something about...themselves.

They couldn't forever go walking along beaches in the moonlight, hand in hand like love-struck youngsters. They were beyond that. They, and their passions, had acquired the depth and needs of maturity.

Maturity?

There were moments, Sharon thought, when she felt younger than Tonette in trying to get through her personal obstacle course with Scott. Younger, and much more vulnerable.

CHAPTER FOURTEEN

"I'VE MADE a few plans I hope you'll have time for," Diane said to Sharon, a couple of days before Easter.

"Oh?" Sharon knew her twin so well she automatically went on the alert when Diane made a seemingly casual comment like that.

"I've asked Ricardo and Scott to come over Saturday night and help us dye eggs. Then, Sunday morning, we'll have an Easter egg hunt for Tonette and a couple of her friends from school. Tony and Genevieve will drop by, too."

"How absolutely *congenial*," Sharon managed.

"Do I detect a note of sarcasm in your dulcet tones, loving sister?"

"Sarcasm, no. Astonishment, maybe. I guess I'm just not contemporary enough. If I were in your shoes, I don't think I could handle having Rick and Tony and Genevieve on the premises at the same time."

Diane chuckled. "Well, they're all coming back later for the open house," she added, as if that made the difference.

"I give up," Sharon confessed, flinging up her palms in mock despair.

Nevertheless, the Easter weekend proved to be one of the most enjoyable times she could ever remember spending with her sister. Along with Rick and Scott, they dyed the eggs late Saturday night after Tonette was in

bed—just as though Tonette still believed in the proverbial Easter Bunny. Then, using flashlights, they hid
the eggs around the patio and all around the garden.

Ten o'clock Sunday morning was the official hour for
the egg hunt to begin. By then, Tonette, three other little girls and two little boys—all classmates of hers—were
champing to go, and the grown-ups were taking their
stances on the sidelines to serve as "judges."

Genevieve Landry looked lovely in a flowing white
dress...and younger, with only a touch of makeup in
contrast to her stage face. Tony was smitten, anyone
could see that. But Diane captured Rick's attention in a
similar fashion, and the atmosphere wasn't strained in
the least. In fact, everyone seemed to be enjoying themselves immensely.

At one point, Sharon murmured to Scott, "Is it a
crazy world, or am I just old-fashioned?"

"Frankly, I think it's great," he whispered back.
"One thing's for sure, Tonette's not going to grow up
with any extra traumas, like a lot of children of divorced parents. I think she just feels she's expanded her
family by adding Genevieve and Rick, and you..."

"And you?" Sharon prompted.

"I'd like to think so," he said very softly.

Sharon caught her breath. In a way, this was the most
significant thing he'd ever said to her. Yet she didn't
want to attach a meaning to his words that perhaps he'd
not meant at all.

At the conclusion of the hunt, the eggs each child had
garnered were solemnly counted by the adults, and prizes
distributed. Diane had selected prizes that were each
special in their own way, so the youthful participants all
went home happy.

Tonette, clutching the plush, pale blue rabbit she had won, said to her mother, "I'm glad this isn't a chocolate bunny, Mommy." She looked up at Rick and added, "I wouldn't want to be allergic sick again, Doctor Rick."

He burst out laughing. "I'm sure you wouldn't," he agreed, giving Tonette an impulsive hug and kissing the top of her dark curls.

Around noon, Rick and Scott bade everyone goodbye, saying they would return in a few hours for the open house. Sylvie and Maria arrived, followed shortly thereafter by the same caterers Diane had hired before. Soon, the house and patio were transformed into a flowery wonderland, with pots of Easter lilies and tulips and jonquils blooming all over the place.

"This," said Diane, as she paused to have a glass of iced tea with Sharon on the patio, "is all tax deductible, thank heavens."

"What do you mean?"

"It's a business expense," Diane informed her sister, quite seriously. "Most of the people you'll see here this afternoon are involved in one way or another with Di-Tone. At least, Tony and I hope they will be. We've invited quite a few media people, too. One magazine writer is very much interested in interviewing you, though that'll have to wait for another time, of course."

"Interviewing *me*?"

"That's what I said, Sharon. Tony's dropped a few hints hither and yon about the cover design, and naturally a lot of people want to meet this artist he's raving about."

"Di, I didn't intend anything like that."

"Shar, will you kindly learn at some point in your life that it doesn't pay to always keep your light hidden inside a brown paper bag. Naturally, you're going to get your share of publicity. It would be selfish of Tony and me to keep you entirely to ourselves. All we want is for you to give us first priority in your commissions."

"You're out of your mind, twin. You sound like I've suddenly started my own business."

"You'll be doing exactly that before long, I venture to say... that is, if you want to," Diane amended cryptically. "Now, I've got to be sure everything's set up in the living room."

With that, Diane was off again. Sharon headed to the kitchen to see if she could help Maria or Sylvie do anything. They were deeply involved in finalizing some trays of very fancy appetizers and, in so many words, said thanks but no thanks.

She wandered upstairs and into the screened sun room where she'd been working almost exclusively of late. Earlier, Sylvie bemoaned the fact that they hadn't been on a painting expedition in almost two weeks, and Sharon agreed she missed that very much. But her work for Tony and Diane had demanded her time, which Sylvie understood completely.

"This is just the beginning for you, *cherie*," she had prophesized. "Just the beginning, you'll see."

Wondering about that for perhaps the thousandth time, Sharon went back into her bedroom and took the painting out of her closet, where she'd stashed it after it had dried. Neither Diane nor Tony knew that she'd executed the final brush strokes only yesterday. The cover was ready, or as ready as it would ever be, Sharon amended.

She propped up the canvas against the wall, then walked the width of the room before turning to survey her work. The afternoon sunlight slanted across the face of the painting, giving it a special glow. But even without that special effect, the design was vital and vibrant, and exactly what both Diane and Tony had wanted.

At least, that's what Sharon hoped. Though she had more confidence in this particular work than in anything she'd ever attempted, she knew she still didn't have confidence enough.

I should have more of Diane's assertiveness, she found herself thinking, *and she should have more of my reticence.*

She returned the painting to its hiding place and, as she dressed for the open house, hoped that neither Tony nor Diane would think to ask her just how close to completion the painting was.

To her chagrin, the opposite happened all too quickly. The minute she walked onto the patio, Tony disengaged himself from a group of men with whom he'd been talking and quickly moved to her side.

He kissed her cheek, then said, "You're just the person I want to see, beautiful! Those fellows over there are thinking about investing in Di-Tone, and all we need to make them reach for their checkbooks is to show them your painting. Would you mind if they take a peek at it?"

"Tony, I . . ." Sharon floundered for words, shrinking at the thought of bringing her work out for display in front of these strangers. Suppose she and Tony and Diane had all been wrong about what she was doing?

"Shar, even if you'd let them have a glimpse of the preliminary sketch, it would help," Tony beseeched, his voice low. Sharon could tell by his carefully fixed smile that this was very important to him. "If you could let them see the real thing, of course, it would be even better. How far along with it are you?"

There was no point in hedging any longer. "It's finished," Sharon said flatly.

That did it! Sharon's painting was brought downstairs and soon she, and it, became the center of attention. The magazine writer Diane had spoken about took one look at the design and promptly asked for an interview. "Too much to request an exclusive, I know," he said, "but I'd like to be the first."

The talk-show host from a local TV station asked her jovially how she'd like to be on his show one morning, soon, and to bring her design with her—as if there was any chance she could dare say no to him. And so it went.

Sharon felt as if she'd been smiling for hours at people she'd just met, and virtually saying the same thing over and over again as she answered their questions. Then, like a hypnotist's snap of the fingers, a very familiar voice said, "Might there be a chance of my getting your autograph, Mrs. Williams? I'm starting a collection of celebrity autographs and I want yours to take up the whole first page of my album."

Scott was smiling down at her. To her surprise, he added, "I'm very proud of you, darling. I just had a look at your cover design myself, and it's pretty fantastic. But it took your twin to point out to me that I, evidently, was the model for the man in the picture. I'm flattered, to say the least."

"Scott, stop teasing me!"

"I'm not teasing you. I *am* flattered." Scott glanced around him. "Whew," he said, "this is getting to be even more of a mob scene than the first party your sister had for you."

"This isn't for me, Scott. It's mostly business."

"What?"

"This is mostly business. Diane has a few of her personal friends here, but most of these people have been invited because of some connection with Di-Tone. Either actual, potential, or because they're media."

"You're beginning to sound like a real pro."

"I'm not a pro. As a matter of fact, I feel like a hapless amateur who's stumbled into something over her head."

"Sharon...do you suppose we could cut out of here?"

"I don't see how," she said helplessly. "Tony and Diane are counting on me."

"And you're telling me you're not reacting like a pro?" He stood back a bit, surveying her. "Frankly," he said, "I've been watching you with the various members of the media you've been talking to, and I'd say you were eating up the attention."

Before Sharon could respond, Diane stepped up with someone who wanted to meet her. Almost instantly, Scott faded backward. He watched Sharon greet the newcomer—a staff writer from a music trade publication—and the words he'd just spoken echoed in his ears. He didn't like their sound. He hadn't meant to come on like that. Still, his pride in her was definitely mixed with a feeling that was, he supposed, part jealousy and part envy.

Still, Sharon had this attention coming to her; he would be the first to concede that. She was talented, very talented, and entirely too modest about her work. About herself, as well. Almost too self-effacing, sometimes, too inclined to retreat.

But those character traits could change. Scott recalled seeing them change quite drastically in Claudia.

Thinking this, bitter memories surged. When he'd been an Air Force cadet, and dating Claudia, she'd been a regular shrinking violet. Blond and beautiful, with huge blue eyes and a beguilingly shy manner. She'd always let him take the lead. Even, for a while, after they'd been married. Then . . . that had begun to change.

Claudia had come into her own. Oh, how she had come into her own! He couldn't pinpoint exactly when her moods and mannerisms had started to veer away from the Claudia he thought he was in love with. It didn't happen overnight. Nor could he state, specifically, the date when he realized that she'd begun to drink too much, too often.

Then, to top it all, she had started carping about his career. Especially when he'd received orders to transfer from the base outside Washington where he was then stationed, to a fairly remote base out west, where Claudia really didn't want to go.

So near the Capitol, Claudia had tasted the fringes of Washington's glamorous social life. Tasted, digested and digested. They'd been invited to several diplomatic receptions—as a promising young officer and son of a well-known general, Scott's name found its way onto certain lists—and once even to an affair at the White House. Claudia had spent the better part of a day preening for that one!

The latter invitation, Scott knew, had come more because of his father's prestige than his own. In fact, General Williams had been among the guests. Claudia had really cottoned up to his father that night, and the General, unfortunately, had been delighted by his coy and charming daughter-in-law. So much so that when Scott had finally informed his parents he was filing for divorce, his father had been adamantly against it. Later, he'd relented somewhat, maybe because—within the limited periphery of Washington military gossip—a few stories about that same daughter-in-law found their way back to his ears.

His mother had been more understanding, though she had pointed out that the divorce might have an adverse effect on his career. Scott had countered that things had changed in that respect, even in the military.

Still . . . Claudia had caused him so damned much anguish over the years, after seeming so sweet and innocent in the beginning. Try as he might, Scott couldn't help but wonder if Sharon might change, too. She certainly had more reason to, he decided.

When he'd first met Sharon and she'd gotten a little bit tipsy on the train, he'd initially been put off. Then he'd told himself he had no right to judge this lovely stranger because his ex-wife was an alcoholic.

Now he tried to tell himself again that he had no right—no cause whatsoever—to measure Claudia and Sharon with the same yardstick.

The writer moved on, and Sharon turned to face him. There was real concern in her voice as she asked softly, "What's happened, Scott?"

Suddenly, Scott felt ashamed of himself. But he said only, "Nothing. Look, let's have some more champagne punch, shall we?"

"All right."

She watched him closely as they made their way to the crystal punch bowl that dominated the center of Diane's dining room table. His hand trembled slightly as he filled their cups, and this worried her all the more. She searched his face for signs of fatigue, yet she had to admit he didn't look tired. He looked . . . agitated.

"Did anything go wrong today?" she demanded abruptly.

He raised a quizzical eyebrow as he handed her a cup of pale yellow sparkling punch. "What could have gone wrong today?" he asked reasonably. "I've been here most of it."

"You and Rick left for a few hours," Sharon reminded him as they moved through the dining room's French doors out onto the patio.

"We went back to Rick's place and watched some sports on TV," Scott reported. "Any more questions?"

He knew he sounded abrupt and, seeing Sharon's reaction, tried to make amends for his tone. "Sharon, I'm really not at my best in situations like this."

She smiled rather whimsically. "I thought that was my line," she pointed out. "I keep saying I'm not a party person. You, on the other hand, as a career officer, must have all sorts of social obligations."

"That depends where I am."

"Nevertheless—"

"Okay, I do have my share of functions and so-called parties to attend," he admitted grimly. Again he thought of Claudia and the misery she'd caused him during the execution of some of those obligations, and of the number he'd later sidestepped because, regardless of how that might look to his superior officers, he had no intention of having a drunken wife on his hands yet again.

The "official" hours of the open house had been given as five to seven. Most of the guests did leave by seven, but a few lingered. Finally, there were only Scott, Rick, Sylvie and Greg Dubrinski left with Diane and Sharon. After a time Diane's affable real estate colleague roared at Sylvie, "Come on, woman, I'll take you home!" and she raised her eyebrows and said, in exaggerated horror, "I was afraid you were going to say that."

They were both laughing lightheartedly as they departed the house on Pine Tree Drive. Diane, who had seen them to the door, returned to the patio. "Sometimes I could shake Sylvie. I think Greg's crazy about her, and she won't even look at him. Seriously, I mean."

"It takes two," Scott observed quietly.

"Do tell, philosopher!" Diane kidded him. Turning to Rick, she said, "I want something to drink, Doctor, but I can't stand the thought of any more punch. What would you prescribe?"

"A very small brandy for each of us," Rich suggested. "Then, Scott and I will be off. I have to be in the hospital in the morning and you have a pretty important session ahead of you yourself, don't you, Scott?"

Sharon looked at him questioningly. He had said nothing to her about anything important coming up, but he nodded.

"I have to meet with several senior officers at ten o'clock sharp to present my plans for the special training program I've developed," he said. "I just hope they go for it without putting up too many obstacles."

"What kind of obstacles?" Sharon queried.

Scott stirred restlessly. "Well, it's just that I'd like to get started *doing* something," he confessed. "I was never cut out for idleness."

"Will you get an answer right away, do you think?" Rick asked. "Or is this one of those things that has to be referred to Washington?"

"I'm sure a decision will be made promptly," Scott said firmly. "There's no reason why we need any further clearance. At least, that's what I've been told. So...cross your collective fingers for me."

CROSSING THEIR COLLECTIVE FINGERS didn't prove to be good enough, Sharon learned late Monday afternoon. But it wasn't Scott who told her that. It was Diane, who'd gotten the word from Rick.

"As Rick put it," Diane said, "Scott had been given every reason to think this was an all-systems-go situation, and that approval was a mere formality. Instead, the powers that be suddenly decided to cancel the entire program, for reasons that Scott felt were pretty vague. Rick says he's afraid Scott is taking it very personally. He seems to think it's an indication that, as far as the Air Force is concerned, he's already being put on the shelf, without their waiting for the results of his tests."

Sharon had visited Sylvie's studio for a cup of tea and some "art talk," and had just returned to Diane's house when her twin tugged her into the living room and told her what Rick had relayed to her over the phone.

She listened, aghast, imagining how Scott must feel and knowing that this was the last kind of blow he needed. But even though she could appreciate his feelings—and the mood his superiors' decision must have plunged him into—it hurt to be hearing the news third-hand.

"When did Rick find out?" she asked.

"Scott was through with his session by eleven o'clock this morning," Diane reported. "Evidently he called Rick at the hospital as soon as he could get to a phone. Rick was in surgery, but when he got the message he called Scott back right away."

"Where was Scott?"

"At the—what do they call it?—at the BOQ at Homestead," Diane said. "I gather he'd gone to his room there and hadn't really seen or spoken to anyone." After a moment, she asked cautiously, "Were you around here this morning?"

"At the time when Scott might have called, do you mean?" Sharon asked. "Yes. I promised Tony last night that I'd try to sketch another design. He told me you two want to do an all-waltz disk. Really sentimental old waltzes. And I really like your idea for an all-tango disk. So many people love those brooding, sultry Latin tangos."

"Am I hearing what I think I'm hearing?" Diane queried, tapping her ear. "Has Tony convinced you to stay around and work for Di-Tone?"

"No, he hasn't," Sharon said a shade too shortly. "I told Tony I'd try a waltz design, that's all. It can still be Deco-ish in context. I mean, it will be a companion piece to the first cover, though different." Sharon's mind was not entirely on what she was saying, and she sighed. "You know what I mean," she finished.

"Yes," Diane said. "Yes, I think I do." She paused for a moment, then added, "I'm sorry Scott didn't call you this morning when he found out, Sharon. But I'm sure he will before the day's over, so don't take it too much to heart. Give him a chance. This must have been quite a dreadful blow. It must be terrible for a man to have his whole future hanging in the balance, as Scott's is, and then to have the one small straw he's clutching snatched away."

"He could have told me about it, Di." There was no point in mincing words, Sharon decided, especially with her twin.

"Yes, he could have, that's true. But don't jump to conclusions, okay?"

"If I were as important to him as he's indicated, he would have called me," Sharon insisted stubbornly. "I know we're not on the same wavelength where his flying is concerned. And I don't happen to agree with you about Scott's entire future hanging in the balance. His *flying* future, maybe . . . but not his career with the Air Force. After all, the majority of men and women in the Air Force aren't pilots.''

As she made this statement, Sharon was sharply aware of her own ambivalent feelings about Scott's future. How could she feel anything but elated if, in the final analysis, Scott was told he could no longer fly? On the other hand, how could she honestly wish that terrible verdict upon him? If her love for him was really as deep as she believed, how could she wish his greatest thrill in life permanently denied to him?

She went on, ''Scott is young and strong and intelligent. There are dozens of successful careers that he could pursue. His knowledge of electronics alone would open up all kinds of doors to him. I mean, it's not as if he's going to lose an arm or a leg or go blind, Diane. He won't be forced to cope with a severe disability that really *could* limit his career choices, you know.''

''In some ways,'' Diane said softly, ''that might be easier.''

''What?'' Sharon snapped. ''How...how can you say that?'' She blurted out the words, and then suddenly her eyes filled with tears, the tears started down her cheeks, and she began to sob uncontrollably.

Diane sat on the couch next to her twin and cuddled her, acting more like a mother than a sister.

''Come on, ninny,'' she chided softly. ''Scott's going to have a good reason for not calling you yet, I promise.''

As comforting as Diane was, Sharon couldn't imagine what reason that could be.

THE SPLITTING HEADACHE she developed later that evening was valid enough, however. She ate two bites of her dinner, then pushed her plate away, grimacing.

"Are you sure you're not coming down with something?" Diane asked, alarmed.

Sharon shook her head. "I'm just...exhausted, that's all."

At Sharon's elbow, Tonette piped up, "You didn't eat too much chocolate candy, did you, Sharon?"

"No, honey," Sharon said unsteadily. "I didn't eat any candy at all." She pushed back her chair and stood up. "Di, excuse me, but I think the best thing for me right now is to go to bed," she announced.

Diane nodded and promised, "I'll be up as soon as you're settled in."

A few minutes later, she appeared in Sharon's bedroom. "If you need anything in the night, call me, please," Diane told her. She bent down and kissed her twin on the forehead, then turned off her bedside light. "Try and get some rest," she urged. "Everything will look better in the morning, Shar. Things always do."

This time, they didn't.

The day was bright and blue, but Sharon's head was still throbbing. She hadn't fallen asleep till the wee hours, after much thrashing about, pacing, and even a midnight painting session.

She climbed out of bed, dressed, then despite her headache, began to work feverishly on the cover design once again.

She wasn't one to renege on a promise, and she'd promised Tony that's she'd do this design for him. But once the cover was finished, she was heading back to Providence.

CHAPTER FIFTEEN

"SAY SOMETHING!" Scott implored, reining in his impatience with difficulty. "Shout at me, throw something at me! But don't just stand there looking at me with those huge, woeful eyes of yours as if I've sabotaged you!"

"What do you expect me to say?" Sharon asked coolly. "My, it's nice to see you, Scott. I'm so glad you could stop by." She'd carefully held her resentment toward him in check for the past twenty-four hours, but now it was reaching a boil.

"Sarcasm sure as hell doesn't become you," he growled.

"You may be wrong about that."

"Am I?" he challenged.

They were facing each other across the table on Diane's patio, squared off like two sparring partners about to start throwing punches—except that these punches would be purely verbal.

Reluctantly Scott accepted that. In a way it would be easier if Sharon picked up a flowerpot and heaved it at him. She seemed angry enough, but she was just too blasted polite—too repressed, too inhibited. He tried to think of a few more uncomplimentary adjectives to label her with, but looking at her, he failed.

Since coming to Miami, Sharon had taken the sun cautiously whenever she'd gone to the beach or ven-

tured out to paint. She had succeeded in protecting her
fair skin, but had remained almost as pale as the day
she'd stepped off the train. Now, there were dark circles
of fatigue under her eyes, and Scott knew that she hadn't
slept much last night. But then neither had he. He'd been
tormented by too many things to remember.

He should have called her, of course, and told her
personally about the training program being cancelled.
When he'd phoned Rick instead, he hadn't expected that
his words would be transmitted to Diane, and thence to
Sharon. He had no idea that Rick and Diane were keeping up that kind of communication. Regardless, he'd
been an idiot in staving off talking to Sharon. He'd told
himself this repeatedly ever since this morning when,
upon arising, he'd finally mustered the necessary courage to call her and tell her what had happened.

Maria, sounding decidedly chilly, had informed him
that Sharon was working and could not be disturbed. He
had accepted that without any great degree of displea-
sure, asking only that Maria have Sharon call him back
once she was free.

He'd wondered why Maria had sounded so cool. It
wasn't until later, when he learned the way the grapev-
ine was growing, that he realized Maria was in on his
"secret," too.

The outcome of his meeting had never been a secret,
of course, which was the ridiculous part of it. His superiors had decided to cancel the training program, cit-
ing lack of available funds and insufficient personnel as
their rationale for doing so.

There was no protesting the decision. Scott had sa-
luted stiffly then marched from the conference room as
quickly as possible, waiting until he was well out of earshot before uttering a string of choice oaths under his

breath. It was only after he'd walked briskly back to his quarters, managing to simmer down some along the way, that it occurred to him the reasons for the decision might really be valid.

It also occurred to him that maybe he was taking things too personally these days. Maybe he'd simply become unduly sensitive about just about everything. But none of this struck him until he'd spent the better part of two hours brooding by himself in his room at the BOQ. Finally, he'd gone to a movie theater in neighboring Homestead and sat through the film twice. Still, he could barely remember what he'd watched on the screen.

Emerging into one of south Florida's famous moonlit nights, Scott began to realize that he'd been reacting like a frustrated adolescent, and he knew he should have gotten in touch with Sharon first. Sharon, of all people. He should have let it all out with her, told her honestly how he felt and how he was becoming downright neurotic about rejection.

By then it had been almost 11:00 p.m. Too late to phone her, he'd thought, considering that he'd probably wake the whole house up if he did. So, he decided to wait until the morning.

Now he was paying for his vacillation. He knew that part of Sharon's problem was hurt pride, and he couldn't blame her for that. No one liked to hear, third-hand, important news concerning someone they cared about.

Also...she'd been worried about him. He'd caught glimpses of that worry etched on her lovely face from time to time, and he'd been deeply moved by it. He couldn't remember any woman—even his mother, once he'd passed his teens—actually worrying about him. It was a warm and wonderful feeling to know that you meant that much to someone . . . as he knew he did to Sharon, and as she surely did to him.

Which makes me all kinds of a damned fool, Scott thought grimly, *for having phoned Rick first.*

He didn't blame Rick for conveying the information to Diane. It just hadn't occurred to him that that would happen. He had the utmost faith in his friend's ability to keep a confidence. But there again, there'd been nothing confidential about what had been decided. It all boiled down to the simple fact that he should have called Sharon first. She should have heard the news from him.

He wished he could atone for his mistake. She still hadn't answered the challenge he'd flung at her about being sarcastic, so he began, "Look, Sharon—"

Unexpectedly, she pulled out a chair, sat down, and propped her elbows on the table top. She looked drained.

Scott asked carefully, "Did you get any sleep last night?"

"Not very much."

"Why?"

"Because I decided to work rather than stare at the ceiling and count sheep, that's why."

"What were you working on?"

"I promised Tony a second design, and I wanted to get it done."

"Is Tony pressing you with that much of a deadline?"

"Tony isn't pressing me with a deadline at all."

Scott pulled out a chair himself, and sat down across from Sharon. "Is there really such a need for hurry?"

"I want to get it finished before I leave."

"Leave?"

"Leave," she stated flatly.

Scott was tired, too. His fatigue mixed with exasperation and made his tone sharper than he intended. "You're not going to start in on that bit about heading back north, are you?" he demanded.

"I'm not going to start in on anything. I am going back north. No ifs or buts, this time. I've already called Gary Freeman and told him when I'll be back."

"You mean to say you're quitting on Tony and Diane?"

"I wouldn't put it that way."

"All right, do you mean to say you're giving up your job with them at what certainly must be a crucial point in their scheme of things? Couldn't you even wait to find out how your first cover goes over?"

"That will be quite a while," Sharon said coolly. "And just to set the record straight, I am not giving up my *job* with Tony and Diane. I've never had a job with them. I agreed to do the first cover design, and subsequently I agreed to the second."

"Didn't you say something about other cover ideas in the works? Tangos, I think you said, among other things?"

Sharon surveyed Scott levelly. "My, you do have a good memory about some things, don't you?"

He winced. "Look," he said, desperately desiring to make peace with her, "I don't blame you for being annoyed at me."

"Annoyed is an extremely mild word," she pointed out.

"All right. Like I told you, be furious, or murderous, or whatever you want to be. Even your sarcasm is better than the accusing indifference with which I was greeted."

"Accusing indifference," she mused. "I like that."

"Sharon!"

There was nothing woeful about her eyes now. They scorched his face as she said, "It's not amusing hearing information that seriously affects someone you *thought* you were very close to, from someone else. Even when that someone else is your twin sister."

"I understand that, sweetheart," Scott said gently. "But you're not giving me a chance to tell my side of the story."

"Okay, what is your side of the story?"

Scott's mouth tightened. "I think that you're making a mountain out of the proverbial molehill."

"*That's* your side of the story?"

"No, Sharon. What I'm saying is . . . well, I goofed in not calling you first. I admit that, so do we really have to make a federal case out of it? Look, I'd been given every reason to think that I was going to have the chance to do something useful during the balance of my stay at Homestead. I worked up an innovative training program that had preliminary approval. In fact, I was told that it was excellent in every aspect. Then the rug was pulled out from under me and, rightly or wrongly, I took it as a personal defeat. I wasn't ready to handle another personal defeat . . ."

Scott paused, but Sharon said nothing.

"I suppose," he continued after a moment, knowing full well how inept he'd probably sound, "I somewhat automatically contacted Rick because I still think of him as my doctor."

"You considered this a medical problem?"

"I wasn't thinking straight. It was a blow to my ego. Can't you understand that?"

When she didn't immediately answer, he went on, "Once I'd simmered down a little, I began to see that maybe the reason for the decision was really what I'd been told—not enough money, not enough men. In short, that it was nothing personal. Something about a budget *was* mentioned ... fiscal expenses, whatever. All of that went in one ear and out the other when, of course, I should have been listening."

Sharon was as still as a statue, and about as talkative.

"Look," Scott said helplessly, "I never intended to keep anything from you. Now for you to suddenly decide to pack up and return to Rhode Island, just because I delayed telling you something that actually isn't all that important—"

Sharon stirred at that. "Isn't it?" she asked icily.

"No, it honestly isn't. It took some serious soul searching for me to see that myself. Whether or not the training program is activated has absolutely no bearing upon my competence as a professional pilot. I realize that now, and I admit I was being unduly sensitive. Couldn't you bring yourself to try to understand that ... and then let's move on?"

Sharon let his words fade out into the short space between them. An amazingly chilly space, considering the air temperature was pushing eighty-five degrees.

Finally, she said, "I am not going back to Rhode Island, Scott, just because you didn't call me about your program being cancelled."

"Correction," he put in. "I did call you, quite early this morning. As soon as I thought you'd be up, as a matter of fact. Unfortunately, I was informed that you were working and couldn't be disturbed. So kindly don't make my delay any longer than it actually was."

"I'm not," Sharon responded tersely. "But it really doesn't make any difference. Last night I decided what

I'm going to do. You see...this just isn't my world," she finished rather feebly.

"Just what is your world, Sharon?" Scott demanded.

His voice suddenly matched hers in coldness, because the things she was saying were beginning to remind him of Claudia. The way Claudia had always thought of herself first, refused to consider anyone else's viewpoint, made so few allowances...at least for him.

She said, "I've made a small niche for myself in Providence. I have my job there, and my home there—"

"Your home? You've never mentioned having a home in Providence."

"I have my apartment there. I consider it my home."

She didn't add that it was a furnished apartment in an old triple decker in a rather indifferent neighborhood. Or that, in all honesty, she'd never thought of it as a "home," until now.

"Do Diane and Tony know you're planning to leave?" Scott asked suddenly.

"I told Diane at lunch today, and right after that I went over to Tony's office at the club and I told him. I only got back here a few minutes before you pulled into the driveway."

"I would imagine they're disappointed."

"Diane is quite disappointed, yes. Tony is more...philosophical. He suggested that we might work out an arrangement whereby I can do the covers in Providence and have them sent down by bonded carrier."

"I have nothing against Providence," Scott said steadily, "but I can't picture your capturing this Miami mood—as you did so well in the first design—if you're living in New England."

"That's for me to worry about, Scott. There is such a thing as imagination, you know."

"So there is," he agreed, ignoring Sharon's tone. Suddenly, he wanted to kiss her, and throttle her, and talk sense into her all at the same time. He'd seen her warm and caring side. That's what had deepened a simple sexual attraction toward her into love. He'd also witnessed what he was coming to term the "Claudia side" of her, though he hated the inference. This disturbed him, but he had no intention of falling into the trap of equating Sharon with his ex-wife, unless she somehow proved that she really *was* as self-centered as she was painting herself to be.

He said quietly, "All I can think of is that old song, Sharon. The one that poses the question, What can a person say after they've said they're sorry? What can I say to you, now that I've said I'm sorry?"

"I'm not expecting you to say anything, Scott."

"That's not the point, darling. The point is—"

Sharon turned away, stopping Scott short.

He began again. "Look . . . let's drive up to Sunday's and sit on the deck and have a piña colada or something. Let's just relax and talk."

"Thank you," Sharon told him politely, "but I really have to get back to work."

"Now?"

"Now."

She was allowing absolutely no room for discussion, and Scott's anger brimmed. "I didn't know you were so stubborn," he accused her.

"There's a lot you don't know about me, Scott."

"Yes, I'm beginning to think that's true." He pushed back his chair, got to his feet. "Okay," he said. "I won't keep you from your work. Is there a chance you might take a break later, and go out for a drink with me?"

"Not tonight, thank you."

"Very well, then. I'll call you tomorrow."

SCOTT LEFT the house quickly, quietly, without the slightest of backward glances. Not five minutes passed before Sharon desperately wished that she'd handled their meeting differently—much differently.

She would have given anything to be able to take back the last few minutes, especially the last few seconds. Anything, to hold Scott, kiss him, just be with him, like before. If she'd known where he was going, she would have followed him somehow. She would have borrowed a car....

She tried to get back to her work, but neither her mind nor her fingers were functioning properly. Finally, she gave up and called Sylvie, and asked her if she might be free to take a ride out to the Haulover Marina for a drink at Sunday's.

Sylvie arrived a half hour later, and they started up Collins Avenue. Once again, the traffic was heavy, and the drive seemed to take forever.

"We will just about be in time to see the sunset over Biscayne Bay," Sylvie said as they pulled into the parking lot.

This evening, Sharon couldn't have cared less about seeing the sunset, though normally she thrilled to such a display of natural beauty. As they walked into the waterfront restaurant, her eyes were sweeping every inch of the familiar low-ceilinged room, hoping to get a glimpse of Scott, hoping he'd be at one of the tables by the water's edge or occupying a stool at the bar.

She'd prayed that maybe, just maybe, he had decided to come out here anyway...then realized she should have known better. Sunday's would evoke memories for him, just as it was for her right now. Memories of a wonderful time they'd shared. He wouldn't want to sit here by himself any more than she wanted to sit here without him. But she'd invited Sylvie, so she tried to make the best of it as she sipped a frozen strawberry margarita.

Sylvie, though, was her usual perceptive self. After a spate of silence she prodded, "I hope you will excuse my curiosity, *cherie*. It is provoked only by my fondness for you. But I sense something has gone very wrong in your life. Is it Scott?"

Sharon nodded miserably. "Yes."

Under Sylvie's coaxing, she related her feelings about what had happened, ending with, "And you don't have to point it out to me, Sylvie. I know I've been behaving like an idiot."

"No, no," Sylvie admonished gently. "You were hurt, Sharon. You were hurt because you love him, so you are especially vulnerable where he is concerned. But this matter of your leaving for Rhode Island and quitting the work you have started here just because of a fairly small omission on Scott's part—that, I do think, is childish, yes."

"It isn't just because of Scott's omission, as you put it," Sharon said. "Last night, I couldn't sleep, so I thought the whole thing through."

"*Cherie*, don't you know that the poorest possible time to think seriously about anything is in the middle of the night, when you are wide-eyed awake and already frenetic?"

A faint smile tugged at Sharon's mouth. "I always love your word choices," she admitted, almost shyly, "but you are right, of course. I was in a mental frenzy in the middle of the night. I *was* wide-eyed, staring out at the street. But that's why I had to think things through, don't you see? I was going around in circles and getting nowhere."

"You think you solved your problems by thrashing around in the dark, your mind all muddled?"

"Not solved them, no," Sharon confessed. "But at least I came to a decision."

"Are you not afraid it is the wrong decision, *cherie*? Are you so sure it is right to walk out on him?"

"I don't feel I'm walking out on him," Sharon protested.

"No?"

"Sylvie . . . believe me, I've thought this through, and through again. Scott's calling Rick before he called me was only the tip of the iceberg. Sort of a catalyst, really. It crystallized things I should have seen sooner and more clearly. You see . . . there's no future for Scott and me. That's what it comes down to. We're just too different."

"People do not have to be alike to love, Sharon."

"Yes, I know that. But they do have to be able to accept each other's differences."

"You think Scott cannot accept your differences?"

"I think he would grow very tired of them after a while. After the shine had faded," Sharon decided. "He already got into a discussion with me the other night about the fear of flying."

"Yes, you have told me about your problem."

"It isn't just a casual thing, Sylvie. It's deep-rooted. Something that was there long before my husband died.

It isn't just that I'm afraid of flying *myself*. It's that I am terrified—more terrified than you can imagine—by the thought of Scott flying. Yet being a pilot is the most vital part of his life."

"Suppose he is not permitted to fly again?" Sylvie suggested. "You've mentioned that possibility."

"It's a very real possibility, but I can't wish for that to happen. I simply can't. Even though that would remove a very large concern for me, I cannot wish Scott that fate. I . . . I'm just not that selfish," Sharon concluded, her eyes misty.

"You are going to have me in tears in another moment. I am a ridiculous sentimentalist, you know. With the experiences I've had, no one would think I am still a believer in true love. But I am, though it has come to me only once, as I have told you. Maybe because it was just that once, and because I lost my love, that I caution you not to move too swiftly, Sharon. You could spend the rest of your life regretting your actions."

"Yes, I know."

"No two people are entirely the same, *cherie*. Need I tell you that? We all have our strengths and our weaknesses. I think you fear that Scott would become bored with you, because of what you feel he would consider your weakness."

Sharon nodded, and asked, "How could it be otherwise? His first wife was an alcoholic, Sylvie. She caused him many problems. How could he stand to have a second wife who's paranoid about the very thing he loves most to do, and evidently does so well?"

"Love has certain softening effects," Sylvie answered. "I think real love, which is what we are talking about, involves accepting another person's failings without undue censure. I am not saying that Scott would look at you and say, 'Oh never mind that you don't like flying and that you will be cringing whenever you know I am up in the sky... it doesn't matter.' Of course it will matter. But if he loves you enough, he will learn the way to deal with that. So will you, with his weaknesses."

"I don't think he has any weaknesses," Sharon said morosely.

"We all have weaknesses," Sylvie stated patiently. "The physical ones are more obvious, that is all. The others are kept deeply hidden. We all go around wearing false faces much of the time, you know that. Look at your own twin sister, how she hides her insecurities by giving big parties and pretending to be such an extrovert. Look at Tony, who is not nearly as sure of himself as he acts. Yes, we all have our weaknesses, most of which we go to great lengths to conceal. That is why we so desperately need a... kindred spirit, I think you say, to share life with," Sylvie said. She shrugged. "My English is deserting me. But you will know my meaning."

"Your English is scarcely deserting you," Sharon told her, smiling ever so slightly. "And your meaning is very clear. The problem is... I'm not strong enough to take the risk. I'm not strong enough to take a chance with Scott, even if he were willing to take a chance with me. He'd only find out, too late, that I couldn't handle what he does—to say nothing of never having a home to call my own."

"What is a home to call your own?"

"Please, Sylvie..."

"All right, all right. I know what you mean, of course. So the question of what a home is we will save for another occasion." Sylvie paused, then asked, "You are absolutely determined to go back to Providence?"

"Yes."

"Then how would you like me to come with you?"

"Are you serious?" Sharon managed, shocked.

"Yes, very much so." Sylvie nodded. "I have never been in the New England section of your country, and I would like to visit it. Also, just now I am becoming bored here. With all the work you have been doing for Tony, you and I have not been going out to paint together."

"Yes, I know. I've missed that, too. But what about that latest man in your life?"

"He became dreary very quickly," Sylvie conceded. "At my age, that becomes a problem. With most men, it is all the same. The same words, the same promises, the same desires. It is like a broken record. I get tired of hearing the scratches."

"Honestly, Sylvie!"

"Well, it is true. I would like this change."

"Then why don't I try to get a compartment on the train for both of us?"

Suddenly, Sharon had a vision of her trip to Miami on the *Silver Comet*. She recalled standing in the doorway of bedroom four and seeing Scott sitting by the window. He turned toward her, and she felt the impact of his presence. Then he looked up at her with those astonishingly blue eyes...

It hurt. It hurt deep down inside. It hurt very much.

Sylvie had said something, but Sharon hadn't really heard her. Trying to shake off her vision, she said, "Pardon?"

"I was saying that if it is all right with you, I would prefer to drive. It is past the season of snow. We would not need to be in any particular hurry, would we?"

"No, not really. And I can always phone Gary and tell him I'm going to be a few more days getting back. The work will be waiting for me, I'm sure."

Sylvie nodded and said, "My car is not the most opulent vehicle in the world, but it runs better than it looks. Do you drive, Sharon?"

"Yes."

"Then we could take turns with the wheel?"

"Yes, of course we could."

The more Sharon thought about it, the more the idea of driving back north with Sylvie appealed to her. Sylvie was the one person she felt she could tolerate—the one person whose companionship she might even enjoy—on a trip that would not be easy for her. Diane would never keep off the subject of Scott, or what she was leaving behind in Miami. Sylvie wouldn't do that. Sylvie, in her time, had cast a few dies of her own. She knew how to respect a person's space, how to accept.

"You are agreeable, then?" Sylvie asked now.

"More than agreeable. It would be great, really great."

"So, when do you want to leave?"

"If I go back to work tonight and work most of tomorrow, I should have the design finished for Tony by midafternoon," Sharon calculated. Meeting Sylvie's gaze, she asked, "How about early the next morning?"

CHAPTER SIXTEEN

DIANE WAS FURIOUS. "For one thing," she exploded, "it would be absolutely unsafe to drive all the way to Providence, Rhode Island, in that excuse of a vehicle Sylvie calls a car! For another thing, aren't you even pausing to consider the fact that you're really leaving Tony and me in the lurch? And what about Scott?"

At Scott's name, Sharon held up a commanding hand. "Stop it, Diane!" she shouted, determined to make herself heard. "Please...just stop," she repeated, forcing herself to sound considerably more calm than she felt.

Tears started to fill Diane's green eyes as she stared at her twin. "Oh, damn it all!" she blurted miserably.

It was nearly midnight. Diane had come home from a dinner date with Rick to find the lights blazing, and Sharon working at her easel. That, in itself, had been enough to set her off.

"You're behaving as if Tony and I are a couple of slave drivers," she'd accused.

To mollify her, Sharon agreed to take a break over a cup of herb tea. It was still quite warm in the kitchen, which faced west and felt the lingering effects of the tropical sun long after the sun had set. So they took their teacups into the dining room and faced each other over the clutter spread across the table.

There, the tension had begun to mount. It culminated when Sharon had told her twin that Sylvie wanted to make the trip north with her.

Now Sharon drew a deep breath and said, "Look... I can appreciate how this must seem to you."

"How it must *seem* to me?" Diane challenged, wiping away the trace of tears. "It seems to me that you're going off in a huff because Scott hurt your feelings. And if that isn't behaving like a ninny I don't know what is!"

The childhood epithet brought a wry smile to Sharon's lips. She said, more gently, "It isn't like that at all, Di. Honestly it isn't. But frankly I'm too tired to get into a deep discussion over this tonight. What you were saying, though, about Sylvie's car... I admit it doesn't look like much, but it's perfectly safe. Also, we're planning to take our time. We're not out to set any speed records. When we get tired, we'll stop over someplace. There are endless motels along Interstate 95, as I hear it."

"So?"

"So I'm trying to tell you that we're not going to push it. Also..."

"Yes?"

"I do not feel that I am leaving you and Tony in the lurch. I'll have the second design finished by noon tomorrow, and I think it's working out very well. The waltz theme is there, but so is that Miami Deco atmosphere that we're featuring as your trademark. I think you'll like it."

"So?" Diane repeated annoyingly.

"Must you speak in monosyllables?" Sharon demanded. Her fatigue was catching up with her and, though she tried to push back her irritation, it still showed.

Realizing this, Diane conceded, "All right, I took a peek at your design just now, and . . . well, okay, it's terrific, Shar. As smashing as the first one."

"Thank you."

"But that doesn't change the situation."

Sharon sighed. "I think Tony is the one person who's believed all along that I was serious about going back north. He understood that I was just taking a two-week extension to my vacation. I'll admit he's told me he was hoping I'd decide to give Gary my resignation and come in with you two full-time. He seems to think we might even start a small gallery—"

"Exactly!" Diane pounced. "Believe me, Sharon, Tony is a very clever businessman. He knows Miami, and he knows what he's talking about. He sees that special quality in what you do, and he knows it would go over big here. If you'd just listen to him . . ."

If only she could listen to Tony, Sharon thought wearily. If only her relationship with Scott—or lack thereof—did not have to be considered. It *was* because of Scott that she was leaving. Actually *for* Scott, because she'd come to realize only too well that she was not the right person for him.

Again trying to mollify Diane, she said, "Tony has mentioned the possibility of my doing your designs anyway, even if I'm in Providence. There's no reason why we couldn't handle that."

"If you'd fly, there'd be no reason," Diane stated. "If you'd get on a plane, like millions of people do every day, you could come down here for conferences, when we needed to talk out ideas."

"There is a little thing called the telephone, Di."

"That's no substitute for personal confrontation."

"In other words, everything must be eye to eye?"

"Oh, come on, Shar. You know what I'm saying."

"You're saying you want me to stay here, that's what you're saying," Sharon told her twin. "I know you have the best intentions in the world, but just now it wouldn't be right. Please accept that, will you?"

"No, I won't."

"Must you be so stubborn, Diane?"

Stubborn. The word echoed in Sharon's mind. Scott had accused her of being stubborn.

She finished her tea, then said, "I don't like to leave it like this between us, but I've got to get some sleep. I'm bushed, and I want to get back to work early in the morning. I told Tony I'll have the design over to the club hopefully around lunchtime."

"Fine," Diane said stiffly. "Go ahead upstairs. I'll turn out the lights and lock up."

Sharon felt as if her sister's disapproval was trailing in her wake as she ascended the spiral stairway. She was on the verge of tears herself when, a short while later, she slid under the bed sheets. But she was so tired even her misery didn't keep her awake. She fell asleep within minutes after her head touched the pillow, and when she awakened, golden sunlight was streaming through the windows.

She had her usual *café con leche* and a Cuban sweet roll on the patio, then moved her easel into the sunlight and got to work on the design again. Evidently, Diane was still sleeping. At least, she hadn't made an appearance yet.

Later in the morning, Sharon heard her sister's voice coming from the kitchen, but walked into the living room just in time to see her heading out the front door. She was tempted to call after her, but she didn't. Diane, obviously, was still annoyed about last night, or she would have stopped by the patio on her way out.

Maria was making gazpacho, and Sharon had a bowl of the chilled vegetable soup for lunch. Then she showered, slipped on a cool cotton dress and called for a taxi to take her to Tony's office.

There had been moments when Sharon considered renting a car while in Miami, but there'd never been a need . . . until the past couple of days. Sylvie had been around. And so had Scott.

Thinking about Scott, seeing a vision of his handsome face, remembering his gentle touch, sent poignant waves of sadness sweeping through Sharon.

She was still brooding when she reached Tony's nightclub, and she had to paste on a smile as she was admitted through a service door and ushered to his office.

Tony, in short sleeves, was sitting behind a desk piled high with papers, poised to dial the phone. But he quickly replaced the receiver when he saw Sharon, and got to his feet.

"Hey there, beautiful," he greeted her, coming around the end of his desk to bestow a tender kiss on her cheek. "How's it going?"

Sharon couldn't repress a grimace. Because she knew Tony so well, she dispensed with false cheeriness to say honestly, "Not too well, personally. But I think you'll like the design."

"So let's take a look at it," Tony said, beaming.

They propped up the painting on a straight-backed chair against one wall. Then Tony stepped back and surveyed it from the open doorway. When he didn't say anything, Sharon's spirits began to sag. Diane had said she thought it was smashing. But was there a chance they'd both been wrong? Was there a chance Tony didn't like it?

She held her breath until she heard him exhale, sharply, "Whew!" Then he turned toward her, his dark eyes glowing. "I can't believe it," he told her, "but you've surpassed yourself, Sis. I mean, this painting is even better than the first one."

It was Sharon's turn to exhale sharply... with relief.

Tony glanced at his watch and said, "I have a meeting in an hour. Have you got time for a coffee break or some iced tea? There's a little hole in the wall around the corner."

"I'd like that," Sharon said. Still, she was dreading sitting down at a table and having iced coffee or anything else with Tony, right now, because there would be no way around telling him that she'd be leaving Miami first thing in the morning.

Once they were seated, though, Tony surprised her by commenting, almost casually, "So, you're skipping out."

"You know?"

Tony nodded. "Diane phoned me about an hour before you got here," he said. "She knew you were coming, and I guess she wanted to tell me her side of the story first. What's with this, Sharon? Is it true that you got irked over something Scott Williams did and decided to pack your bags and take off?"

"It's not that simple," Sharon managed.

"I didn't expect it would be. Still, the bottom line is you *are* going, right?"

"Yes."

Tony frowned. "I wish you wouldn't, Sis," he said honestly. "For one thing, Di needs you. For another thing, I need you." He concentrated on stirring his coffee, then he looked up and laughed. "That sounds crazy, doesn't it?" he admitted. "But you're a stabilizing influence, you really are."

"Me?" Sharon asked, astonished.

"Yes, you. Deep under that fair skin of yours, you and Di are very much alike. The thing is, I think you've learned to handle what life deals out better than Di has. She either explodes or glosses things over. You think things through. You're not fooled by surface appearances, the way Di sometimes is. I worry about her, in that respect." He paused. "You like this guy Rick, don't you?"

"He's a very fine person, Tony," Sharon said sincerely, more than a little amazed by the turn this conversation was taking.

"Good." Tony nodded. "That's the way he came across to me, but I haven't seen that much of him. I think Di is pretty taken with him, and it seems to work both ways. I'm not saying that it's going to amount to anything, but—" Tony shrugged "—you never know.

"Now, as for you and Scott..." he continued. "I guess I pictured the two of you as a team the minute I saw you together. But your sister says you're walking out on him."

Sharon felt her nerves beginning to unravel. "Look, Tony, I just can't go through another long explanation about why I'm doing what I'm doing where Scott is concerned. I've told Diane, but she just won't hear me, that's all. She wants to believe what she wants to believe."

"Yes, Di does tend to be that way sometimes," Tony conceded. "But once she cools down, I'll guarantee you she'll see things your way. I think Di loves you more than you probably know."

"I love her very much, too," Sharon said unsteadily.

Tony smiled. "Well, in my opinion, the two of you are certainly the greatest pair of twins the world has ever produced. Now, as to the work you've done for Di-Tone..."

"I'm not sure I'm up to talking about that, either," Sharon confessed.

"I don't expect you to be. I just want you to know the way it is, that's all. We can go back to my office and I'll give you a check for the second design now, if you like. Or, I can mail it to Providence."

"It's fine by me if you mail it to Providence."

"Consider it done." Tony paused, then he said carefully, "Once you're in Providence, once you're settled down again and sort of have your act back together, I hope you'll do some serious thinking about working with Di-Tone, Shar. We need your talent. I don't want to pressure you, but it wouldn't be fair to any of us to skip saying that. We want you on our team. But I don't intend to rush you into making a decision. I think too much of you for that."

Again, Tony glanced at his watch. "I have to head back," he said reluctantly.

"And I have to get back to Diane's house and start putting my things together," Sharon told him. "Tony?"

"Yes?"

"Thanks for being so understanding. And thanks for not lecturing me."

Tony grinned. "Me lecture you? Didn't you ever hear that old saw that people in glass houses shouldn't throw stones? I'm the last guy in the world who should lecture anybody!"

"You're a pretty wonderful guy," Sharon said shakily.

"Hold to that thought, will you?" Tony quipped. Then he sobered. "You know, Sis, a trip back north doesn't have to be the end of the line."

"What do you mean?"

"You can always reverse directions," he pointed out. "You can always come back to Miami Beach, once you've had some peace and quiet and a chance to think things through. Just remember, if you ever want to do that, you've got Diane, Tonette, Di-Tone and me waiting for you."

THAT EVENING, the twins ate their dinner in a constrained silence. Afterward, Sharon went upstairs to finish her packing. Sylvie was planning to come by very early in the morning so they could get under way.

As she packed, Sharon kept listening for the sound of the telephone. As far as she knew, Scott had not called all day. If he had called, he hadn't left a message. Maria would have recognized his voice and left word. Certainly, Diane would have, or even Tonette.

The night wore on. When finally the phone did ring, the call was for Diane. Later, there were two more calls for Diane, who evidently was handling some real estate matter from the privacy of her bedroom, but otherwise keeping herself incommunicado.

It was midnight before Sharon finally went to bed . . . without a word from Scott.

In the morning, Diane suddenly and swiftly relented. At the last minute, she tried to be as helpful as possible. Sharon even invented a few things Diane could do for her, because she'd never felt more in tune with her twin than she did right now.

By the time Sylvie arrived, both Sharon and Diane were biting their lips as if doing so would guarantee calluses and no tears. Nevertheless, tears prevailed. And tears were still streaming down Sharon's cheeks as she and Sylvie drove away from the house on Pine Tree Drive, with Sylvie at the wheel.

She'd spent almost seven weeks of her life there, Sharon thought emotionally. Seven weeks that had been the most significant weeks of her life. Only then did Sharon begin to think that maybe her twin was right. Maybe she really *was* wrong to be leaving. Maybe she and Scott...

Sharon quickly closed her mind to that thought and reached for her handkerchief. The other afternoon, Scott had told her he would call. He never did.

That night, Sylvie and Sharon stopped just over the Georgia border in Brunswick. It had been a long trek up the coast of Florida, and Sylvie had done more than her share of the driving. Whenever Sharon offered to spell her, she'd said more often that not, "In a few more miles." Then the few more miles had stretched to a fair number, and Sharon hadn't protested. She was totally done in, physically and emotionally, and Sylvie knew it.

She did better the next day, as they wended their way through Georgia and into the Carolinas. They'd lingered at their motel that morning to eat a hearty breakfast before hitting the road, so their start had been later than anticipated. By the time they were into North Carolina, both women were willing to call it quits for the day.

Sharon, watching the passing scenery, remembered traveling through the Carolinas years ago with her parents and Diane, when they always seemed to be moving from one place to the next. The countryside was not unfamiliar to her, but it was all new to Sylvie, who was fascinated with the cotton fields, then the tobacco fields, and the South's muddy rivers and tall pines.

The next day they decided to bypass the Washington metropolitan area and take the slower route up Maryland's eastern shore, heading north to Delaware. They stopped in a seafood restaurant for an early supper, and feasted on Maryland oysters and soft-shell crab. And Sharon found herself thinking how wonderful and magical it would be to share this experience with Scott.

She'd been trying to keep him at the very back of her mind, but he was refusing to stay there.

They made it into Providence late the following afternoon, and were almost at the door of the old house in which Sharon had her apartment before she fully realized what a letdown this homecoming was going to be. The street looked dingier than she remembered it, the house shabbier. Maybe it was the contrast to the pastel-and-white brilliance of Miami Beach. Whatever it was, she felt a sharp sense of sadness...and was more thankful than ever that she had Sylvie here with her.

She led the way up the steps to the front porch, then unlocked the door leading to her second floor apartment. Inside, a steep stairwell greeted them immediately, a stairwell badly in need of paint and a new light bulb, Sharon discovered, as she flipped the switch and got no response.

She'd left her apartment in reasonably good order. Still, it looked plain to her as she turned the key in the door and they stepped into her living room, furnished—as furnished places often are—with a variety of mismated castoffs. Her plants—the cheeriest aspect of her decor—had either faded or died for lack of watering, even though her landlady had agreed to check them once in a while.

She wondered how all of this was striking Sylvie, whose studio, though much smaller, was so unique. But

Sylvie, looking around, was her usual imperturbable self. The only thing she said was, "Things will look brighter once we hang those paintings you did in Miami."

Sylvie shivered as she spoke, and Sharon realized that it was chilly in the apartment. Along their journey, they'd noticed the signs of spring becoming less and less frequent. By the time they'd reached Virginia, the trees were just beginning to bud. Here in Rhode Island, the willows were sprouting their mellow green leaves, and the crocuses were popping up wherever there was earth to sustain them. Even a few jonquils were beginning to emerge, and an occasional forsythia, here and there. Still, the land looked bare.

But then spring was never the best of seasons in New England, Sharon remembered. It seemed to hover on the cool doorstep of summer until, very quickly, summer arrived. That was still many weeks away.

Gazing out at the early evening street scene—a grayish vista of houses marching along in drab rows—Sylvie said, "It is not about to snow, is it?"

Sharon chuckled. "No, but I'll turn up the heat just in case."

Suddenly, it occurred to her that Gary Freeman had given her a bottle of brandy at Christmastime. If she recalled correctly, it was nearly full. She went into her kitchen and pried the bottle from the upper shelf of the cupboard. Then she filled two miniature snifters, also gifts from Gary, and returned to the living room where Sylvie was still standing at the window, gazing outside.

"Here," Sharon said, handing a glass to her friend. Then, bravely, she proposed a toast. "Here's to the beginning of your newest . . . adventure," she managed, faltering on the last word, and hoping she wouldn't cry.

Sylvie clicked her glass to Sharon's decisively, and said in her throaty, accented voice, "I will drink to that." Then she added tenderly, "Sharon, my dear, believe me . . . it will get better."

The sympathy nearly sent Sharon over the edge.

Seeing this, Sylvie turned back to the window. "I suppose we should unpack the car tonight," she commented. "For my part, I would leave the task until morning, assuming it is safe to do so."

"It's safe enough," Sharon decided. Like Sylvie, the last thing she felt like doing was unpacking the car. It would be enough to heat up a can of beef stew for their supper, then shower and go to bed.

Tomorrow literally *had* to be another day!

THINGS DID GET BETTER once Sharon went back to work. Gary Freeman was so relieved to see her that he bypassed chastising her for having taken extra time off. Instead, he presented Sharon with a staggering work load, much of which he had been saving especially for her.

Still, Sharon was glad to be so busy. It bothered her to leave Sylvie to her own devices so much, but Sylvie was completely intrigued with everything around her, and very quickly established a schedule of her own. The weather coöperated nicely, for the most part, so she spent her days exploring Providence, searching for scenes to paint.

Soon, Sylvie met all sorts of people who offered all sorts of suggestions. One night she told Sharon, "In another week or two, when I think my hands will not freeze, I will set up my easel and start painting again. Do you think you could possibly take some time now and then and join me? I hate to see you give it up, *cherie*."

Sharon, still struggling to catch up with her work at the printing firm, didn't see how she could find the time. But she said, "I'll try."

The work at Gary's only increased, though. After Sharon finished the backlog of jobs Gary had dumped on her, he promptly presented her with a new pile. To handle these, Sharon went in on Saturday, for which her boss was more than willing to pay overtime. But this soon became the custom, and the extra money, though welcome, really didn't compensate for the frazzled feeling Sharon was beginning to wear home each night.

Then Tony called one evening to ask if she was prepared to do the tango cover for the next disk. At that point, Sharon knew something had to give.

She sat down with Gary in his office the next morning, wondering if she looked as tired as she felt. She hoped she did...because when she'd asked for this meeting with him it had been with a definite objective in mind.

Gary's desk was a faded old rolltop, littered with paper and all sorts of junk. Every time he tried to find something it was like going on a treasure hunt. Sharon, sitting at the side of the desk, watched him probe for some bit of miscellany as she said, "Gary, I have a friend who is an artist. A very good artist, I might add."

"Oh?" Gary said vaguely, absorbed in his search.

"And I want you to hire her as a part-time assistant to me."

"Hmm?"

"Gary, I'm going to slam that rolltop down on your fingers if you don't stop fumbling around and listen to me!" Sharon threatened.

She tried to keep a certain employer-employee tone between them in the office, hoping this would discourage him from asking her out. At this rather personal outburst, though, Gary looked up.

Swiveling around in his chair to face her, he asked equably, "What's on your mind, Sharon?"

"My friend who is staying with me, Sylvie Grenda, is an accomplished artist. She also has a terrific eye for design," Sharon stated firmly. "She's not a person you can lock into a job, by which I mean there's no guarantee how long she'll want to stay around Providence. But while she's here, I'd like you to hire her for a few hours each day to help me out. I'm consistently falling behind, Gary. There's simply too much to do."

"That's because you're so good," Gary replied easily. "Which is why I saved so much stuff for you. The customers like your work, Sharon. They say you have a special touch."

"Well Sylvie Grenda has an even more special touch. If anything, she'll improve on whatever style I have."

Gary frowned dubiously. "Well, it might be okay...but then again it might not be," he concluded indecisively. "I'd have to meet this Sylvie person."

"That can easily be arranged. Come over and have dinner with us tonight."

Gary brightened. He often mentioned that it was seldom he ate "home cooking" these days, and verified as much by saying, "That *would* be a real treat!"

Sharon, knowing that it would be at least five before she could get out of the office, wondered how much she could achieve in the way of home cooking by the time Gary arrived for a reasonably early dinner. Nevertheless, it was worth a good attempt.

Before she went back to work, she called Sylvie, almost certain she'd be home. It was a raw, drizzly day, not the kind of weather for strolling around Providence, and Sylvie answered on the third ring.

"Can you cook anything except fancy hors d'oeuvres?" Sharon demanded in a urgent whisper.

"But of course," Sylvie responded instantly, sounding faintly insulted.

"Then will you go out and buy something and start dinner for three? I'll help you finish as soon as I can get out of here," Sharon said quickly. "I've asked Gary to dinner. I told him I want him to hire you to work here for a while."

"With your company?"

"Yes, with my company. Gary's company, that is."

Always hesitant at the thought of being trapped in a situation, Sylvie hedged, "Sharon, I don't know..."

"Wait till tonight, will you?" Sharon pleaded. "You and Gary and I can talk the whole thing over then."

BY THE TIME Sharon got home late that afternoon, Sylvie had done remarkable things with the drab little apartment. They'd hung Sharon's paintings on the walls not long after they'd arrived in town. Now, Sylvie had picked up the color splashes by strategically placing vases of fresh-cut flowers around the room. Next, she'd moved Sharon's modest wooden table out from the wall, covered it with a red cloth, and added ivory candles in brass holders.

"Where did you get this stuff?" Sharon said, gasping, at the same time sniffing the marvelous aromas that were emanating from her tiny kitchen.

"I went to a—what do you call it?—a flea market," Sylvie informed her. "The cloth was fine, but the candle holders needed a bit of polish. Anyway, for three dollars I decided not to argue."

"You are without a doubt the most miraculous person I have ever known," Sharon told her.

"But of course, *cherie*! Now, when is this ogre you work for going to descend on us?"

"Gary's anything but an ogre, and he should be here in about an hour," Sharon said. "What can I do?"

"Go take a shower, put on a pretty dress, and make yourself presentable," Sylvie advised.

"I'm not trying to make points with Gary, Sylvie. I want *you* to make points with him, so he'll give you a job."

This said, Sharon took a second look at her houseguest. Sylvie was wearing a white skirt, a red satin blouse and black sandals with improbably high heels. Her blond hair was swept into a chignon, and gold earrings studded with rubies that could have been real or fake—one never knew with Sylvie—dangled from her lobes. To top it all off, she smelled fantastic.

"What's that perfume?" Sharon demanded abruptly.

Sylvie smiled disarmingly. "My secret," she said. "But maybe I'll tell you someday."

"Well whatever it is, Gary's going to be overwhelmed."

Gary was exactly that, when Sharon introduced him to Sylvie a short while later. He seemed to back off ten feet, then barely managed an awestruck, "Hello."

All through dinner, in fact, Gary was as taciturn as the most stoic of New Englanders. But he did full justice to the fantastic meal Sylvie had concocted.

When Sharon brought up the subject of Sylvie working part-time at the printing firm, Gary looked as if he'd been struck with lightning. All he could manage to say was, "Yes, I think that would work out fine."

Sharon held her breath for fear that Sylvie would suddenly announce that she didn't want to work for him. But remarkably, Sylvie didn't say anything at all.

When the door closed behind Gary, though, she turned to Sharon, her eyes sparkling mischievously. "Who was that artist who painted the marvelous all-American pictures for the magazine covers that were so famous?"

"Norman Rockwell."

"Ah, yes, Norman Rockwell. Gary, he would have made a fabulous model for Norman Rockwell, don't you think? I mean, he is *exactly* as I imagined a Yankee man should be!" she proclaimed.

CHAPTER SEVENTEEN

"HELLO, SHARON?"

"Yes?" she answered hesitantly, not immediately recognizing the masculine voice at the other end of what was obviously a long-distance connection.

"Sharon, are you there?"

"Rick?"

"Yes. How are you?"

Rick didn't have an accent, as Sylvie did, yet there was something different and delightful in the way he spoke. By his own admission, English was his second language. But even though he was totally fluent—having gone to American schools—his English retained a certain Latin flavor.

"Oh, Rick!" Sharon gasped, a wave of emotion washing over her. She gripped the receiver tightly, her throat suddenly constricted.

"Hey, now! Is there something wrong?" Rick asked swiftly.

"No, no. It's just wonderful to hear your voice, that's all."

"Had I known that would be your reaction, I would have called sooner," he teased. "Incidentally, I hope I am not calling too late. I didn't wake you up, did I?"

It was barely ten o'clock, and Sharon quickly assured him, "No, of course not."

"I had an early dinner with your sister," Rick reported, "and I just got back to the hospital. So, I have a few minutes of peace before people discover I am here. This is a very busy place lately."

"I can imagine."

"Sharon, do you and Scott communicate at all?" Rick inquired bluntly.

Sharon's throat constricted all the more. She said huskily, "Scott and I haven't been in touch since a couple of days before I left Miami Beach." It was not quite a month, but it already seemed like years to Sharon. The problem was, with every passing day she missed Scott more, instead of less.

"I see," Rick mused. "I have been wondering. Scott is not very vocal these days. Which brings me to something I must ask you."

"Yes?"

"Well, as you know, I consider Scott one of my closest friends. He's also still my patient, in a sense. But I must ask you, if you do speak to him, not to say anything about this call."

It was not like Rick Fabrega to be so mysterious, and Sharon was frowning as he continued, "I must ask that this be a completely off-the-record conversation. Scott would be very annoyed with me, to say the least, if he knew I was calling you about him."

Instantly Sharon was clutched by worry. "Has something happened to Scott?" she managed, wondering how she could possibly handle it if Rick answered affirmatively.

"No," Rick reassured her quickly. "Nothing has actually happened to him. That is…physically, he is fine. But I am concerned about his . . . well, his mental disposition, let's call it."

"Why, Rick?"

"Well, it's difficult to be specific," Rick admitted. "I'd say Scott has been in a deep depression, though. To be honest, I've done my damnedest to shake him out of it. So has Diane. We've tried to include him with us when we've gone out. A couple of times, we've gotten him to tag along with us to the movies, but he usually cuts out early after that, and . . . well, he's just not with us, Sharon."

"Oh."

"I guess part of my own problem with this is that I can see Scott getting healthier all the time," Rick went on. "In fact, I would say that he has an excellent chance of regaining his flying status once this interim period is over. If, that is, he gets back on track mentally and emotionally. Right now, I'm afraid that this depression he has fallen into is impeding his recovery. I don't want him to reach the point where he requires psychiatric counseling, because he doesn't need that on his service record."

"Psychiatric counseling?" Sharon repeated, shocked.

There was a pause on the line. Then Rick said slowly, "You know, Sharon, we humans are a strange mass of contradictions. But there's no denying that the body and the mind work pretty closely together. I'd say that Scott's mind and his body are in conflict. As I've said, he gets physically more healthy every day. But emotionally, he's regressing."

Sharon was trying to digest everything Rick was saying while her thoughts and emotions whirled around visions of Scott. Finally she said, "I can't imagine that the training program being canceled could have this much effect on him, Rick. The last time we talked—"

"When was that, did you say?"

"A couple of days before I left. Even so, Scott sounded like he'd come to terms with the Air Force's decision."

"I don't think Scott's present problem has anything to do with his career, Sharon."

"What, then?"

"I think Scott misses you more than you can possibly imagine," Rick told her. "But he's too stupidly proud to ask you to come back to him. In his book, you totally rejected him when you left Miami without so much as a goodbye."

"He told me he'd call me, Rick. He never did." All Sharon's own feelings of rejection surfaced, and the words tumbled out.

"Didn't Diane tell you that he called about fifteen minutes after you left her house?" Rick demanded. "He had no idea you were going so soon."

"No, Diane didn't tell me," Sharon said slowly. "But then, Diane and I haven't been in touch since I left Miami Beach. She was pretty angry with me. She relented, somewhat, at the last minute. But I can imagine that after I actually left, her anger returned."

"Perhaps," Rick said enigmatically. He paused, then added, "Frankly, Sharon, Diane felt she needed you here and you were letting her down. But things are working out all right with her."

Thanks to you, probably, Sharon thought silently.

"With Scott, though..."

"Yes?"

"Damn it!" Rick said impatiently, "Scott should be doing his own talking. The reason I'm interceding is because the doctors at Homestead will be giving him a preliminary physical in a couple of weeks, and the results may have considerable bearing on his future as a

pilot. He's scheduled to put in another three and a half
months at Homestead, roughly speaking, before his case
comes up for review. Believe me, they'll pull out all the
stops. He'll be thoroughly evaluated psychiatrically, as
well as physically tested to the max. Meantime, I would
like to see him come through this first session with flying
colors. And when I look at him these days, I just can't
envision that happening.''

"I'm sorry, Rick. I don't know what to say.''

"Don't say anything, Sharon. Just get on a plane and
fly down here.''

"What did you say?''

"Sharon, I know I'm asking a lot,'' Rick went on
slowly. "In fact, I'm stepping way out of bounds. But
someone's got to do something for Scott. Diane and I
talked it over, and if you could fly down here—even if
it's only for a day or two—and just talk things out with
Scott. For myself, I think you both deserve a little honest dialogue with each other.''

Sharon would have sworn that her pulse stopped entirely. Then, just as quickly, it began to pound hard.
Didn't Rick know how she felt about flying? Hadn't
Diane told him? Was this some kind of test? Were they
trying to see whether or not she could brush aside her
fear of flying? Whether or not, if sufficiently motivated, she could hop on a plane like most people would,
and in three hours be walking into Scott's arms?

The thought of walking into Scott's arms made Sharon giddy. It was easy to imagine that she could actually
smell his special scent and feel the tenderness of his
touch.

She shivered, speechless.

After a moment, Rick queried, "Sharon? Are you still
there?''

"Yes, I'm here."

"Look, Diane mentioned you don't care for flying," Rick said, and Sharon wondered if he was aware of what a gross understatement that was! "But this is a very special circumstance. If you'd ask your physician, I'm sure he'd give you some tranquilizers that would make the flight a lot easier for you. I honestly feel that if Scott could just see you, and talk to you, it would make an awfully big difference in the way he's approaching life."

Rick laughed wryly. "I'm beginning to sound like a professional matchmaker," he confessed, "and that's not my intention at all. I'm not trying to bring the two of you together in that way, believe me. That's your business. All I ask is that you face up to each other. From then on, it's entirely your ball game. Yours, and Scott's."

Sharon closed her eyes tightly. If only courage could be purchased in bottles, she thought. If only fear, and horror, and terrible memories could be whisked away, like the wind blowing away autumn leaves. If only it was that easy.

Even if she could somehow force herself to get aboard an airliner and fly to Miami—with or without tranquilizers—their problems, hers and Scott's, would not be solved. True, she would have taken a supremely significant step as far as her own life was concerned. But whether or not she arrived in Miami in any shape to talk was another thing. In fact, the more Sharon thought about it, the more she became certain that even with pills to help her, she'd still freak out the second the plane started roaring down the runway.

It was ironic, but only that afternoon she had read a want ad in the *Boston Globe* for a graphic design post with a big publishing house in Boston. She'd torn out the ad, and planned to call the personnel department in question first thing in the morning to make an appointment for an interview.

Now, she snatched at this as a ready excuse. "I don't think that's possible, Rick," she temporized. "I have something... well, I have something in the works. I couldn't possibly get away for quite a while. Maybe later..."

Disappointment underscored Rick's voice as he said reluctantly. "Okay, then. If it is possible for you to come, it would be wonderful. Meanwhile..." He sighed. Then, with an obvious attempt to conclude their conversation on a lighter note, he asked, "How is Sylvie doing? Diane thought by now she would have tired of Providence and probably started back to Florida."

Sharon felt an instant sense of relief at this reprieve, this chance to get off the subject of Scott and flying. "Sylvie's working with me for Gary Freeman, as my assistant," she reported. "In fact, I wouldn't be at all surprised if one of these days Sylvie takes over my job entirely."

"How would you feel about that?"

"Well, I *have* been thinking of moving on, Rick."

"I see."

"The thing is, Sylvie and Gary have hit if off amazingly well. They really seem like they might become seriously interested in each other, and it would be pretty terrific, if I'm right. I'm sure Diane will tell you they're the two most opposite people in the world, which is true. Yet somehow they mesh. For all their differences, they seem to have so much in common. You should see them together. It's a riot, sometimes. Gary is the ultimate New Englander—Sylvie thinks he should have been a Norman Rockwell model—and, as you know, Sylvie is so absolutely exotic. But they complement each other.''

"That is the way it should be," Rick commented gravely.

Was he thinking of himself and Diane, or of her and Scott? Sharon was not about to ask and, after a few more words, they rang off. Then all the things she'd been trying so hard not to think about swirled in on her.

Could she really be the cause of Scott's depression? Was this moodiness of his really serious enough to affect his upcoming physical?

As she asked herself these questions, one answer stood out. Jeopardizing Scott's future was the very last thing she wanted to do.

WORK HAD ALWAYS been a panacea for Sharon. The day after Rick's phone call, she plunged into her assignments so fervently that by late morning Sylvie was raising her eyebrows and protesting, "*Cherie*, what are you trying to do? Show me up, or wear yourself out completely?"

"Neither," Sharon retorted.

She slowed down for the balance of the day and let Sylvie handle a number of new chores. Using work as a cure, she realized, was not accomplishing what it usually did. She could scarcely get her mind off Scott, and absently doodled little scenes of Miami while she thought about him.

It was Friday, and Friday was payday. Gary Freeman seemed especially exuberant as he passed out checks to his employees late that afternoon, and Sharon discovered, to her surprise, that he'd given her a bonus.

"I don't know how I would have gotten along without you this past year," he told her, taking her aside.

"Thanks, Gary," she managed. "I've learned a lot."

Gary favored her with a skeptical glance and said, "I'd say you're the one who's done the teaching around here." He paused, then added, "Anyway, I know you're not going to stay with this job forever, Sharon. Sylvie and I have had a couple of talks about that, and I want you to know that as long as you want to stay here, you're number one. Make no mistake about that! But if you ever decide to push on to greener pastures, there won't be any hard feelings, okay?"

"Okay," Sharon agreed.

She watched Gary as he moved on to talk with Sylvie, and the smile that curved his lips spoke volumes. Sylvie, for her part, seemed totally smitten as she smiled back at her boss. Maybe they were an odd couple, but they were a couple, nonetheless.

As she stashed away the jobs she'd been working on, Sharon began to feel something of a third wheel in Gary's printing business. She didn't doubt his sincerity in saying that her job was hers as long as she wanted it. He was giving her an option, that was all, whereas previously he'd balked at even the slightest suggestion that she might not be staying in Providence forever.

If you ever decide to push on to greener pastures . . .

The phrase echoed in Sharon's mind, and she suddenly remembered that she'd completely forgotten to phone the Boston publishing firm about setting up an interview for their graphic designer position.

She glanced at the clock. It was after five. Too late.

My own damn fault! Sharon scolded herself.

A few minutes later, she and Sylvie left the office and drove home together. They were almost at the door of Sharon's apartment before Sylvie said mysteriously, "I have something to tell you, *cherie*."

"What's that?" Sharon asked, intrigued.

"Gary and I are going away for the weekend. Just to the coast, you know, where we will find some quaint inn to stay at. We will go in Gary's car, so I will not leave you without transportation. You do not mind, do you?" she asked anxiously.

"Mind?" Sharon asked. "Frankly, Sylvie, I think it's high time."

It *was* time for them to get away and be alone, Sharon thought, time to explore their relationship. Still, their "togetherness" only made Sharon feel all the more alone, once the two of them had gone off Saturday morning.

By noon, the apartment was closing in on her. She got out her paints and her easel, packed them in Sylvie's car and started out with no precise idea of where she might go.

She stayed on back roads, winding her way across the Rhode Island hills, through picturesque little towns and farms and forests. Everywhere, plants of all types were finally coming into full bloom, now that they were almost through the allegedly merry month of May.

Sharon didn't feel very merry about anything. She was lonely, she was dispirited, she was annoyed with herself. She found it impossible to choose a decent subject to paint, though subjects were all around her. Still, the idea of lingering in one spot for a couple of hours was the last thing that appealed to her now, even if she could get something down on canvas.

She wound up in the coastal town of Port Judith, from which the mass of Block Island, well offshore, was plainly visible. There was a ferry due to leave for the island in less than half an hour. Sharon had always wanted to take this trip, but the thought of going alone made her sad.

She stopped at a small seafood restaurant for a bowl of chowder, then wandered on, driving back inland. The towns were all so pretty, so charming, and near enough to Providence and Boston so one would have the excitement of a big city within reach.

She'd always wanted to live in a town exactly like these towns she was passing through. She'd wanted to own a gracious home on a tree-lined street, where the best of New England's changing seasons would forever be putting on a show.

She pictured "her" house in the snow, with a giant Christmas wreath on the door. She pictured it in spring, with the golden forsythia blooming like captured rays of sunlight. She could see it in summer, with a swing suspended from a tree, and barbecues on the Fourth of July. And in the fall, with a traditional bunch of Indian corn fixed to the door and a big pumpkin on the doorstep.

She saw herself, waiting for her children to come home from school. The girl would look a little like her. The boy...she suddenly had a vision of the boy, and he looked more than a little like Scott!

As she came around a bend in the road a few moments later, Sharon saw a For Sale sign on the thick green lawn of the house just ahead. Impulsively, she pulled off the road and stopped the car.

She was looking at the house of her dreams. A life-size doll house of painted white clapboard, cedar-shingled roof, barn-red trim and shutters. A weathered split rail fence covered with wild rose vines surrounded the yard, and pink hyacinths bordered the sloping brick wall that led up to the front door.

Sharon, as if in a dream, found herself getting out of Sylvie's car and walking slowly up the front walk, beckoned by the promise of what was to be found inside. She lifted the shiny brass door knocker and let it fall. And even before its clang died out, the door opened.

The woman standing before her was tall and slim, and wore a beautifully tailored gray suit that almost exactly matched her closely cropped silvery hair.

She seemed puzzled. "I'm sorry," she said. "I'm afraid they didn't put you down."

"I beg your pardon?"

The woman smiled. "Let's begin again," she suggested. "Are you here to see the house?"

"Well . . . I'd like to see the house," Sharon admitted. "I was just driving by and I spotted the For Sale sign—"

"Ah, that explains it. We're only showing by appointment, you see. That's what I was wondering about. My last client left fifteen minutes ago, and I didn't think there was anyone else scheduled this afternoon."

"Oh."

Sharon started to turn around, but the woman quickly stopped her. "I'm Betty MacNeal, of Daniels and MacNeal," she introduced herself. "We have an exclusive on this property. Since you're here, why don't you come in and look around."

"Thank you," Sharon managed.

"I should tell you, though, I think the property just sold." The realtor moved back to let Sharon in, and added, "I'm going to make a few phone calls, but if you have any questions, I'll be glad to answer them."

"Okay."

"Oh yes, there was an estate sale just before we began to show the property," Mrs. MacNeal explained,

"so, as you'll see, the rooms are only partially furnished. The pieces remaining will be sold with the
house—unless the purchaser really doesn't want them. I
think they rather fit, though," she said decisively.
"Anyway, please wander."

"Thank you," Sharon said again, because that was
precisely what she wanted to do: wander around this
beautiful house and pretend it was hers.

She moved into a large central foyer, noticing the
staircase leading up to the second floor, and for the next
thirty minutes, she roamed from room to room. She
tried to imagine the rooms as they must have been when
they were fully furnished, with curtains framing the
windows, paintings on the walls, antiques and bric-a-
brac and china and books all in position.

As it was, the emptiness began to gnaw at her. With
only a few basic furniture items left in the house, there
was a certain lack of warmth, a bleakness. People must
have lived here for years, Sharon realized. But as she
wandered upstairs and looked out across a magnificent
stretch of back forty, alive with spring, Sharon wondered where those people were now. Had the owners
died? Had they retired and moved elsewhere? Who was
selling the house, and why? How could anyone who
owned a place like this possibly bear to give it up?

The questions tumbled.

People had loved here, as well as lived here, no doubt.
But had there ever been a wedding in that beautiful
drawing room downstairs? Had a baby ever been born
in that corner bedroom? Had that other, smaller bedroom once been a nursery? Had life ended here, as well?

Had there been the continuity that spelled *home*?

Sharon looked around her. The walls were mute, the windows were blank. There were no voices, echoes or answers.

Suddenly, an overwhelming feeling of emptiness, of loneliness, came over her. She stood at the top of the stairs, and her fantasy came to an abrupt finale. She couldn't wait to leave.

The real estate agent was still on the phone. As she descended the stairs, Sharon could hear the woman's crisp voice and was glad that she was occupied. She didn't want to say anything about the house. She didn't want to be asked anything about the house.

Once in the car, though, she sat at the curb for several minutes without driving off, posing new questions to herself. Why was she reacting like this? Why was she so shaken? It was just a *house*, that was all.

There was the answer, staring her in the face. Empty rooms, silent halls...were slated to remain that way until transformed by the magic of love into a home. And a home, a true home, could be anywhere. Anywhere at all. It only needed creating.

It was people that mattered!

In a moment of almost blinding revelation, Sharon knew that no place on the entire globe could ever be home to her without Scott. With him, home could be anywhere.

The sudden surge of love she felt for Scott threatened to overwhelm her. She gripped the steering wheel tightly as she started off down the road, watching the realtor emerge to lock the door behind her. It put a symbolic end to a dream that in no way measured up to reality, once she'd tested it out.

As she drove away, Sharon knew what reality was for her, and what she had to do about it.

She had to reach Scott . . . as quickly as she could.

CHAPTER EIGHTEEN

IT WAS DUSK when Sharon turned onto the street where she lived. Her usual parking space was taken, so she pulled up in the spot beside it. Preoccupied, she was mounting the porch steps and fumbling in her handbag for her apartment keys when she sensed the presence of someone just behind her.

This was not the best of neighborhoods, but thus far she hadn't encountered any trouble, even when occasionally coming home alone late at night. Nevertheless, a little icy chill coursed down her spine before, chin tilted defiantly, she turned to confront whomever it might be.

She found herself staring down at Scott.

The breath went out of her. Sagging, Sharon clutched for the porch railing, unable to speak.

"I didn't mean to frighten you," Scott said instantly, alarmed. He nodded back toward the curb. "I was parked right there," he explained. "I thought maybe you saw me when you drove by."

"No," Sharon managed. "No, I didn't," she repeated, as if her reaffirmation would cause this scene in front of her to swing back into focus.

Scott made no move to come closer. He was standing at the bottom of the steps, she was at the top. The dusk was merging into a blue-toned twilight presaging darkness, so his features were obscured. He was a blur to Sharon in this light, but still she could sense his tension.

She snapped to. Straightening up, she crossed the short distance to her door and fitted the key into the keyhole with fingers that were surprisingly steady. Then she called over her shoulder, "Come on up."

Scott got as far as the porch. Then, standing in the open doorway, he stared at Sharon as she ascended the steep flight of stairs to her apartment. She was fitting another key into another lock when she realized Scott was still standing on the threshold below her.

"Please...come in," she called down to him.

She flipped on the light just inside her tiny foyer, and heard Scott's heavy footsteps coming up the stairs. When he stepped into her apartment, and into the light, she was shocked by her first real glimpse of him. He looked so gaunt, so weary, so much in pain.

Her heart ached for him as she murmured, brokenly, "Scott, what have you been doing to yourself?"

Maybe it was the expression on her face. Maybe it was the tone of her voice. Whatever it was...something that Scott had been holding inside suddenly broke. With a groan, he closed the gap that separated them, and Sharon fell into his arms.

He held her close, so close he was afraid he might be hurting her. But he wanted her nearness so desperately. This tangible evidence of her, captured within the circle of his embrace. He felt the softness of her beautiful coppery hair against his cheek, smelled the special, wondrous fragrance of her. And all the doubts, all the uncertainties, all the awful skepticism that had been plaguing him unmercifully since that terrible day when he'd learned she'd left Miami...all these feelings began to evaporate.

What mattered was now. What mattered was this moment.

Scott seized it. He moved back just enough to cup Sharon's chin with one palm, tilting her face upward. With his other arm he continued to hold her, because he couldn't bear to let her go. Not for a second did he wish to lose her touch. Tired, and maybe a little incoherent from fatigue—he couldn't remember when he'd last had a decent night's sleep—he knew only that he never wanted to let her go again. Never, never again.

He brushed her mouth with his lips, testing her response, trying to determine if this was what she wanted from him. Or if there was a chance, just a chance that, despite her seeming compliance, she'd shut him out of her life. He didn't think he could handle that. He'd handled a lot of things, but he didn't think he could handle that.

Then...Sharon raised tender arms to encircle his neck. Scott felt her fingers entwining in his hair. He felt her tug, as she tried to bring him even closer against her. And at last their lips meshed.

At that point, nothing else mattered for either of them. They stood, swaying slightly, gripping each other. Scott murmured low, hoarse words in Sharon's ears. Words that didn't really make much sense. But that didn't matter. It wasn't a time to make sense. It was a time to feel, without reservation, without restraint.

She listened, half-laughing, half-sobbing, to his nearly incomprehensible words. But had he been speaking Sanskrit, she would have known what he was saying. She pushed away from him ever so slightly, sensing his resistance when she did, knowing that he wasn't about to let her leave him, and not wanting to leave him...ever again.

She touched Scott's face with her fingers, outlined his features, traced the strong line of his jaw, the bridge of his nose, the smoothness of his forehead, the softness of his closed eyes.

Her hands moved past his face to wander down his neck and across his shoulders. Then they followed the taut lines of his back and his waist, as if she was a sculptor and he was the clay she must mold, must bring to life. He stood very still, stock-still, as she came to the masculine core of him and paused, her fingers suddenly as still as he was.

He began saying her name half under his breath, repeating it over and over again. And within a few moments they were tangled in each others' arms, possessed of a consuming urgency to shed clothes, possessed of an unrestrained desire to feel the heat of their naked bodies, loving and caressing.

For a second or two, they stood silently apart, visually feasting upon each other in the soft bronze light cast from a nearby lamp. Then they tumbled onto Sharon's old chintz-covered couch, eyes open as they began to physically devour each other...two starving people suddenly brought before a feast.

Sharon gazed deeply into Scott's gaunt and weary face, and this time it was she who brought him surcease first. On that single, other occasion when they'd come together on Diane's couch, it was he who had been patient, he who had led her to first discover the full meaning of passion.

Now, on this early evening in May, she was content to wait. She wanted to make love to Scott until he soared into the stratosphere of his own sensual release. Not to prove that she could exercise the same remarkable restraint that he had, but because she loved him so totally. She wanted to give herself without reserve, with only him in mind, with only the idea that love would re-store him to the man he was before.

Later, as they lay together on her bed, bathed in flickering candlelight, it was Sharon's turn. And Scott taught her, all over again, the wonderful lessons of love.

MORNING CAME. Sharon rolled over on her side and stared at the man lying next to her in bed. He was still asleep, but as she watched, he moaned softly, struggling through a dream. Instinctively, she reached out to clasp his hand. And, like a child made to feel safe in the dark, he subsided back into a deep slumber.

After a while, she slipped out of bed and showered. Then, wrapped in her comfortable old terry robe, she put on some coffee. At that moment, she heard some-thing behind her, and turned to see Scott standing in the kitchen doorway, wearing only his slacks, needing a shave, his hair tousled. Across the space they looked at each other. He shook his head dazedly, then he held out his arms.

Sharon went into those arms without a word, pillow-ing her head against his shoulder as he caressed her. Not as a prelude to sex, this time, but with an infinite, car-ing gentleness.

Later, after they'd talked quietly over two cups of coffee, Scott mentioned, "I thought Sylvie was staying with you."

"She is," Sharon told him. "But she and Gary took off for the weekend."

"Gary, your employer?"

"Our employer," Sharon corrected. "Sylvie's work-ing for him, too." She giggled. "And would you believe it? I think they're falling in love with each other."

"It must be catching," Scott said. "I think Tony and Genevieve are falling in love, too. And perhaps your sister and Rick, as well. And..."

Sharon shook her head. "No," she said. "You can't include us."

Scott's eyes opened wide. "Are you telling me something?" he asked, his eyebrows arched warily.

"Only that there's no chance of my falling in love with you, darling. I did that a long time ago. Now...oh, Scott, I love you so much."

Slowly, Scott said, "I know that, Sharon. That's the crazy part of it."

"What do you mean?"

"I know you love me. And you must know I love you. What I feel for you goes way beyond anything I've ever felt before. It's not just the fact that we're as physically compatible as two people possibly could be. It's, well..."

"Yes?"

"It's that our love for each other is the one thing we're both really adult about."

"That's a funny thing to say."

"I suppose it is."

Scott stood and went over to the kitchen window. He looked out onto the narrow street. The old frame houses—most of them painted dull tones of gray or tan or a somewhat sickly green—created a drab scene, even on a bright sunny morning such as this one.

"You know," he said, "I pictured you living in an entirely different sort of place. I mean...I know how home conscious you are."

Sharon smiled faintly, tempted to tell him about yesterday, about the truths that had come over her as she toured that house of her dreams. But this wasn't the moment.

She said, wryly, "I haven't had scads of money these past few years. I think I must have told you at some point that Jerry left me with almost no insurance and quite a stack of bills. Well, I've caught up with all of that. So, even though I can afford to upgrade my living quarters somewhat, I haven't made any move in that direction for the simple reason that I don't think I'm going to be at Gary Freeman's much longer. I've decided to change house and job at the same time."

"Have you been job hunting?"

"Actually, no. I meant to answer an ad in a Boston newspaper the other day, but I didn't get around to it. Anyway..."

"Yes?"

"Aren't we digressing?"

"Yes, I suppose we are." Scott turned, and with the daylight behind him, he was mostly in silhouette. Sharon couldn't see his features clearly as he said, "Our problem is that the same obstacles that have always been in our way are still looming up. However...there is something I have to tell you, Sharon Williams. Do you suppose we could get out, though? Maybe drive around and get a little fresh air?"

Scott sounded distracted, and Sharon frowned. She'd assumed that he'd come to Providence because his need to see her had become as overwhelming as her need to be with him. She'd driven back here last night with the single thought in mind of going to him as soon as she could make the necessary arrangements. She'd assumed that it was that need, and nothing more, that had caused him to put his pride in his pocket—as she would have done, had he not acted first.

Now, she realized it was something more. Something important. Something crucial.

It took all her willpower to straighten up the kitchen as Scott shaved and dressed. Then she slipped on a pair of slacks and a blouse, brushed her hair and touched her lips with gloss, trying to sound bright and cheerful as she announced that she was ready to go.

They took the car Scott had rented at the airport the day before, and started forth with no particular place in mind. But when they headed south out of the city, Sharon suggested, "If we cut over to Westerly we'll be right by the shore. The beaches are really beautiful. I don't know how much will be opened, but there's a long stretch of beach at Misquamicut where we could walk."

The season wasn't in full swing yet at Misquamicut Beach, so Scott drove slowly down the full length of the long parking lot. There were a number of sun worshippers sprawled on the sand, several people strolling and a few surfers wearing sleek black wet suits as protection against the still-icy water.

"This is relatively uncrowded," Sharon told Scott. "I came down here last summer with Gary and it was quite a mob scene."

"I can imagine," he replied dutifully.

His mind was obviously on other things. After a time, when they'd walked a ways in silence without his broaching whatever it was he had on his mind, she said, direct as her sister Diane would have been in such a situation, "Why don't you come right out and tell me, Scott?"

He paused, looking down at her. They were standing near the water's edge, where the waves spilled onto the glistening sand. This became a picture etched in Sharon's mind, this scene of Scott with the water behind him and a near-cloudless sky, as blue as his eyes, overhead.

He said, his voice knot tight, "It's almost a certainty that I'll be able to fly again, Sharon."

Up the beach, three youngsters were molding a sand figure at the tide line. Sharon felt as rigid as that supine facsimile of a human form. Compressed sand, but in her case the sand could easily be granite. She suddenly felt made of stone . . . with a heart of lead.

She wanted to say, "That's wonderful," but she couldn't find the words. Despite all she'd said to Diane—and to herself—about not wishing anything but the best for Scott, she wasn't able to verbally congratulate him.

She tried to rally. It wasn't that simple. Scott stood staring down at her, motionless, waiting for her to speak. She was only too painfully aware of how vitally important whatever she might say would be to both of them.

She moistened her lips. Again, she tried to say, "That's wonderful." But she choked on the words. And suddenly her emotions spun out of control. She, too, had lived through nights when sleep was a stranger. She, too, was tired, her nerves frayed, the tension of these past weeks finally catching up with her. The tears came in a torrent. She stood before Scott, helpless, as they streamed down her face. Then she turned and ran, ran up the beach along the tide line, where the sand was firm and wet with the shine left by the water ebbing out to the open sea.

She ran until she felt her lungs were going to burst, her breath coming in great, heaving gasps. In another minute, she knew she'd sprawl on the sand, collapsed. She had the crazy wish that maybe the tide would rush in and sweep her out with it, because she felt such a coward. Such a coward!

Then Scott's arms grasped her. No one else's touch felt as his did. He swung her around to face him, panting from the chase. His eyes blazed, angry blue fire raking her face. She shrank from what she labeled contempt for her weakness, disgust at her lack of understanding, her ability to rejoice with him.

"Damn it," he rasped, "why did you do that? Why didn't you hear me out?"

Finally, she managed the words. "It's . . . it's wonderful," she stammered.

"*What's* wonderful, for heaven's sake?"

"That . . . you're going to fly again."

"That's not what I said, Sharon."

She stared at him dumbly. "But you did. You did. Just now. Back there."

"No," he contradicted. "That's not what I said. I said it's almost a certainty that I'll be able to fly again. That's to say, it's practically a sure thing I'll be fit enough to be placed back on active flying status. That doesn't mean I'm going to do it."

"What are you talking about?"

He drew her arm though his and urged her to start walking. She felt herself moving along stiff gaited like a wooden puppet with stilts for legs.

Scott said, "The preliminary physical comes up in ten days. The one that'll finally settle matters is still three months away. But I could no longer sit back and wait. So the day before yesterday, Rick went over me completely—at my request. At the conclusion," Scott said, managing the shadow of a smile, "he told me the only thing wrong with me was, and I quote, my 'brain is going soft.'"

"What?"

"In other words," Scott explained, "there's a ninety-nine percent chance I'll pass all my Air Force physicals with those proverbial flying colors. That means that by around Labor Day, I can be looking for an activated status and a transfer. I'll amend that. It means that around Labor Day I *could* be looking for an activated status and a transfer. Except I'm not going to wait till then. I'm going to resign from the service, Sharon."

She stopped in her tracks. "What are you saying?"

"Exactly what you just heard me say. I've had a month since you left Miami to think about this. A month that's been like a century. Believe me, I've reviewed every detail of my life. And what I want, more than anything, is to make a new life with you . . . in Miami, maybe. Where you could be near Diane and Tonette, and maybe do your work for Di-Tone, if that's what you want. I'm sure there'd be job opportunities for me, too, in Miami. Aside from being a pilot, I do have expertise in certain areas that have their counterparts in civilian life."

Sharon shook her head dully. "It's out of the question, Scott."

"No, it's not out of the question. I want to settle down, Sharon. I want to marry you. I want us to have children."

His words were like a magic potion. Sharon said, almost dreamily, "A girl who looks sort of like me, and a boy who looks exactly like you."

"Whatever you want...as long as we have kids. I want kids. And we'll find a big old house on some nice shaded street where we can bring them up. You can join the PTA and be a Girl Scout mother... You can do whatever you want to do. And every night, I'll come home to you."

She actually laughed. "You're dreaming, Scott."

"I'm not dreaming," he said soberly. "I've thought it through. I've made up my mind. That's why I came here. To tell you that if you'll have me, I'm ready to remove those obstacles in our path."

"And leave some insurmountable ghosts?" she asked him.

"No, no ghosts."

"That would be impossible." She looked up into his beloved face and knew she'd never forget today...when he'd actually offered to make a sacrifice for her that she was sure would cost even more than he now realized.

She said softly, "Have you ever wondered why Tony and Diane broke up when they are so fond of each other and apparently get along so well?"

"Yes, I have. Why did they?"

"They both told me, on separate occasions, that they made up their minds to dissolve their marriage while they were still friends, still had common interests, and could build a different kind of mutual future for Tonette's sake. Otherwise, as they both said, they were sure they would have come to hate each other."

"There's no relevancy there to us," Scott said quickly.

"Ah, but there is. It might work for a time. The big house. The children. Coming home at five every night. Going to PTA pot-luck suppers. Doing whatever it is that people who live in big houses on shaded streets do." Sharon laughed shakily. "I don't really know," she admitted. "I've never lived that way."

"Nor have I. Which is all the more reason—"

"All the more reason why it's something we should stave off, for maybe another twenty years or so," Sharon said quietly. "Please," she added, as Scott started to speak, "hear me out. Yesterday I was driving around because I was so lonely. I missed you so much. I saw a big house on a country road with a For Sale sign on the front lawn—exactly the kind of house I've dreamed about ever since I can remember. I went in. I went all through it. And I couldn't wait to leave. Because whatever had been there before wasn't there any longer, Scott. It was empty, not alive."

He frowned. "I don't understand."

"It wasn't a home any longer, don't you see? It isn't a house that makes a home. It's the people who live in it. The love they share. Their happiness, their sorrow. The comedy in their lives . . . and their tragedy. All of it, wrapped together. Maybe I'm not saying this very well, I don't know."

He looked at her, his blue eyes curious. "I think you're saying it quite beautifully."

"Well, I'm trying to explain to you that all at once I learned a lesson. It was my parents who were wrong for each other, who probably should have divorced each other when they were young enough to start new lives, just as Diane and Tony are doing. It was because of them that I never felt I had a home, not because we moved around all the time. It was the same way with Jerry and me. If we had lived in a palace, we would never have had a home. But with you . . ."

Scott held his breath, waiting for her to finish.

Sharon said raggedly, "When I got back to Providence last night, the first thing I intended to do was call an airline and book a flight to Miami. Then you appeared on my doorstep."

"What did you say?" Scott asked hoarsely, sure that he'd heard wrong.

Sharon nearly blurted that Rick had phoned and suggested that she consult a physician and get a prescription for tranquilizers before she flew. Just in time, she said, "I was going to get in touch with Gary's doctor to see if he could give me something that would...well, sort of knock me out so that I wouldn't go all to pieces as soon as I put a foot in the plane."

Scott stared down at her, and his eyes misted. "What am I going to do with you?" he whispered huskily, shaking his head. "What ever am I going to do with you?"

He drew her into his embrace and lifted her off her feet, holding her tightly and kissing her until she moaned, "Help!"

With that, he set her down again, laughing. But the laughter faded into a solemn tone as he said, "Sweetheart, I'm never going to urge you to fly. It would be the wrong thing to do. Who knows, maybe someday you'll feel differently. But until that time comes, you can be as earthbound as you like."

"Then that has to work both ways, Scott. I never want to keep you earthbound. You wouldn't be you."

"Maybe not, I don't know. I've changed since I've met you, sweetheart ... more than I think even I realize. Also, there does come a time when one should step down and let younger men take over the actual controls—when all the knowledge and experience gained over the years can be channeled to better uses, let's say. Where I'm concerned, that may not be for a while yet. So...let's just take it as it comes, okay? Do you think you could live like that for a little while longer, darling?"

Sharon looked out toward the horizon, where the sky met the sea. She could not say that the sky looked friendly. It never had. Possibly, it never would. But she could look at it without flinching now. She could begin to see its beauty.

And each day I live with Scott, I will learn to see more of that beauty, she promised the stars hiding behind the blue. *I will live life in wonder, not fear. Because my heart has found a home.*

EPILOGUE

THE TRAIN ATTENDANT knocked on the door of bedroom four and, when bade to enter, opened it and prepared to give his usual spiel.

"Welcome aboard," he said, his voice rich and mellow. "My name is Thomas Chalmers the Third, and I will be serving you aboard the *Silver Comet* all the way to New York—"

He broke off as he recognized the handsome man and beautiful woman smiling up at him.

"Why, it's Mr. and Mrs. Williams," he murmured, surprised.

Scott nodded. "Good to see you again, Thomas."

"And you, sir."

The train was due to depart the Miami station at any second. But now Thomas became aware of a commotion on the platform outside bedroom four's window. Three men, three women and a small girl were grouped in a line, holding a wide, white satin banner emblazoned with bright blue letters that read, Just Married.

As if to verify the fact that someone had, indeed, just been married, the young girl suddenly broke away from the others, danced closer to the window and raised her hand. A rain of small particles showered forth from a blue satin cone, pelting the glass.

Thomas Chalmers the Third cleared his throat. "Sir," he said to Scott, "I think someone is trying to attract your attention."

Scott and Sharon turned simultaneously to see Diane, Rick, Tony, Genevieve Landry, Sylvie and Gary Freeman waving the banner frantically, while Tonette prepared to toss another cone full of particles at the window.

Scott grinned. "Looks like they've still got wedding fever."

Sharon's eyes misted. "It was such a beautiful wedding," she said dreamily. "By the time Diane finished having her patio decorated it could have doubled as a movie set. And wasn't it terrific of Gary to pinch hit for my father at the last minute and come down and give me away? Incidentally, did you notice that Diane and Sylvie both grabbed my bouquet at the same time?"

"Poor Genevieve," Scott murmured.

They heard the conductor calling, "All Aboard," and they pressed close to the window, waving at their friends and family on the platform. The small group waved back. Tonette prepared to launch another attack. Sharon noticed Thomas Chalmers the Third wincing, and said quickly, "It's only bird seed, Mr. Chalmers. People are using it these days instead of rice, because it's supposed to be better for the environment."

"I see," Thomas Chalmers said, nodding gravely.

Car 714 lurched, the wheels began to turn. The *Silver Comet* slowly moved out of the Miami station.

Thomas found himself leaning forward to watch until the Just Married banner faded from sight. Then he glanced a bit apprehensively at Mr. and Mrs. Williams. You couldn't tell what was about to happen with those two. And he hated to imagine the fit the conductor would have if they suddenly insisted they'd booked separate bedrooms, the way they had the first time they'd traveled on the *Comet*.

"You can reserve your dinner time, if you like," he began again, leaving out the rest of his routine speech because the Williamses were familiar with it anyway. "Meantime, if there's anything you require..."

Scott Williams smiled in a way that spoke volumes to Thomas. Meeting the public on a daily basis as he did, he'd long ago become an expert on the meaning of smiles.

"I think we'll skip making a dinner reservation, Thomas," Scott said. "You might bring us a split of chilled champagne, though. After that, how about posting the Do Not Disturb sign?"

Thomas nodded, but he was puzzled. Then it occurred to him that maybe the Just Married banner was for real, after all. Even though he didn't see how that could be, since he remembered—vividly—the trip this couple had made down from the north early last March. On the other hand...Mr. and Mrs. Williams certainly did *look* like newlyweds!

"I'll get the champagne to you just as soon as I make sure everyone's settled," Thomas promised, and discreetly withdrew.

Sharon waited until the door was closed, then she flashed her new husband an impish smile. "I think we've thrown him a real curve, darling," she said.

"It'll make his day," Scott retorted. "I'd bet my last cent that Thomas is a real romantic at heart."

"Are you?"

"Am I what?"

"A real romantic at heart?"

He surveyed her with mock dismay. "Do I have to prove that, Mrs. Williams?"

"No." Sharon sat down in the chair by the window, slipped off her slim, taupe leather pumps and wiggled her toes. Glancing at the passing vista of palm trees and a cloudless blue sky, she said, "It's going to be odd to see autumn foliage tomorrow afternoon."

"The leaves should be beautiful in the Shenandoah Valley," Scott mused. "That's a nice day trip from Washington. Maybe next weekend we can escape for a forty-eight hour honeymoon. You're not getting a real honeymoon out of this marriage, come to think of it."

"We're going to be honeymooning for years and years," Sharon corrected lazily. "Anyway, first we'll have to house hunt, if you're really going to be stationed at the Pentagon for two whole years."

"I'm really going to be stationed at the Pentagon for two whole years," Scott assured her.

They both knew this didn't mean he wouldn't be flying. He would be—frequently. But the major thrust of this assignment would be making full use of his knowledge, his technical background, not of his flying skills. Thinking about it, Scott mused that if the Air Force had deliberately calculated every aspect of his next assignment they could not have come up with anything better. Being based in the Washington area in a job that was part desk, part flying, would make it a lot easier for Sharon to adjust to his way of life. She would have had to face a lot more, sooner, if he'd been assigned to a position and a base where planes would have been a constant part of the picture.

"We're going to need to find exactly the right kind of house, with work space for you," he reminded her.

"We will," she said, obviously unperturbed. "I don't need a lot of space to do my designs, anyway."

"I'm glad you've worked it out so you can handle your job with Di-Tone long-distance, without anyone having to sacrifice anything," Scott told her.

She'd been working for Di-Tone throughout the summer and into the fall. The compact disk market was steadily increasing, but Di-Tone was more than holding its own, and the company's future looked very bright.

"I'm also glad that your father was able to make that phone call to you himself, before we left," Scott said.

"So am I. When Diane and I got word that he'd had a heart attack, I can't begin to tell you what we both went through," Sharon confessed. "All the guilt about not getting to see him, about not really letting ourselves get to know our stepmother. Well...that's behind us now. Fortunately, the heart attack was minor, a warning more than anything else." She laughed. "He told me on the phone that the doctors say he's good for another century. So I told him..."

"Yes?"

"I said," Sharon reported, phrasing the words very carefully, "that maybe when you have a leave coming we'll fly out and see him."

She was looking out the window as she said this, still watching the palm fronds waving languidly in the tropical breeze, and Scott smiled at her tenderly. He'd come to know her so well. He knew it wouldn't be easy for her to fly to California with him to see her father. It would, in fact, be very difficult. Yet he was convinced that she'd do it, when the time came, and it would be an all important first step. The first of many, many first steps they'd be taking together.

Harlequin Superromance

COMING NEXT MONTH

#278 NIGHT INTO DAY • Sandra Canfield
When their eyes meet across a crowded New Orleans
dance floor, travel agent Alex Farrell and sports
celebrity Patrick O'Casey learn the meaning of
Kismet. Alex, a semi-invalid stricken with
rheumatoid arthritis, refuses to burden Patrick with
her illness, but he decides she'll be his wife—
no matter what the obstacles!

#279 ROOM FOR ONE MORE • Virginia Nielson
Brock Morley loves Charlotte Emlyn and is
determined to marry her—until her teenage son
reveals he's fathered a child. Brock is ready to
be a husband and stepfather, but a grandfather...?

#280 THE WHOLE TRUTH • Jenny Loring
Besides integrity, Susannah Ross brings a certain
poise to her judgeship—and nothing threatens that
more than seeing lawyer Dan Sullivan in her
courtroom. Difficult as the situation seems, this time
they are both determined to make their love work.
Ten years has been too long.

#281 THE ARRANGEMENT • Sally Bradford
Juliet Cavanagh is a no-nonsense lawyer with a
practical approach to motherhood—she wants a
child but not the complications of a marriage. She
advertises for a prospective father and attracts a
candidate with his own conditions. Brady Talcott is
handsome, wealthy, intelligent and healthy, and he
insists on living with Juliet—especially when he
learns he can't live without her!

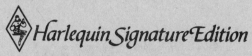

Penny Jordan

Stronger Than Yearning

He was the man of her dreams!

The same dark hair, the same mocking eyes; it was as if the
Regency rake of the portrait, the seducer of Jenna's dream, had
come to life. Jenna, believing the last of the Deverils dead, was
determined to buy the great old Yorkshire Hall—to claim it for
her daughter, Lucy, and put to rest some of the painful memories of Lucy's birth. She had no way of knowing that a direct des-
cendant of the black sheep Deveril even existed—or that James
Allingham and his own powerful yearnings would disrupt her
plan entirely.

Penny Jordan's first Harlequin Signature Edition *Love's Choices* was an
outstanding success. Penny Jordan has written more than 40 best-sell-
ing titles—more than 4 million copies sold.

Now, be sure to buy her latest bestseller, *Stronger Than Yearning*. Available wherever paperbacks are sold—in October.

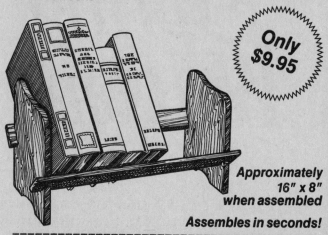

What the press says about Harlequin romance fiction...

"When it comes to romantic novels...
Harlequin is the indisputable king."
— *New York Times*

"...always with an upbeat, happy ending."
— *San Francisco Chronicle*

"Women have come to trust these
stories about contemporary people,
set in exciting foreign places."
— *Best Sellers*, New York

"The most popular reading matter of
American women today."
— *Detroit News*

"...a work of art."
— *Globe & Mail*, Toronto